The
Cursed Half Moon

The Cursed Half Moon – Book 1
The Cursed Half Moon – Book 2

Other books by
Danielle N. McDonough

THE LEGACY SERIES

BOOK 1: THE PREPARATIONS
BOOK 2: THE TRIALS
BOOK 3: THE RETURN
BOOK 4: THE BROKEN

www.thecursedhalfmoonbookseries.com

The
Cursed Half Moon
Book 2

Danielle N. McDonough

Story by
Danielle N. McDonough & Charles Gilbreath

Ideas contributed by
Collin Glaess, Makenna Glaess, Anna Castro,
& Joe Martinez

Illustrated by
Aleasha Ford, Rebecca Coker, & Danielle N.
McDonough

Edited by
Terry McDonough & Rebecca Martinez

The Cursed Half Moon – Book 2
by Danielle N. McDonough

Printed in the United States of America
ISBN (Paperback): 978-1-950296-15-6
ISBN (Hardcover): 978-1-950296-16-3
ISBN (eBook): 978-1-950296-17-0

Written by Danielle N. McDonough
Story by Danielle N. McDonough & Charles Gilbreath
Ideas contributed by Collin Glaess, Makenna Glaess, Anna Castro, & Joe Martinez
Illustrated by Aleasha Ford, Rebecca Coker, & Danielle N. McDonough
Edited by Terry McDonough & Rebecca Martinez

This series and other books by Danielle N. McDonough are available online at www.daniellenmcdonough.com.

Again, for my party and our Dungeon Master:

Collin, who is like a brother to me.

Makenna, who is like a sister to me and married to someone who is like a brother to me.

Anna, who is also like a sister to me but not married to anyone.

Joe, who is literally my brother-in-law and married to my sister.

And Charles.

Planosia

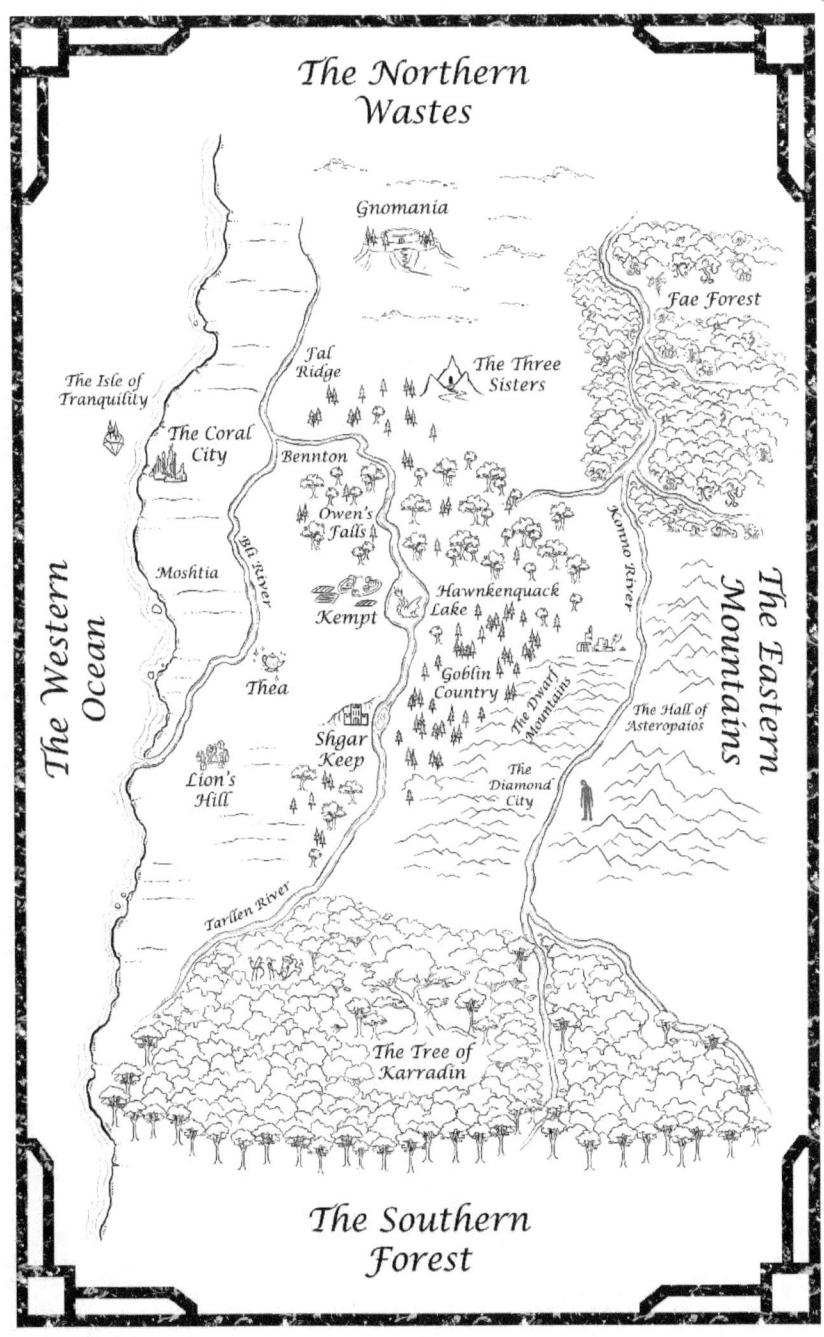

The Northern Wastes

Gnomania

Fae Forest

Tal Ridge

The Three Sisters

The Isle of Tranquility

The Coral City

Bennton

Owen's Falls

Moshtia

Bli River

Konno River

Kempt

Hawnkenquack Lake

The Western Ocean

Thea

Goblin Country

The Dwarf Mountains

The Hall of Asteropaios

The Eastern Mountains

Shgar Keep

Lion's Hill

The Diamond City

Tarilen River

The Tree of Karradin

The Southern Forest

Chapter 1

The Cloud

The ground was strewn with the corpses of high elves. Hundreds of them.

I don't know how long I stood there, staring open-mouthed as I took in the devastation.

"What– happened?" Wren breathed.

I looked back at her and saw tears filling my half-elf friend's large, brown eyes.

These were her kin, I reminded myself, *even if they did reject her.*

I was a half-elf too, but I was descended from wood elves instead of high elves.

"There must have been a battle," Gnombie said softly from where he sat on my black gelding, Tempest. The gnome didn't have a horse of his own, but ever since he'd somehow brought Tempest back from the dead, I'd let him ride double with me.

Tempest wasn't quite the same as before, and I was still concerned about what dark ritual might have been used in his restoration. However, continuing our journey without a horse would have proved nearly impossible, so I hadn't asked too many questions.

"There wasn't a battle," Kraster, my half-brother, said. "There are no wounds on the bodies."

Kraster and I had the same father, a man who had stepped away from his family and into my mother's arms just long enough to create me. I'd lived fifteen years in the same tiny town with him, his wife, and their dozen or so children.

Kraster, who was a few months younger than I, was the only one of my half-siblings to acknowledge my existence. He'd spent many years trying to befriend me when we were children, but I had resisted. Only once we found ourselves placed in the same army unit did I relent and allow my brother to become the first friend I'd ever had.

Mentored by General Greyward, Kraster had risen steadily in the ranks of the Kempt army. He was one of the rare humans naturally gifted with magical abilities, which ensured that he was selected for special assignments and promotions.

I'd spent my military career in his shadow, the only half-breed in the entire army.

To be fair, it would have been much worse for me without him, because as my brother rose, he pulled me up with him.

For a while, our relationship was strained, but now I considered him my only true family. Even my mother was cold with resentment, as though it was my fault for being born an illegitimate half-breed.

"What's that stuff on their faces?" Wren asked, motioning toward the fallen high elves.

Looking more carefully at the body on the ground before me, I could see a dark, purplish dust on his clothes and skin. The largest concentration of the substance was around the mouth and nose. As I studied it closely, some of it stirred, despite the lack of wind. For a moment, I thought the elf had returned to life; then I realized it was some sort of dark purple growth slowly emerging from his nose.

Valor, Wren's enormous chestnut horse, moved a step forward.

"No!" I called out, backing away. "Don't get any closer."

Wren gave me a look of confusion as I hurried back to Tempest and mounted in front of Gnombie. Quickly, I backed us away from the dead bodies. In my haste, we nearly bumped into Raspberry, Kraster's bay warhorse.

"They're dead, and we need to get out of here or we might be too," I warned, steering Tempest away from the clearing filled with bodies. Thankfully, the others followed.

I didn't tell them what I had seen. We'd faced many terrors in the past few days. For all I knew, the moving growth could have been nothing but my mind creating fresh horrors that weren't really there.

In the late afternoon, we stopped in a meadow to give the horses a breather. I was looking back over the trees the way we'd come when a cry of surprise escaped my lips. Approaching steadily from behind was a gray cloud swirling with purple specks. The colors were the same shade as the dust I'd seen on the high elf's corpse.

"We need to move!" I cried, running to Tempest as the others hurried to their own mounts.

At first, we pulled ahead of the cloud, but each time we slowed to let the horses walk, the gray and purple mist loomed closer. It felt like we were in a race against time, a race we were certain to lose.

As we dashed through the trees, I felt a twinge of worry for Valor and Raspberry. Unlike Tempest, who no longer required rest or food, the pair were covered in lather and blowing hard. Both had been bred for long hours of toil, but we'd been on the road many days with little rest.

Throughout the remainder of the afternoon, the cloud continued to advance. Even once it grew dark, we dared not stop our desperate flight. I had excellent night vision, a gift from my wood elf ancestors. Tempest also seemed to be able to see as well in the dark as if it had been sunhigh. With us in the lead, we continued on for many hours. Finally, we were forced to stop for fear one of the horses' hearts might burst.

We dismounted, and I checked Tempest. He showed no signs of fatigue and clearly could have continued. Feeling a slight chill, which I was getting used to, I stored the horse in my shadow. I didn't know how it worked exactly, but Gnombie had said it was because of our bond. The strange creature would remain there, nothing but a cold prickle at the base of my skull, until I summoned him.

An idea started forming in my mind. The only trouble was, we wouldn't all fit on Tempest, and it would be very hard to pick from among my companions.

Kraster was my brother and more dear to me than any of the others, but Wren was the most necessary to our mission. She had been chosen specifically by Shal'eth, one of the great dragons of old. Wren also carried two of the eight stones we were seeking. Kraster had another, as did I, leaving us with four more to find and precious little idea of how to locate most of them.

These thoughts churned chaotically in my mind while the others lay down to sleep. I knew there was no point in trying to join them. Instead, I paced among the trees, ears and eyes ever searching for signs that the cloud was closing in on us.

Dawn found me still alert and watchful. I was about to rouse Kraster and Wren from where they lay when I realized I couldn't see Gnombie.

Softly, I called his name.

"Yes?"

I whipped around to find the gnome standing behind me.

"There you are," I sighed. "I was worried you'd wandered off and gotten lost."

It wasn't quite true, but it sounded plausible enough. Gnombie hadn't been part of our party from the beginning, and I sometimes questioned his reasons for coming with us.

"It is not unusual for those of your height to overlook us small folk," Gnombie said.

I wasn't sure if he was trying to make a joke or actually being serious. I never found out, because at that moment I heard the sound of ripping bark and cracking trunks.

Both of us raced to the others.

"Get up! Get up!" I yelled, shaking Wren awake as Kraster clambered to his feet.

I glanced over my shoulder and saw that I was too late. The mist was less than thirty feet away from us. As the trees were engulfed, they began to erupt. Strange purplish gray growths, crystal-like in nature, broke through their trunks, each releasing a spray of spores.

We had less than thirty seconds before we would be inside the cloud, leaving me almost no time to react. Mentally, I summoned Tempest, who was by my side in an instant. I was closest to Wren and, through sheer adrenaline, threw her onto the horse.

"Kraster!" I screamed, turning and seizing his arm. "Get up behind her!"

"But—"

"There's no time!" I cut him off. "Take this and go!"

I fumbled in my pouch for the green stone I'd had for only a few short days.

It didn't matter what happened to me; I just wanted them to live! If any of us could complete our quest, it was Kraster and Wren. I might die here, but they would survive. They had to. The world needed them.

The instant my fingers touched the stone, warmth washed over me. What's more, a transparent green aura, fifteen feet in diameter, spread out around us. When the cloud of spores met it a second later, it did not penetrate the barrier.

I stared in shock, then turned to look at the others. All of them appeared similarly confused.

"Did you do that with the stone?" Wren asked breathlessly.

"I think I may have," I whispered, glancing down at where it glowed in my hand. This one was called The Heart of Jong and had the rune for life engraved on the top.

"Whatever you are doing, don't stop," Kraster told me.

I nodded, afraid to even draw breath lest the enchantment falter. The cloud had completely surrounded us. Every tree outside the bubble was afflicted by the crystalline growths.

"What now?" Gnombie asked after a minute had passed, and the mist around us did not dissipate. If anything, it seemed to have gotten thicker.

Carefully, I took one step forward. The ethereal walls surrounding us moved too, pushing the spores back. Several trees passed through. The purple growths on their trunks turned completely black and didn't release any spores.

"Get your horses," I ordered. "We need to get out of here before this stone runs out of magic."

"I don't think it will," Wren said, sliding down from Tempest.

"Why not?" Kraster asked. He was quickly saddling Raspberry.

"It powered Jong for a long, long time," Wren explained while tacking up Valor. "Then it kept the half-elf town under Morana's spell for centuries. I seriously doubt it'll stop working in the next few minutes."

"Well, it might take longer than that to get out of here," I argued, wondering if I would have to stay awake the whole time. "And I don't even know what the stone is doing exactly."

"It's giving life," Wren replied as if it was the most obvious thing in the world. Of course, once she said that, it made perfect sense.

We moved more slowly than yesterday. I didn't dare let go of the stone and held it tightly clenched in my fist. Kraster and Wren kept their horses close to Tempest. Gnombie rode behind me as usual. He hadn't said a word, and I hoped he wasn't angry that I'd tried to save the others instead of him.

An hour after noon, I heard cries coming from ahead. I alerted the others and pushed Tempest into a trot. We emerged from the trees into a clearing. There were several high elves on the ground. As we drew near, the aura of the stone pushed the spores away from their bodies, and I saw that one of them was still alive.

He was an adult, but young, probably less than fifty years old. I dismounted and approached cautiously. He'd been writhing but now lay still. When I was only a few feet away, he coughed up a mouthful of dark, clotted blood and opened his eyes. They were shot with black veins, and I knew we were too late.

"How did this happen?" I breathed, not sure if he could answer. I knelt beside him and took his hand. It was as cold as death. I was vaguely aware of Wren and Kraster checking the others.

"The tree," the young elf croaked, black blood escaping his lips. "The Tree of Karradin— it started there, and— and the poison

6

spread to the others. The cloud kept getting bigger– and more– potent."

I glanced up at my brother, who had come to stand beside me. He shook his head solemnly, and I knew that none of the elf's companions were still alive.

"We fled. We ran all day and night– trying to catch the others, but– but they had horses, and we fell behind," he choked. "We– we couldn't escape."

"Wren, summon Puvva," I ordered, realizing that there was a slight chance the genie might be able to save the elf's life.

Puvva was some sort of water spirit who had been bound to a vessel long ago. Wren was her current master. She'd received possession of the genie from Shal'eth when he sent us to see The Oracle and begin searching for the stones.

Wren nodded and raced to Valor's saddlebags. She was by my side a moment later with Puvva's vessel, which was a teapot. However, it was too late. The elf had gone still.

"Do you think any of them survived?" Wren asked in a small voice. I knew she was thinking of Aki, the high elf who had helped us and might very well be Wren's grandfather.

"Many of the elves had magic, so there's a good chance," Kraster told her, then nodded to the elf on the ground. "He did say there were others ahead of him with horses."

"But if they were exposed–" Wren cut off, unable to say more. No one had any words to comfort her.

We departed a few minutes later. My shoulders were heavy with sorrow and the fatigue of the last twenty-four hours. The horses were weary too but still managed to keep plodding forward.

Just before nightfall, we made it to the edge of the forest. The land ahead was visible since the deadly mist ended at the treeline. It wasn't until we had completely cleared the woods that I was able to take a deep breath and release the tension that had pressed down on me since the day before.

I still waited until we'd put nearly a hundred yards between us and the forest before I unclenched my hand and returned The

Heart of Jong to my pouch. As soon as I did, the green aura faded from around us, and I suddenly felt very cold.

The evening was a blur as we unsaddled the horses and built a fire from the grass and scrub of the plain. As I was laying out my bedroll, I rested my head for a moment and fell asleep almost immediately.

However, my slumber was short-lived.

Chapter 2
The Survivors

"It's them! Get them!"

I awoke instantly as the cry shattered the silence. Hastily, I fumbled for my weapons while dark forms poured out of the shadows.

The fire was mostly dead, but a word from Kraster set it blazing again, revealing that the twenty figures surrounding us were high elves. Most were armed with bows or long knives. A few others held their hands at the ready, unspoken incantations on their lips.

"Keep back!" Kraster bellowed, making the flames flare up in a blinding flash.

"What do you want from us?" Wren asked. Her voice was filled with confusion and terror.

"Our leaders wish to speak with you," replied one of the high elves, a female with waist-length, blonde hair.

"I think not," I spat, turning in her direction. "We have nothing to say to your leaders."

"You must answer for the disaster you have brought upon us," called a voice from the other side of the fire.

"You have caused the deaths of thousands of our people!" cried another.

"We did not!" Wren protested.

"Actually, we tried to warn your leaders," I couldn't help adding.

"I think we might have to go with them," Kraster whispered to me. "They have at least three casters, and their bows are faster than your swords."

I hesitated. I didn't think I'd ever backed down from a fight of any kind before, not counting one instance of twisted magic and terror. However, I was so tired and still felt strangely cold. Despite

9

that, if the high elves were determined to engage us, I wasn't going down easily.

"We will meet with your leaders if you guarantee safe passage back here after," I offered.

"Not a chance," the blonde female snarled at me. "The council means to pass judgment on you."

"Then if our options are to die now or to die later, we will choose now," I warned. "You might be able to defeat us, but not all of you will survive. How will your families deal with losing more members this night?"

There was a moment of silence.

"We haven't done anything wrong!" Wren exclaimed.

"If that is found to be true, then the council will let you go," the blonde vowed.

"We will agree to those terms," Kraster told her.

I shot him a furious glare. I did *not* agree to those terms.

Kraster met my gaze and shook his head ever so slightly. It never ceased to amaze me how he could remain level-headed in nearly every situation. Admittedly, it had saved my life on more than one occasion.

Slowly, I sheathed my swords, half expecting to be asked to give them up. Fortunately, the high elves seemed to understand how useless that request would be.

Kraster and Wren left their horses behind, but I put Tempest into my shadow, making the elves shudder. The experience was hard to describe. To observers, it appeared that Tempest vanished into darkness. But even after he'd faded from sight, I could still sense him. Gnombie said that was normal, but it unnerved me a little.

As I thought about the gnome, I suddenly realized he was nowhere to be found. He must have scampered off when he heard the elves coming. Maybe he was making his escape, or maybe he was planning to rescue us. I had no idea what to expect from him.

We walked for nearly half an hour before the lights of the high elf camp came into view. They had built makeshift shelters of the bushes and plants growing on the plain. While I'm sure the whole process had been rushed, there was still a refined grace to the structures. It was to be expected; high elves could bring elegance to any circumstance.

Even though there were still several hours until sunrise, we found the camp wide awake. Hundreds of infected elves lay on the ground and were being tended.

As we passed one who was coughing up red blood, I put my hand in my pouch and gripped The Heart of Jong tightly. The familiar warm feeling returned, and I could almost make out a shimmering green aura in the air. The elf stopped mid-cough. Slowly, he sat up and took a few deep breaths. Our escorts noticed and gave each other confused looks.

The elders, most of whom I recognized from our last meeting under The Tree of Karradin, stood in a half circle near the edge of the camp. Elhanan was in the center of the others.

Of course, I thought bitterly. *I could have done without seeing his sneering face ever again.*

Beside me, Wren craned her neck, looking at each elf in turn. I felt her shoulders slump when she realized Aki wasn't with them. More than half the council was missing, so it wasn't a surprise. However, it would have been nice to have an ally among so many hostile faces.

"We found the strangers of whom you spoke," the blonde female elf told Elhanan, giving him a small bow.

He turned on us with a look of utter disgust.

"You are alive for one reason and one reason only," Elhanan began. "You will tell us how to undo the curse you have brought to our land, or you will all die."

I raised my chin in defiance, but before I could say anything foolish, Kraster spoke up.

"We brought no curse upon your land. In fact, we ended one that you allowed to linger for hundreds of years. A curse that I believe you knew of and yet took no action to remedy, despite the suffering of many. If anything ill has befallen you, perhaps it is the judgment you deserve."

11

I nodded at my brother. I couldn't have said it any better myself. Actually, I could pretty much guarantee it would have come out way worse. Plus, there would have been more insults and name-calling.

Elhanan curled his lip. "If the curse is not of your making, how have you survived it?"

"I think you know that," Kraster replied.

There were several murmurs from the gathered elders giving me the impression that most of them knew what my brother was talking about.

"If you have the stone, then hand it over," Elhanan demanded.

"Not a chance," I told him. "You knew where it was and could have gone and gotten it long ago."

"We can always take it off your corpses," Elhanan threatened.

My hand went to my knife, and, unlike at our last meeting, there was no chair behind him where I could aim my blade.

"Why are you doing this?" Wren asked from behind me. Her soft, tearful words were met with complete silence. The raw sorrow in her voice stilled me before I could finish drawing the blade.

"Your people are suffering and without a home," she went on. "Why are you trying to make enemies of those who would aid you? We were sent by dragons, and you refused to hear us. We offered you news of possible danger, and you spurned us. Now, we have completed our mission on our own, and you seek to stand in our way. After all we have come through, must we come through you as well?

"So much is wrong in the world right now. All we want is to fix it. If that is also your desire, should you not be helping us?

"Everything looks dark this day, but I have walked in dreams of a darker future yet to come, one without the light of a single star. If our quest fails, that is the future I fear will follow."

Wren's powerful words and tears didn't seem to have much effect on Elhanan, but it did on those around him. The mage, who had impaled my leg with a shard of ice at our first disastrous meeting with the council, covered her face with her hand to conceal tears. One of the younger males turned and walked slowly out of sight. Several others sank to the ground, overwhelmed. A few spoke out loudly, their elvish words so quick even I didn't catch much of it. They seemed to be arguing with Elhanan, who was glaring daggers at us all the while.

"The council has spoken," Elhanan spat at last in the common tongue. "You are free to go."

He turned and stalked away.

Before the rest of the council could break up, Wren approached the nearest high elf and started making inquiries about Aki.

"He took a scouting party farther east to look for more survivors," the elf answered.

I felt relief fill my heart. Maybe someday, when all of this was over, Wren might have a chance to get to know her grandfather.

Wren began to press the elf with more questions as Kraster approached me.

"Let's get back to camp," he said softly.

"Go ahead. I'll be there in a minute," I told him.

It was longer than a minute, nearly two hours in reality, before I joined him. When I did, I was drooping with weariness. I had walked the entirety of the high elf camp, The Heart of Jong clutched in my palm as life radiated from it.

Some were beyond saving, like the young elf we'd found in the woods, but if I helped even just one survive, then I felt it was worth it.

Wren and Kraster were talking when I reached our campsite mounted on Tempest. Without the horse, I don't think I would have made it back.

"She said the cloud was small and moved slowly at first. That was how they were able to outdistance it and escape, but many of those infected died as they fled," Wren was telling my brother. "They don't know about the outer villages, but thousands are dead. Nothing like this has ever happened before.

"The fact that it started with The Tree of Karradin is what bothers them the most. It was the oldest tree in the forest, planted by Karradin the Wise hundreds of years ago, before the dragon went missing."

I didn't speak to them, my tongue too heavy to form words. Instead, I dropped onto my bedroll. Idly, I considered Wren's words.

What would it take for a great dragon to go missing? My thoughts didn't make it very far.

When I woke, it seemed to be midday. The sun was choked by thick cloud cover, and the air was downright chilly. Someone, probably Kraster, had draped a blanket over me during the night.

Slowly, I sat up and glanced to the east, where the high elf camp stood.

"They're gone," Kraster said. He was sitting on a log next to the remains of last night's fire. I could see Wren a dozen yards away, brushing Valor while he grazed beside Raspberry.

"All of them?" I asked.

Kraster nodded. "Wren went at first light to see if Aki had returned. She found their camp deserted."

"And they didn't invite us to come along?" I gasped in mock surprise.

"I don't think we were their type," he replied.

I sighed. Normally, this was the kind of thing that made my blood boil, but I was far too tired to waste the energy. Wren had been warned against using The Scrying Stone too much, lest it cause her harm. It seemed I would also have to be careful, since I felt completely drained from wielding The Heart of Jong for so many hours.

"Wren was pretty disappointed," Kraster told me.

"Aki will find her again," I said confidently.

If anyone survives this, I added mentally, because if I had ever imagined what the end of the world would look like, this was it.

14

"Where's Gnombie?" I asked suddenly.

For a moment, a shadow passed over my brother's face, then it cleared. "He hid when he heard the elves last night and followed us without giving himself away in case we needed help."

I nodded slowly and glanced around. Wren was still with the horses, but the gnome was nowhere to be seen.

"And now?" I arched an eyebrow at Kraster.

"He went to see if the elves left anything useful behind," my brother answered.

"He certainly does like to wander off," I observed.

"I think Gnombie's used to working alone," Kraster chuckled.

"And what kind of work was he doing, do you think?" I wondered.

"Who knows?" Kraster replied lightly. "I'm just happy we have him along. You never know when an arrow from the dark might save one of our lives."

Clearly, my brother trusted the gnome more than I did.

We stayed put the remainder of the day. Despite the urgency of our quest, the horses were still recovering. Wren spent much of the afternoon caring for them and even treated Valor and Raspberry with a few of the apricots still in her pack.

Gnombie returned just before dark. He hadn't managed to scavenge anything, which wasn't a surprise since the elves had escaped with nothing but the clothes on their backs.

I took the first watch, but had to wake Kraster early because my eyes were so heavy I couldn't keep them open.

Kraster didn't say anything, but he gave me a worried look as I lay down, hoping that the weariness would be gone for good in the morning.

Chapter 3
The Plan

I woke with the dawn, feeling refreshed. Raspberry and Valor also seemed to have benefited greatly from having a whole day's rest. The sky was clear, and the sun was warm, although not nearly as warm as I remembered it from past years. Three of the last five summers had been unusually cold, and I dreaded the thought of having another. Cold summers led to bitter winters with more snow and less food.

We set off to the north, heading directly for Kempt to begin our search for the stone called Baarthagon's Collar. On our journey south, we'd been coming from the eastern edge of Planosia. This time, we would miss the valley and travel along the western side of the mountains of the dwarves.

The land here was barren compared to that inside the valley. The scraggly grass was short and more brown than green. There were no trees and no animals. When night came, we struggled to find anything to burn and soon gave up the idea of a fire.

Wren poked me at dawn. I looked at her groggily. Something in her expression made me sit up instantly. I glanced around, glad to see Kraster and Gnombie were still asleep.

"What did you dream?" I asked softly, pulling her down beside me.

"There was an island," she started, seeming confused. "It wasn't in water, but floating, in the sky."

"The Isle of Tranquility," I whispered.

"What is that?" Wren asked in bewilderment.

"It's just a legend, or so I thought," I told her. "The people of The Coral City claim that, on the very clearest of days, if you look to the sea, you can make out the shape of an island floating above the horizon."

Wren gaped at me.

"Occasionally, they also find the bodies of strange creatures washed up on their shores," I continued. "Large beasts with feathered wings."

Wren nodded slowly, brow furrowed.

"Now, what did you see?" I pressed.

"Pretty much everything you described," Wren replied. "Except, there was something dark in the water under the island."

"The monster from your other dreams?" I asked

"No," Wren shook her head. "It wasn't a monster. It was a tendril of darkness. It reached up out of the depths and latched onto the rocky bottom of the island, spreading out like the roots of a tree."

"Then what?" I wondered.

"That's all I saw," Wren answered. "But it made me feel cold inside. The darkness kept spreading and digging into the isle."

"Well, our journey might take us that way after Kempt," I said. "Maybe we can help them."

"Help them?" Wren laughed bitterly. "Everywhere we go, tragedy follows."

There was a moment of silence between us before she continued. "We told Elhanan that we didn't bring disaster to his people, but what if we did?

"Look what's happened to Gnomania, The Hall of Asteropaios, and now the forest of the high elves. I can't shake the feeling that destruction is following us everywhere we go."

A lump suddenly formed in my throat. "If you are right, then it started with your village, Thea," I said softly.

Wren blinked, and her eyes widened.

"Maybe it's not following you but Kraster and me. Maybe– maybe you should go on without us," I suggested.

"No!" Wren nearly shouted. "Don't leave me! I can't do this alone. I would never have made it this far without you and Kraster."

I reached out and gripped her shoulder tightly. She looked at me as I stared intently into her eyes.

"Wren, Shal'eth chose you. At some point, you might have to leave us behind. If that day comes, don't look back, just do what you need to do. We aren't the important ones, you are."

I held her gaze for a moment longer, then let my hand slide from her shoulder. We spoke no more and woke the others a short time later.

While we were saddling the horses, the wind picked up sharply. Conversation was all but impossible, leaving us to ride in silence for hour after hour.

The horses' manes and tails were hopelessly tangled by the time we stopped for the night. Wren spent thirty minutes working on Valor, attempting to pick all the knots out, but soon gave up. There was no chance of keeping a fire going in such a gale, so we huddled in our cloaks and tried to get some sleep.

The intense wind went on for the next few days, making them the most miserable of the trip, except, maybe, when we'd ridden through a thunderstorm on the plateau. No one was in a good mood. We didn't so much talk as growl at each other.

At last, we reached the Tarllen River. It ran almost parallel to our path, wide and fast-moving. The banks on both sides were steep, and I doubted the horses would ever be able to climb out if they fell in.

"Is there a better place to cross further ahead?" Gnombie asked, as though he was reading my mind.

"I'm not sure," Kraster admitted. "I've never been this far south of the human territories."

"Well, we obviously can't cross here," I said, feeling greatly relieved. Even if I wasn't the kind of person who had nearly drowned in a puddle more than once, I would never have thought trying to swim this section of the river was a good idea.

"Then we should keep going until we find a safer spot," Wren suggested.

Her solution was the best we had.

"We do need to be careful how far north we go following the river," I warned.

"Because of the Hawnkenquack?" Wren giggled.

I shot her a playful scowl.

"Because of goblins," Kraster explained. "It is well known that they have a stronghold in the foothills. They and the dwarves take turns raiding each other's towns."

"I wouldn't mind running into some goblins," I heard Gnombie mutter.

"What?" I asked, turning to him.

"I'm just saying, goblins aren't all that strong, and we could take them," Gnombie explained. "Plus, they smell bad."

I laughed.

"I had no idea you disliked goblins," Wren said.

"I mean, does anyone really *like* goblins?" Gnombie asked.

"He's got a point," Kraster grinned.

I laughed again. The gnome was often so quiet I couldn't even fathom a guess at what he was thinking. This might be the first time he'd spoken without it being totally necessary. It made me feel a little warmer toward him, like he was finally letting his barriers down slightly.

For the next few days, we followed the river. The farther we went, the less confident I was that we would be able to cross before reaching goblin country. Our time traveling was spent debating possible solutions but to no avail.

Kraster mentioned using the same spell that had gotten him, Raspberry, and me out of a pit when we were attacked by harpies, but he wasn't sure he could keep it powered long enough. The idea of the magic giving out above the raging water was terrifying.

Gnombie thought that if we could get one person across with a rope tethered to them, they could tie it to a tree and somehow use that to transport the horses over. Either he didn't describe it well, or his gnomish brain was much more developed than mine, but I never fully understood the logistics of what he was saying.

At last, we reached a small forest, which was a relief. We were able to have fires and hot food again. I brought down a deer the first night, and we enjoyed fresh meat instead of our stale rations, which were nearly gone. The horses also found the grass more plentiful and grazed late into the evening.

The next afternoon, I spotted the smoke of a campfire ahead. We left the horses and went to investigate. Before long, I could hear the harsh prattle of high-pitched voices.

"Goblins," Gnombie hissed from beside me.

"Lovely," I muttered, turning back to Kraster. "They are loud enough to wake the dead. I think we should be able to slip by unnoticed."

He nodded. "If we stay close to the gorge, the noise from the river will cover the sound of the horses' hooves."

Both of us started to back away, Wren following.

"Where's Gnombie?" she whispered.

"He was right here," I replied, glancing to my left.

The gnome had vanished.

"He's probably moved into an attack position," Kraster sighed.

"But why?" Wren asked.

"He did seem keen on fighting some goblins," I reminded them. "I'm starting to think it's personal."

"What do we do?" asked Wren.

"We go and get him," I told her.

Once more, we crept forward as quietly as possible. I saw the goblins before I saw Gnombie. There were three of them, all on the smaller side. One sat by the fire, roasting some sort of meat on a spit. Close by, the others were pawing through several piles of clothing on the ground. I couldn't understand their speech, but every once in a while, one of them would hold up a piece of jewelry or other trinket with a gleeful cry.

Before I quite understood what was going on, two more goblins arrived, dragging a bloody bundle of clothing. Those in the clearing leapt forward and began ripping the cloth away to search through the belongings within.

Murderers and thieves, I thought grimly. *The world would be better off without them.*

Before I could draw my sword and charge, which was something I was strongly considering, an arrow struck one of the original three goblins in the throat. It went down, gurgling in surprise as it died.

The others sprang to life, two of them racing toward the location the arrow had come from. The remaining pair stood back to back, weapons drawn.

Without hesitation, I sprinted into the clearing. I'm sure Kraster was rolling his eyes behind me, but it didn't matter. These were goblins and shouldn't pose much of a threat.

Being short, with stubby arms, the goblins had no way to deflect my first two blows. One I killed, and the other I left wounded. A bolt of fire from the undergrowth behind me finished him off. Without waiting for Kraster to catch up, I chased after the second pair.

I found them in a small clearing with Gnombie. One was dead, an arrow in his eye socket. The other was grappling with the gnome on the ground. I'd never seen such an expression of intense hatred on Gnombie's face. He appeared to have the upper hand, and I felt that he would not thank me for interfering.

A moment later, Gnombie slipped the blade of his knife between the goblin's ribs. The creature let out a squeal, then went limp. Gnombie shoved the body aside and sat up.

"You all right?" I asked.

He looked up at me, hostility still hot in his eyes. Slowly, the anger faded.

"I'm fine," he answered, getting to his feet and cleaning his knife.

"What did they do to you?" I asked.

"Nothing," he replied without meeting my gaze.

I waited to see if he would go on. It took a moment, but he eventually did. "These goblins didn't do anything to me, and the ones who did haven't drawn breath for a long time."

Again, I was silent, but this time, the gnome said no more.

We rejoined Wren and Kraster a little while later. They had gathered the most valuable of the trinkets.

"What should we do with them?" Wren asked.

"Sell them," Kraster replied. "We'll have to purchase more supplies when we get to Kempt."

"But that's stealing!" Wren objected.

"The only other option we have is to leave them here," I pointed out to her. "We don't have any idea who this stuff belongs to. There are no human cities nearby, and dwarves make it a point to conceal the entrances to their tunnels."

Wren looked away but didn't argue as we gathered the valuables.

I turned to Kraster. "We need to get to the other side of the river sooner rather than later," I told him. "These goblins weren't much of a problem, but there were only five of them."

My brother nodded. Both of us had fought against goblins a few times when they'd tried to raid the southern part of Kempt's territory. Their strength wasn't in skill, training, or superior weapons but in numbers.

"We'll figure something out," he promised. "For now, we should keep moving."

After our encounter with the goblins, we traveled more carefully, keeping an eye out for other camps or signs of an ambush. The trees grew right up to the gorge's edge. I would have suggested cutting a few down to make a bridge, but the expanse was wide enough that I didn't even think three trees lying end to end would span the distance.

In the late afternoon on the next day, the forest began thinning out, and I saw that the cliffs on the far bank moved away from the river, leaving a strip of land about two hundred feet long. In this space, a fortress had been built. Inside its massive stone walls there was an earthen ramp leading up to the top of the gorge.

The fortress was of dwarven make. However, I could see several goblins patrolling its grounds. The wall that ran along the river had been partially knocked down. Rubble still littered the area where it once stood, making me think the damage was recent.

"Well, isn't this interesting?" Kraster said, bringing Raspberry to a stop behind me.

"There are boats down there," Wren observed, pointing to where our side of the bank turned into a gentle slope leading to the water's edge.

As Wren had said, several boats were moored on both sides of the river. Clearly, this was a well-traveled crossing.

"Look there." Kraster gestured at two chain nets that spanned the broad river. The first one was placed at the start of the level ground and the second at the end of the fort. Getting a boat past them would be all but impossible, which I assumed was their purpose.

"I don't like this. It feels like a trap." I motioned to the far side of the water. "If we cross here, we'll have nowhere to go but through the fortress."

Even missing one wall, the structure blocked all access to the lands beyond.

"It's clever, really," Gnombie observed.

"A good way to hold the crossing for sure," Kraster added.

"Should we keep moving and look for another place to cross?" Wren asked.

"I vote yes," I announced.

"But it's only a few handfuls of goblins," my brother protested.

"We don't know that," I countered. "There could be over a hundred of them in there."

"We could probably take that many," Kraster insisted. "Especially if we went quickly and took them by surprise."

"I think it would be smarter to look for a better spot," I argued.

"If there was a better spot, why would anyone have built this fortress?" he countered. "Its very existence makes it pretty clear to me that there will be no other crossings anytime soon."

I scowled at him.

"Is this because you're scared of water?" Kraster asked gently.

"No!" I practically shouted. "It's because I don't think this is a good place to cross."

I could tell from the way he looked at me that he didn't believe me. The others seemed to feel the same way, and I wasn't even sure I believed myself. All I knew was that I didn't want to have anything to do with that water.

"There are boats," Kraster tried to persuade me. "Big boats. Solid boats. Safe boats."

"Not helping," I scoffed at his words.

My brother sighed.

"Maybe she's right," Wren put in. "We could go a little further and see–"

"There's no point," Kraster cut her off. "Like I said, if there was another place to cross, no one would have bothered building a fort here."

Our discussion went on for nearly an hour. Finally, I conceded and agreed that crossing here did make the most sense. With that debate settled, we started making our plan, which took another hour. At last, it was decided that just before dawn, we would slip down to the boats, take the biggest one, and cross the river under the cover of darkness.

With goblins being nocturnal, our hope was that most of them would be heading to bed at twilight. We would hide just outside the walls until the sun started to rise, then rush the gate.

From the large opening in the wall facing us, we could see most of the path leading up to a second gate at the end of the earthen ramp, which was where we would escape.

After that, there would be nothing between us and Kempt. Wren suggested we enter through the hole in the wall, but the shallows there were filled with jagged rocks, making the front gate seem like an easier path.

We argued over, talked through, and rehashed the execution of our plan a dozen times before everyone was satisfied. When I lay down to get some sleep, I even found myself walking through each step in my dreams.

Chapter 4

The Fortress

Gnombie had the last watch. He woke me just as I was dreaming about falling out of the boat for the sixteenth time. I jerked awake and staggered to my feet.

Looking at the dark liquid made my heart race. Wren gave me a sympathetic glance, and Kraster patted my arm. I glared at both of them in response.

While the others saddled their horses, I drew Tempest into my shadow. As quietly as possible, we crept down the slope to the riverside.

Using some form of his fire spell, Kraster melted through the chain securing the boat we'd selected. Together, he and I pushed it toward the water. I stopped just as I reached the muddy part of the bank.

"Better get in," my brother whispered to me.

I clambered over the side, already feeling nauseous even though the boat was still mostly on dry land. Wren followed a moment later leading Valor. I held him while she went back for Raspberry.

With both horses in the center, the boat was starting to feel very small.

Wren squinted as she looked up and down the river curiously. We still had at least an hour before dawn. The thinnest of crescent moons was our only light.

"This place seems familiar," she whispered.

"What do you mean?" I asked.

Wren shook her head slightly. "I know I haven't been here before, but it feels–" she cut off as the boat gave a sudden lurch.

If I'd eaten any breakfast, I was certain I would have immediately lost it. Wren and I each grabbed an oar and started paddling. Gnombie and Kraster pushed the vessel from behind, then leapt into the back as the boat moved out onto the river. We had already been sitting low in the water due to the horses, but now the wooden sides were less than a foot above the surface. I fought to keep my panic at bay and my breathing even.

Gnombie and Kraster took their places at the second set of oars. Wren counted quietly to help us find our rhythm. As we neared midstream, I felt like we were losing the battle and would be carried away down the river.

After struggling for at least ten minutes, we managed to escape the worst of the current. The other bank was less than a dozen yards away when a particularly unruly wave washed over the side of the boat and engulfed me. I could feel the dark water trying to pull me down. For a moment, I was slipping and in very real danger of falling into the river. Kraster grabbed my arm from behind, keeping me in place.

"Thanks," I gasped, shivering with cold from my wetting.

"Water really does have something against you," he said in amusement.

I glowered at my brother. It was lovely that he found that fact so humorous. It wasn't like I had almost just died or anything.

Despite the near mishap, we reached the opposite shore quickly. I was the first to jump from the prow onto dry land. Hurriedly, I put several feet between myself and the water. The others quickly unloaded the horses and secured the boat.

I'd almost forgotten about the sentries. Thankfully, no cry was raised as we slipped through the darkness in front of the fortress's portcullis. A fire burned inside the gatehouse, but I didn't see a single goblin. Apparently, they weren't expecting an attack.

We took shelter in the shadowy cleft where the turn of one wall met the stony side of the cliff. Our plan was to wait there for dawn and hope none of the goblins on the ramparts looked over the side. The section of the wall that we were visible from was small, but there was always a chance we might be spotted.

Kraster and Gnombie dozed. I was still damp, and the crisp air left me shivering, so I pressed against Raspberry's flank for warmth. Wren tried to rest, but after twenty minutes, she gave up and came to my side.

"Don't forget to stay in the back with the horses," I couldn't help reminding her softly. We'd been over the plan a million times, but my nerves were getting to me.

"I will," she vowed. "Unless something goes wrong."

I nodded, not even daring to ask what could go wrong when four people, only two of whom had any military training, decided to assault a fortress with an unknown number of goblins who were probably all armed to the teeth.

At last, the sun rose, and I nudged the boys awake. The main gate was around the corner, back the way we had come. I felt exposed as we left the relative safety of the small cleft.

We rounded the corner quickly, reaching the gatehouse a moment later. With one word from Kraster, the wooden shutter over the window caught fire and burned to ash. The opening left behind was so small only a young child would fit through. A young child, or a gnome.

I took hold of Gnombie's arm and helped him swing inside the opening. There was a tense moment, then we heard a high-pitched shriek. The silence that followed was unnerving.

A sudden rumble came from the portcullis as it started rising into the air. On the other side was a pair of enormous, iron doors. These swung open with a loud creak, revealing Gnombie operating the levers.

"Nice work," Kraster congratulated the gnome.

Gnombie nodded, but glanced over his shoulder with a scowl. "I fear our presence is known," he said.

"Couldn't be helped," I told him.

Leaving Wren to bring up the rear with the horses, Kraster and I stole forward, followed closely by Gnombie.

Instead of swords, I held several of the gnomish knives I'd acquired on the plateau. They were the perfect size and weight for throwing.

Beyond the doors, there was an enclosed stone hallway, which led into the fortress. It was long and resembled a tunnel more than anything else. The sides were full of arrow slits. They seemed to be unmanned as not a single shot was fired at us.

It was a different story when we reached the far end. I took a careful step out of the hallway, then pulled back immediately as a volley of shafts rained down on the place I'd been a second before.

"Drat," growled Kraster. "Seems more of them are awake than we'd hoped."

"I can draw their fire," I told him, summoning Tempest.

He nodded, and I leapt on the horse before he was even completely formed. Urging the beast forward, we broke out of the tunnel and raced into the sunlight.

The layout of the fortress was strategic, almost maze-like, making it hard for an invading force to gain the upper hand. We'd been able to see a good deal of the interior from across the river, but this corner had been obscured.

As soon as I left the hallway, I immediately had to make a sharp left as there was a wall in front of me and a dead end less than a hundred feet to my right. On top of the walls surrounding the dead end were dozens of goblins. Unfortunately, they were high enough above my head that my knives would not reach them.

Shrill cries came from the archers as Tempest and I raced up the slope of a small hill. We didn't slow until we'd nearly reached the far side of the fortress. From there, I could easily see the path leading to the second door, which we planned to escape through.

First, we'd have to weave around a few other walls and buildings, but the way was unobstructed. There were several goblins on the walls above the fort's second gate, but I didn't think they would be much of a problem. It was the ones currently pinning my friends down that were the greater setback.

With our escape route confirmed, I turned Tempest, and we galloped back the way we had come. I hoped my antics would be enough of a distraction that the others would be able to slip out of the tunnel and get up the hill. Then we would just need to reach the far gate, get it open, and we'd be free!

An arrow clipped my armor, stinging but not sticking. As I looked up at the goblins, several broke away, fleeing from their posts on the wall and out of sight.

Even still, I saw that we were grievously outnumbered, and I doubted all of us would be able to avoid the barrage of arrows once we were in the open.

Kraster must have realized the same thing. He poked his head out of the tunnel. After sizing up the enemy, he bolted for a narrow staircase carved into the stone wall.

"No, Kraster!" I called, still two dozen yards away. "Stick to the plan!"

As he so often did, my brother ignored me and began throwing fire at the goblins on the walls as he climbed. They rained down arrows in retaliation, but had a hard time shooting straight while dodging the flames.

A few goblins had assembled on the ground and were heading for the hallway. I drew my sword and angled my horse in their direction. A few flicks of my wrist, and the foes were dealt with. I pulled Tempest to a stop just in front of the tunnel opening. Hurriedly, I motioned to Gnombie, who scurried over. I leaned down and attempted to haul the gnome into the saddle behind me.

Suddenly, an arrow struck Tempest. The horse reared, becoming nearly vertical as he kicked out with his front legs. I struggled to remain in the saddle while holding onto Gnombie's arm. My grip began to slip. The gnome's did too, and he fell to the ground. Without warning, Tempest dropped back to all fours and bolted, heading straight for the dead end.

The beast was too strong for me to stop. I feared we were going to slam headfirst into the stone wall. Somehow, the animal managed to turn at the last second. It happened very quickly, but I think Tempest might have taken several steps on the walls themselves as we spun all the way around, shooting off in the opposite direction without losing an ounce of speed.

I clung to the horse's mane for dear life as we pelted away from my companions once more. A few times, I felt my grip slipping, but years of riding helped me find my balance and keep my seat. I'd never experienced such speed or strength from any horse. No matter what I did, I couldn't get the animal to stop. At least, not until I leaned down and managed to pull the arrow from where it was embedded in his shoulder.

Instantly, Tempest slid to a halt. He wasn't breathing hard, as a normal horse would be, but he felt incredibly tense. Checking his side, I saw the place where the arrow had pierced his flesh. No blood came from the wound. I had no idea what that meant.

Looking back, I checked to see how the others were faring. Kraster had finished ascending the stairs and was ducking in and out of the turret where two walls met. He was wielding a lot of fire. The goblins had gotten into formation; half were holding up shields while the others shot arrows. Still, he was depleting their numbers at a rapid rate.

Gnombie didn't appear any worse for wear after his tumble, just a little muddy. He was across from the hallway entrance, crouched behind a water barrel, picking off the goblins on the wall above him one by one with his bow. Wren was still in the hallway with Valor and Raspberry, hovering a few feet from the opening.

I was about to head back toward them when I saw movement out of the corner of my eye. It was the group of goblins who had left the wall. They approached the river on the fortress's open side with almost fearful movements.

One was pushed to the front of the group. He hesitated and was given a shove by a larger goblin who was better dressed than the rest, but that wasn't saying much.

The hapless creature stumbled, but regained his balance, shooting a hateful look over his shoulder. The brute that had pushed him pointed to a large pot with a blunt sword resting against it. Carefully, the small goblin inched forward and took hold of the items, then started striking the sword against the bottom of the pot. It created a reverberating note that made my ears ring.

The rest of the goblins were equally twitchy as they went to a large, wooden wheel. An extremely thick chain was partially wrapped around it. The other end ran to the river and disappeared beneath the water.

Even working together, the group struggled to turn the wheel. At last, it began to move, winding up the chain.

For a moment, nothing happened. The small goblin continued to beat on the pot as the chain was pulled in, link by link. Suddenly, something moved under the surface of the water. My mouth dropped open as the first monstrous head appeared.

Chapter 5
The Horror

The head wasn't as large as a dragon's, but I felt certain the gaping maw could have swallowed me in two bites if it was so inclined. Before I could react, the first head was followed by a second, then a third, a fourth, and a fifth. The body that emerged from the water was clumsy and off-balance from the heads turning rapidly in different directions on their stalk-like necks. One webbed foot bore an iron ring. The end of the chain was attached to it.

When the monster was within two dozen feet of the wheel, the goblins fled, escaping into the nearest building. I hoped that the scaly beast, who seemed none too pleased to find itself on dry land, would return to the river.

Unfortunately, it did not.

Instead, it began to root around with four of its heads while the fifth, the one in the middle, kept a lookout. The heads on the ground found nothing of interest among the crumbled remains of the broken wall, which only made the creature more agitated. I had a feeling it was used to being fed when it was called forth from its watery lair.

The middle head turned toward me. I unfroze, putting my heels into Tempest's sides. The horse leapt forward. Arrows were of no concern to me now. Not when a hungry, fully grown hydra had suddenly stepped into the picture.

I reached the cover of the hallway a moment later.

"You need to run for the other door!" I ordered Wren.

"But–" she started.

"Now!" I yelled. "Don't wait, just go. I'll get the others."

Tempest and I were out of the tunnel before the echoes of my cries had even died away.

"Kraster!" I screamed. "We need to go!"

"I'm a little busy!" he called back, dodging away from the turret's entrance as several goblins fired their bows at him.

I was forced to spur Tempest in a circle to avoid several arrows myself, since my cries had drawn the attention of the archers.

"Gnombie," I hollered, looking to where the gnome crouched in his hiding spot. "Go with Wren!"

Almost faster than my eye could follow, the gnome darted across the open space and into the hallway where Wren still lingered. Somehow, he must have convinced her, because as Tempest and I circled closer to the goblin-covered wall, they made their move. Wren was riding Valor while Gnombie followed on Raspberry, the gnome comically small on the enormous warhorse.

"Kraster! Get down here now!" I bellowed, turning back to my brother.

He looked as if he was about to obey, when, suddenly, every archer on the wall turned their weapons in my direction. As though reading the panic in my thoughts, Tempest bolted away, following after Wren and Gnombie.

As they crested the top of the rise, Wren let out a scream. I reached them a moment later and saw that the hydra was slowly lumbering in our direction. Soon, it would block our escape.

"It's— it's the monster from my dream—" Wren stuttered.

"Head for the upper gate," I ordered. "Find a way to get it open, if you can. I'm going back for Kraster."

Wren didn't move. Her gaze locked on the hydra.

"Gnombie! Go!" I commanded.

The gnome leapt into action, directing Raspberry forward.

I turned, pushing Tempest into a run as we raced back for my brother. He was still pinned down, and I thought I saw an arrow protruding from his leg. I wondered if I would be able to get Tempest to climb the stairs to the parapet of the wall. It wasn't something I would try with a normal horse, but Tempest was far from normal. I pointed him at the steps, but he skidded to a stop and refused. I jumped from the animal's back, pulling him into my shadow with little more than a thought as I began my headlong rush to the top of the wall.

I was halfway there when the goblins scattered and fell back. I turned, knowing what I would find.

The hydra had come into view, cutting Kraster and me off from the rest of the fortress. Since it had followed me, I hoped that meant Wren and Gnombie had made it to safety.

I glanced up at Kraster; his jaw was hanging open.

"Why didn't you tell me there was a hydra?" my brother yelled angrily.

"I tried!" I retorted.

"You did not!" he replied. "You said to 'come down' and 'we needed to go'. You *definitely* did not mention a hydra!"

I rolled my eyes.

"Well, there's a freaking hydra!" I yelled at him.

"Thanks," he muttered.

I studied the landscape for a moment, trying to figure out a way to get around the creature. The wall with the gate in it would take us far too close to the five heads, all of which would easily be able to pick us right off the top. The other path, the one the goblins had taken, seemed like our best bet. I began to climb again, but stopped as I saw the goblins forming ranks. There were three times as many of them as before, but I was still ready to take my chances with the entire horde rather than fight the hydra.

Suddenly, the goblins scrambled back, leaving something that looked like a small bonfire burning in the middle of the wall. A second later, an explosion shook the entire fortress. I hugged the stones on my right to keep from toppling down the stairs. When I looked up, I saw the section of the wall between the goblins and Kraster had been destroyed, eliminating our path of retreat.

The hydra was less than fifty feet away. The explosion seemed to have only made it more eager as it stalked toward us, every inch bringing death closer.

My brain worked double time. We could try to jump down from the wall on the outside of the fortress, but it was frightfully high, and I remembered jagged stones at the bottom.

Tempest was fast. Even burdened with two people, he could get us past the hydra in a few seconds. However, there were too many heads to be sure of dodging them all.

If only I could fight them one at a time, I thought. Then I realized, I could.

"Cover me!" I called to my brother, turning and racing back down the stairs.

"Wait! Candra! Come back!" Kraster called after me, but I didn't stop.

Instead, when I reached the bottom of the steps, I lunged into the hallway leading out of the fortress just as two sets of teeth snapped shut behind me.

Thankfully, the walls of the tunnel were only wide enough for one head to push inside at a time. The pair that had almost caught me had a brief struggle as they both tried to follow me through the opening. Finally, the one on the left gave up and withdrew, leaving me to face a single foe.

I was ready.

With a wild swing, I brought my swords down on the head. The brute gave a snarl of pain and jerked away as both blades found purchase. I stumbled forward a few feet, then had to dodge as the head came surging back. It might have caught me, but I saw a ball of fire strike the creature's body, halting the advancing head. Before it could retreat, I stabbed it just behind the jaw, aiming for a place where there was a gap in the scales.

The head went rigid, then dropped to the ground and began flopping. I hacked at it again as the creature pulled back, dragging the wounded head with it and leaving behind a flood of thick, steaming blood.

I watched in awe as the hydra reached up with one of its own legs and finished the process of severing the dying head.

"Burn it!" I shrieked. My throat was raw from all the yelling I'd been doing. I didn't think Kraster had heard, until a blast of fire hit the stump, which was starting to bubble in a disquieting manner.

I heaved a sigh of relief; however, it was short-lived. As the hydra took a step toward where Kraster stood on the wall, I raced from my cover and slashed at the scaly body.

"Down here!" I called. "Come and get me."

The tactic worked, on two of the heads at least. They turned in my direction, and I held up my swords in challenge before darting back into my shelter once more.

Before I was quite ready, another head was snapping at my heels. I lashed out behind me, my blades raking over the beast's teeth. I stopped and leapt to the right, twisting in the air and raising my swords. The hydra's head shot past me, and I brought both blades down on the back of the creature's exposed neck. They didn't go all the way through, but I instantly wrenched them free and struck twice more until the head fell to the stone floor.

The neck began to bubble, and I suddenly realized my mistake. I had nothing with which to burn the stump. Looking around quickly, I spotted an old lantern hanging on the wall a few feet away. I snatched it, feeling the oil swishing inside. I thumbed the lighter a few times, praying for a spark. On the fourth try, I got one. Without waiting to see if it would catch the wick, I hurled the lantern at the monster's gaping neck wound. The oil splashed everywhere. All was still for a moment, then the entire stump went up in flames.

I might have been engulfed in the fire myself if the creature hadn't reeled back. In its haste, it collided with the fortress wall behind it, shaking the stones around me and causing a few to break loose and clatter to the floor.

Two down, three to go, I thought, wondering for the first time if I might actually be able to kill the creature. I'd hoped another head would enter the tunnel, coming to seek vengeance, but a few spots of oil continued to burn close to the entrance, making a return doubtful. I was sure fire was pretty high on the creature's list of dislikes.

I skirted the flames and peeked out of my shelter. The hydra was still thrashing in pain. It struck the wall across from me again. A stone, twice the size of a horse, came free and plummeted earthward, landing on the hydra's back. The monster was knocked to the ground with the rock pinning it down.

Before it could struggle free, I charged for the nearest head. The beast began to writhe, attempting to shift out from under the stone's weight.

I timed my strike and lunged forward, raking my blades across both eyes. The hydra let out a deafening roar from all three of its remaining throats. At the same time, a violent spasm passed through its body.

The neck of the head I'd just blinded slammed into me. I was thrown back and hit a stone wall hard. My lungs felt like they wouldn't inflate, and the metallic taste of blood filled my mouth. I tried to stand, but found I couldn't. At least, not the first time. Several attempts later, I was on my feet, staggering back into the hallway to take shelter.

The earth behind me shook as the hydra finally managed to get out from under the rock. I glanced over my shoulder and saw the beast coming for me.

Forcing air into my lungs was still a struggle, as I tried to get my wobbly legs to move faster. The monster was right on top of me when the blind head collided with a wall to the right. It let out a shriek of frustration, and the beast stopped. The nearest of the remaining two heads attempted to guide the blinded one, but as it got close, the blind head struck, sinking its teeth into the second head. There was a moment of struggle, and then the bitten head was torn free.

The last undamaged head let out a wail of despair. Before it could do anything more, a fire bolt struck the fresh stump, and a set of reptilian eyes turned upward to the wall where Kraster stood. The beast's legs started moving in that direction, ignoring the blind head, which was bobbing about, mouth open, ready to attack anything that it could.

Instead of taking shelter, my brother stood his ground. He launched more fire, but the good head dodged, and the bad head got lucky. The beast was closer now, less than ten feet away.

37

Kraster tried to hit the creature with a wave of fire this time, but the Hydra ducked its heads below the wall.

"Kraster! Run!" I yelled, my lungs working again.

My feet were finally steady, and I darted forward, racing up the steps. Even as I ran, I knew I couldn't make it in time. The hydra would reach my brother long before I did.

"Get away from there!" I called to him, but he didn't listen. Instead, he summoned another ball of fire.

I made it to the top of the stairs and headed for where Kraster faced the monster. He was waiting for the beast to raise its head, but it never did. Instead, it rammed full-force into the wall.

I stumbled and dropped to my knees as the rampart beneath my feet shuddered. I looked to my left. Kraster had been standing directly above the impact point. The wall beneath him began to crumble.

"Kraster! No!" I screamed.

The fire in my brother's hand went out as the stones on which he stood broke apart. Before Kraster hit the ground, the hydra caught him in a pair of iron jaws.

I jumped then, throwing myself forward, knowing it wouldn't make any difference. I held my swords straight out in front of me as I pushed off the wall. The blades pierced the side of the hydra's head on the way down, opening two terrible gashes from its jaw to its chest as my weight drug the swords through the scaly flesh.

My landing was anything but graceful. Both of my legs gave out on impact, and I ended up sprawled in the pile of stones and debris at the hydra's feet. I looked up to see the monster's body lurch. Blood was pouring from its neck, and a strangled wheeze came from its throat.

Clumsily, I scrambled away from the massive feet as the hydra started to thrash, clawing wildly as it attempted to turn itself around in the narrow space of the dead end. At last, it succeeded, then lumbered unsteadily away. The blind head smacked into several walls as it went, wailing piteously the entire time. The other head bobbed and jerked unevenly as the creature departed the way it had come.

Battered and bruised, I managed to regain my feet.

"Kraster?" I said in a shaky voice.

There was silence.

"Kraster?" I called, voice breaking.

There was no answer.

It was too quiet. Recklessly, I began shifting through stones.

"Kraster!" I yelled. "Kraster! Where are you? You have to be all right!"

But how could he be after what I'd just seen? Tears filled my eyes, but I pushed them back. We'd been in worse scrapes. This wasn't the first time I'd had to look for him after the smoke cleared.

"Where are you, Kraster? Answer me!" I pleaded. Tears escaped my eyes and began to spill down my cheeks.

Desperately, I shoved more stones out of the way as I searched.

"Kras–" I cut off, both my words and my hands frozen, because I had found Kraster. At least, what was left of him.

Chapter 6

The Prisoner

My heart stopped.

Hardly even drawing breath, I stared at the mangled pile of flesh that had once been my brother.

He was gone.

I would never again see Kraster roll his eyes at my outrageous behavior. He wouldn't be there anymore to stand beside me in a fight or, more likely, pull me out of one. The times when we had laughed together and cried together were gone. There would be no more missions, no more days of travel, no more fighting. This was the end of it all, because the one person who had ever really loved me was dead.

As I blinked tears from my eyes, a hand fell on my shoulder. I turned to see Wren standing there. Her eyes were wet too.

"I'm so sorry, Candra," she whispered.

I looked back at Kraster, wishing this moment could last forever because it didn't feel real yet. Some part of my mind still expected him to pop up, laughing at me for falling for one of his magical illusions.

But the body remained where it was and never stirred.

"We need to get moving," I heard Gnombie whisper to Wren behind me.

"I don't know if she's ready," Wren replied softly.

I took a deep breath and wiped away my tears with the sleeve of my shirt, then stood and took a wobbly step forward.

"We need to get the stone," I mumbled, hating the idea of what I was about to do.

"I can–" Wren started to offer, but I didn't let her finish. Instead, I reached for the blood-soaked garment that used to be

Kraster's shirt. Half of it was missing, but I knew there was a secret pocket sewn into the hem.

While I searched, I tried not to look at the body. It was impossible not to see the damage the hydra's teeth had done. My brother was ripped open on the left side. His shoulder, arm, and pretty much everything above them was missing, most likely swallowed. I shuddered and tried not to think about it.

The secret pocket was torn with nothing inside, so I started looking for the pouch Kraster wore on his belt. Gnombie and Wren were beside me, searching as well.

A moment later, I located the pouch. Thankfully, it was mostly intact. Inside was Kraster's journal, his military credentials, his brass pocket watch, a silver-handled comb, a book of letters from his family, a few apricots, and, at the very bottom, the golden stone I was looking for.

"I think I found something," Gnombie announced, before I could tell the others of my discovery.

I turned in his direction, confused.

What lay on Gnombie's palm was a gray charm, carved with a purple rune.

"That's–" I started, but words failed me. It was the message charm Kraster had carried before this mission started. Our commanding officer, General Greyward, had an identical one, allowing them to communicate over long distances. I'd thought Kraster had thrown his away when we'd chosen to help Wren after Greyward attacked her people unprovoked.

Maybe he just kept it, but didn't use it, I hoped silently. *Or maybe he was trying to explain our situation, and Greyward was coming around.*

As much as I wished these thoughts to be the truth, a cold feeling filled my stomach. I reached out and took the charm. It felt heavy in my hand as I closed my eyes.

I'm glad to hear that you've found four of the stones. The goblins in the fort have orders to retreat at your approach. They will do you no harm, so that you may bring the stones to me.

I reeled back as though the charm had stung me.

In that moment, all of my sorrow turned to fury. My brother had betrayed me! He'd been working with Greyward this whole time and had lied to me about it.

Angrily, I shoved the charm into my pocket and turned, walking away up the hill.

"Wait!" Wren called, hurrying after me. "What about Dimble's Legacy?"

"The stone is in here," I told her, holding up the pouch before clipping it to my own belt.

"But don't we need to–" Wren started again.

I whirled on her. "Do what?" I asked. "Bury the body? It doesn't matter. Let the hydra come back and finish him."

"Candra?" Wren's voice was shocked and almost scared.

"It doesn't matter!" I repeated louder. "He's gone! So it doesn't matter!"

We stood there for a long moment looking at each other, then I turned away and started walking up the hill again.

"I need a drink," I said, surprised to realize how long it had been since I'd had one.

Since you even desired one, a voice whispered in the back of my mind.

I rounded the corner on the right, which led to the rest of the fort, and stopped dead in my tracks. Valor and Raspberry were tethered there, surrounded by the bodies of fallen goblins, Gnombie's arrows sticking out of several of them.

My brother's horse turned to look at me. Unconsciously, I walked to him. My hand touched the stallion's velvety nose, and a fresh wave of sorrow washed over me.

I turned to find Wren and Gnombie hovering nearby.

"Let's go," I told them, feeling much calmer. "Before more goblins show up."

"Oh, we took care of *all* of them," the gnome assured me, a sinister undercurrent in his voice.

I nodded slowly, then mounted Raspberry and pulled Gnombie up behind me. Wren got onto Valor, and we turned the horses toward the path that led to the second gate.

As we passed one of the buildings, I heard a thud come from within. It was followed by another.

"Guess you didn't get them all," I murmured, swinging down from Raspberry's back.

The doors were thick and made of solid wood. I nodded to Gnombie, who produced a lock pick. A moment later, there was a click, and the gnome stepped back.

I kicked the doors open much harder than was necessary, but it felt necessary to me. The building was a single room and had no windows. On the opposite wall, iron chains hung down from the ceiling. The air was sharp with the smell of unwashed bodies and moldy hay. There were no goblins inside, but there was a dwarf chained up in the back corner.

He staggered to his feet as we entered, blinking in the sudden light. As he moved, his chains hit the stones of the floor, producing the noise we'd heard.

"Who might you be?" the dwarf croaked. He didn't look too emaciated, but the bruises on his wrists showed that he'd been here for at least a few weeks. Naturally, he had a thick beard and a slightly receding hairline. Both were dark in color, as were his eyes.

"My name is of no importance," I said. "I'd rather know who you are."

While the creature was pretty pathetic in his current state, I'd learned to be careful. Not to mention the fact that dwarves didn't tend to feel kindly toward elves.

"I am Flame Keeper Ingol," the dwarf answered, his voice thick with the accent of his people. "Any chance you'd be willing to help me with these chains, lass?"

"I'll think about it," I replied, narrowing my eyes. "This is a dwarven fort. Were you stationed here when it fell to the goblins?"

Ingol shook his head. "Nay, I don't believe there were any survivors from that battle. This place is called Shgar Keep. My people don't even know that it is under goblin control.

"A little more than a fortnight ago, my company and I were ambushed by goblins, more of them than I'd ever seen before. We escaped and fled here, only to find the fort overrun. Myself and a few others were captured."

"Where are these others?" I asked.

The dwarf was silent.

"I see," I said, slightly more gently. "What about the hydra?" I spat the word.

"The what?" the dwarf asked.

"The hydra penned up in the river. Was that your people's doing?" I pressed.

"Definitely not," Ingol insisted. "We'd never keep such a creature."

"That's probably how the goblins took the fort," Gnombie commented. "I bet they used it to break down one of the walls so they could get in."

"Where were you traveling to?" I asked, quickly changing the subject.

"Do you suppose I might have a wee drink of water if you plan on interrogating me much longer?" the dwarf rasped.

Before I could respond, Wren stepped past me, holding her canteen out to Ingol.

I opened my mouth to object, but she shot me a reproachful glance.

"Please have some of mine," she told the dwarf. "And we certainly won't leave you here for dead."

"Thank you, lassie," Ingol said, giving her a small bow before taking her canteen and drinking deeply.

Gnombie moved forward and took out his lock pick again, then began working to free the dwarf of his chains.

"As I have said, I am A Flame Keeper, a position of utmost importance to my people," Ingol explained. There was a hint of pride in his words.

"It is I and my brethren who are tasked with guarding The King's Forge. We ensure that its embers never go out for The Fire

Drake himself built the forge and set it alight many centuries ago. Ever since, it has burned with pure dragon fire."

"If you're supposed to be guarding a forge, then how did you end up here?" I asked skeptically.

"My king has given me a special task. One I have failed." The dwarf's voice nearly broke, and he ceased speaking. Wren offered him more water, but he shook his head.

"Forgive me. I will start from the beginning," Ingol said. "As summer came upon the lands outside our mountains, a stranger arrived at The King's Forge, which stands at the gates of our capital, The Diamond City."

Wren, still standing beside Ingol, leaned forward eagerly. "Who was the stranger?"

"He said his name was Shal'eth, and I have never known a dragon to lie."

Wren and I gaped at him.

"You've seen The Great Shal'eth?" Wren breathed.

Ingol nodded as Gnombie released the first manacle from his wrist.

"Indeed. He told my brothers and me that time was short and asked for an audience with King Hallkell. Being the youngest, I was elected to act as escort. I took him deep into The Diamond City to the palace, where I presented Shal'eth to King Hallkell.

"They spoke for some time, though I was not privy to anything that was said. However, the king became very grave. He asked me to venture into the royal vault and bring him back a special item that he called the earth vessel. After completing the task, I was dismissed for a time.

"When I was recalled, Shal'eth was gone. Tales of war had reached us in The Diamond City, but not to the extent that Shal'eth had revealed to the king, who took me into his confidence.

"King Hallkell bid me choose a company from the city guard and travel to all the dwarven outposts in and around our mountains, spreading the word and raising the alarm. He also gave me the earth vessel, as Shal'eth had instructed him."

45

The last of Ingol's chains fell away with a clang. Gnombie stepped back as the dwarf began to rub his wrists.

"Alas, our journey was nearly completed when tragedy befell us," Ingol continued. "We were attacked on the road, and many of my companions were struck down. Those who remained fled here in hopes of sanctuary, only to find that the fort had fallen."

"Seems to be a common theme everywhere these days," I murmured.

Ingol turned to me. "Is your homeland besieged as well?"

"I have no homeland," I told him.

Ingol gave Wren a questioning look.

"We've been traveling for a while now," she explained. "Nearly every place is facing invasion."

"I see," Ingol said sadly.

"What is this vessel thing, exactly?" Gnombie wondered.

Ingol glanced at him but didn't answer the question.

"Is it a stone?" I asked eagerly.

The dwarf merely shook his head.

"We are also on a mission for Shal'eth," Wren told him.

"You know Shal'eth?" Ingol didn't seem to quite believe her.

"I was one of his shrine maidens for nearly all my life," Wren assured him.

"What exactly did he look like when you were– ummm– being a shrine maiden?" Ingol asked.

"He was always magnificent!" Wren's eyes glazed slightly. "It was an honor to be in his presence."

Ingol appeared to grow more skeptical as Wren prattled on.

"He's a human with an oversized dragon head," I cut in.

Ingol stared at me in surprise. "You *have* seen him!" he gasped.

"You should show more reverence when you speak of The Great Shal'eth," Wren chided me.

I rolled my eyes.

46

"So, if we are all friends of Shal'eth, can you tell me what your mission is?" the dwarf asked. "You mentioned stones?"

I folded my arms across my chest.

"Right, sorry," Ingol said.

"We've set you free," I told him. "I think that's enough. Come on, Wren, Gnombie."

I turned on my heel and started marching toward the door.

"Wait!" Wren called after me. "We can't leave him here all alone. More goblins could come along at any moment. Can't he come with us, at least, for a little while?"

"Not unless he tells us what the 'vessel' is," I countered, pausing to look back at the dwarf from the door.

"Since you require an act of trust, I will show you," the dwarf promised.

Chapter 7
The Hourglass

Ingol rose and walked to a large, wooden bin in the corner across from where he'd been restrained. Inside were several sets of dwarven armor. He removed one of them, which was silver in color and more ornate than the others. There was a matching staff with gilt ends.

I watched as the dwarf took out an empty pack, then continued to sort through the items. It was easy to see the grief on his face as he sifted through the possessions of his fallen comrades.

I raised an eyebrow as Ingol drew out an hourglass filled with a glowing, reddish sand. He set it down and sat cross-legged before it, placing one hand on either side. The dwarf murmured a few words, then raised his arms, only to bring his palms down hard on the dirt floor a second later. In one smooth movement, he seized the hourglass and turned it over.

Instead of running from the top to the bottom, the sand rose upward and became smoke as it escaped from the glass casing.

"Oh no, not this again," I groaned when the mist started forming into a creature. A moment later, there was a figure made of reddish stone standing in front of me. It was about the height of a dwarf, but even more hefty in build.

"I am Sif of the Sand," a deep voice sounded from the earth elemental. "What does Master wish?"

"That's amazing!" Wren squealed in delight. Before I could think to stop her, she'd pulled out her teapot and summoned Puvva. Two bangle bracelets appeared on Wren's arm as pale green smoke poured from the spout of the teapot.

"I am Puvva of the—" the genie cut off sharply. "What—what is he doing here?" she demanded, glaring at Sif.

"You two know each other?" Wren gasped.

48

"Of course we do," Sif said. "But it has been a long time." He dipped his head respectfully.

"How long?" Ingol asked. His eyes were full of wonder as he took in Puvva.

"Many hundreds of years," Puvva replied.

"Is yours a genie too?" I asked Ingol.

"I suppose," Ingol answered. "He did tell me he could grant wishes to his master, who he says is me, but I'm not sure how that happened…"

"Did you not explain the contract to him?" Puvva asked Sif.

"I did," Sif replied.

"Thoroughly?" Puvva pressed.

"More or less," Sif hedged.

"It is genies like you that give the rest of us a bad name," Puvva retorted through gritted teeth.

"How many more of you are there?" I wondered.

"Is that something Master wishes to know?" Puvva asked, looking at Wren.

"Don't be like that," Sif admonished her, before turning to me. "There are two others. Faleous of the Flute and Lamasku of the Lamp."

"Why are you telling them these things?" Puvva demanded, outraged.

"Don't be so salty," Sif fired back.

"All of my water is quite fresh," snapped Puvva.

"Why are you two fighting?" Wren asked. "Shouldn't you be friends?"

There was a moment of silence as the two genies glowered at each other.

"I apologize," Sif finally said to Wren. "When the two of us get together, things tend to get a bit muddy. Although she is far from the least favorite of my kindred, despite her wishy-washy demeanor."

"Let me guess, you're more *grounded*?" Gnombie asked, suppressing a smile.

"Precisely," Sif told him.

I might have smiled too, on any day except today.

"It would be nice if you two were friends," Wren put in.

"Does Master wish that?" Puvva asked hopefully.

I let out a sigh.

Ignoring the genies, I looked Ingol up and down. "We are headed to Kempt. If you want to travel with us for a while, you can."

The dwarf beamed. "Thank you. I would be happ–"

"However, if you even think of betraying us in any way, I'll kill you," I cut him off.

"I agree to your terms," Ingol said with a bow.

"Then let's get a move on," I ordered, stepping back outside.

Valor and Raspberry were waiting where we had left them.

"Don't suppose there are any other horses here?" I asked Ingol.

"Doubtful," he replied, eyeing the animals. "Neither dwarves nor goblins are too fond of riding these sorts of beasts."

"It's time to get over that," I said.

"You seem to be a few animals short," the dwarf pointed out. "I don't mind walking."

"Put your genies back in their boxes, and I'll get out mine," I told him, glancing at Sif and Puvva, who were arguing again.

A moment later, Wren and Ingol had dismissed them.

The dwarf leapt backward a moment later as I pulled Tempest from my shadow.

"What is that?!" the dwarf exclaimed, continuing to edge away.

"I'm not a hundred percent sure," I admitted with a glance at Gnombie.

"It's your horse," he answered, as though I'd asked a stupid question.

"That's no horse," Ingol protested. "It's a work of evil."

"Well, you don't have to ride it," I told him. "You can borrow Raspberry for now."

50

It took us a while to convince Ingol that riding was a good idea and nearly as long again to get him up in the saddle. Once mounted, he clung to Raspberry's mane for dear life before the stallion had even taken a single step.

I won't lie, it really hurt to see someone else on the back of the mighty warhorse who had fitted Kraster so perfectly.

All was eerily quiet as we finally made our way out of the fort. I'd never be able to think of it as peaceful as long as I knew what lurked just out of sight in the river.

Despite my earlier anger, it was hard to leave without my brother. However, we didn't have the time or tools for a burial.

Ever since I'd discovered the communication charm, my feelings were confused. I would have to sort them out later, when the fate of the world wasn't hanging in the balance. The one emotion that could not be pushed down, but towered high above the others, was a nearly all-consuming grief.

To keep myself together, I tried to focus on the importance of the quest. Truthfully though, if I could have run, I might have. But where would I go? My home didn't want me. My family didn't want me. There was nothing for me except the mission and a growing desire to make Greyward pay.

There was a chance he might not have meant to kill my brother, but to me, it sure felt like he'd drawn Kraster into a trap. Greyward was searching for the same stones we were. Now that I knew my brother had been working with him, it explained why Greyward had taken his army in the opposite direction.

Between the two of them, they could gather stones twice as fast, but something had changed. Maybe, since we held so many, Greyward had started to worry about us growing too powerful and Kraster refusing to turn the stones over to him. Plus, I'm sure Greyward would have been delighted to hear that I had been eaten by a hydra.

I was going to find the general, and I was going to kill him.

How does he know about the stones? I asked myself. Surely, he hadn't somehow forced the information from Shal'eth.

No, that didn't make sense. According to Ingol, after we'd left, Shal'eth had gone straight to the dwarves.

I narrowed my eyes. The dragon-man was partially at fault for all of this too. He'd given us a nearly impossible task with no information and no warnings of how perilous our road would be.

Why had I believed him so easily?

Because of the way he spoke to you, a voice reminded me. *And he is one of the great dragons after all.*

Ingol and Wren were riding just in front of me, talking quietly from time to time. I didn't join them and let my internal debate rage for the next few hours. There were so many people to blame for Kraster's death: Greyward, Shal'eth, the goblins, the hydra, Kraster himself, and me. Somehow, I kept coming back to that last one.

Wasn't I the one who had drug him along on this quest? He'd been reluctant from the start. Maybe I should have listened to him. Some of Wren's people could have gone with her, and Kraster and I... What would we have done? Joined Greyward's invasion of the human cities? Run away and lived in exile as deserters? There had been no good options.

"Let's make camp here," Wren suggested, pulling me out of my thoughts.

I glanced around. We were on a sandy plain, with no trees and very little vegetation besides the short, wispy grass.

"Fine by me," I replied.

We set up our tents but had to eat cold rations for dinner due to a lack of firewood. Despite this, Ingol tucked in delightedly.

"Delicious!" he declared after his second helping of extremely dry meat strips and stale bread.

"Any apricots left?" Gnombie asked Wren, tossing away a nearly rotten apple.

"They aren't much good anymore," Wren lamented, taking one of the fruits from her bag. It was wrinkled and browning.

"That's strange," I said, remembering that there had been some in Kraster's pouch. I reached inside and pulled out a perfectly fresh fruit.

"But how?" Wren asked. "We picked those ages ago."

She came to my side and studied the golden fruit on my palm. "I don't–" I started, but cut off and plunged my hand back into the pouch again, this time drawing forth the golden stone.

Wren and I locked eyes.

"Guess we know what it does now," she breathed.

"It keeps fruit fresh for all eternity. How useful," I half scoffed.

"More like it preserves things," Wren replied. "The gnomes were using it to preserve all of Dimble's knowledge."

"Fair enough," I said, putting it back in the bag.

A few feet away, Ingol was clearly watching us. I met his stare, and he looked away quickly.

"Forgive me," he apologized. "I'm confused about what these stones you keep mentioning are."

"So are we," I told him. "But I think I know someone who can give us a few answers. Will you please summon Sif?"

The dwarf nodded and pulled out the hourglass.

"Do you want me to get Puvva too?" Wren asked eagerly, hand reaching for the teapot.

"No!" I all but yelled at her. "I think Sif will be far more helpful."

When the genie appeared, he gave his customary greeting to Ingol.

"Do you mind having a conversation with us?" I asked, stepping toward Sif.

"Of course not," the earth elemental said warmly. "I have been cooped up in that hourglass for many years with no one to talk to, so some conversation would be most welcome."

"Excellent," I said, surprised at his willingness when Puvva had always resisted our questions as much as possible.

"First, I'd like to know more about you," I began. "Where did you and Puvva and the others come from?"

"We are the four elemental spirits," Sif answered. "We have been alive longer than Planosia has existed. If you mean how did we end up in servitude, that is a different story altogether.

"You see, a great evil fell on the land—"

"Char," I guessed.

Sif nodded. "Char. She would have destroyed the entire world if not imprisoned. Shal'eth knew that the only way to contain her was with the power of the elements. It wasn't an easy feat, but he and the other dragons managed to bind us and, with our power, trap Char deep in the bowels of the earth."

"And that worked?" Gnombie asked.

"It did," Sif confirmed.

"Then why didn't he free you afterward?" Wren wondered, forehead puckering with wrinkles.

"Because if we stopped being as we are, Char would no longer be bound," Sif explained.

"Even with all of us working together, we were never able to contain her power fully. Over the years, small amounts of her essence have slipped past our wards and manifested above ground. This has allowed her to affect the minds of those she touches, as well as control the dark creatures of the world," Sif explained.

"Then Shal'eth is planning to use the genies to bind Char again? Only, better this time?" I asked. "Is that what he was doing in The Diamond City?"

Sif shook his head slowly. "No, quite the opposite, in fact. He plans to release her." We all stared at Sif in shock.

I was on my feet in a moment, backing away from the others, my brother's pouch clutched in one hand, the other on the hilt of my sword.

Chapter 8
The Wastes

"Did you know?" I demanded of Wren.

"No," she said, shaking her head violently before turning to Sif. "You must be mistaken. Shal'eth would never do something like that!"

Sif appeared perplexed by our reactions.

"Why would he release Char?" I growled, narrowing my eyes at the genie.

"I do not know," the earth elemental replied. "I'm assuming Shal'eth has a plan though, since he's already started the process."

"What *exactly* do you mean by 'started the process'?" I asked.

"Shal'eth was the original master of each vessel," Sif explained. "His first wish was that we use our power to bind Char. Only the one who makes the wish can then wish it undone.

"Once the binding was complete, Shal'eth sent all of us away, except for Puvva. We were dispersed to the ends of the earth to keep us hidden.

"Several decades ago, I felt Shal'eth wish Puvva to lift her portion of Char's bonds. When he came to The Diamond City, he wished for me to release mine as well."

"Why now?" Ingol asked.

"I have no idea," Sif admitted. "But he must have his reasons."

"If Char is halfway free, does that mean she can manifest in the world?" Wren wondered.

"Only for brief periods of time," Sif told her. "Shal'eth did warn King Hallkell that she's been preparing for an invasion ever since her first bond was broken by Puvva."

"An invasion!" Wren gasped, eyes wide. "When will that happen?"

"It's *been* happening," I told her darkly. "We've seen it nearly half a dozen times in the last few months."

Wren's mouth made an O shape, but no sound came out.

"So that explains the genies," I started, "but what about the stones?"

"The stones?" Sif gave me an uncertain look.

Carefully, I pulled Dimble's Legacy from Kraster's pouch and showed it to the genie. It was his turn to appear surprised.

"Do you know what this is?" I pressed.

Sif nodded. "I do, but I'm not sure I should tell you."

"Come on, don't turn into a Puvva," I grumbled.

Sif considered for a moment, then seemed to decide he did not want to be a Puvva.

"Each of the great dragons was given a special gift when they were chosen," he began. "The stones are the manifestation of their gifts."

My jaw dropped open. I had not one, but two dragon gifts on my person as did Wren.

"But why wouldn't the dragons keep them?" Wren asked. "Both Shal'eth and Asteropaios gave them to us willingly. Surely, it would have been better for them to have their gifts to fight Char."

"The gifts don't work for the dragons anymore," Sif told her. "Not since their betrayal."

"What betrayal?" Ingol wondered.

"Except for Asteropaios, Char convinced the other great dragons to betray the one who gave them their gifts," I answered, recalling the story I'd heard from a gardener in The Hall of Asteropaios.

"That's right," Sif agreed.

"If Asteropaios isn't a betrayer, then shouldn't she still be able to use her gift?" Ingol asked.

"Technically, yes," Sif replied. "But for some reason, she can't. Although she still retained much more of her power than the

56

others. The rest of the great dragons have diminished and begun to fade. They are great no more."

"But we've been able to use the stones," Wren protested.

"Of course," Sif replied. "You weren't the betrayers."

"What happened to the one who gave the dragons their gifts?" Ingol asked.

I cringed slightly, already knowing the answer.

"She died," Sif whispered.

There was a moment of quiet.

"If Shal'eth can't use the stones– or gifts– or whatever they are now, why does he want them?" I broke the silence.

"Maybe he's found a way they can kill Char," Sif shrugged. "Or maybe he just wants to keep them from her."

We were all silent for a moment.

"Where's Gnombie?" I asked suddenly, realizing for the first time that the gnome had slipped away.

Everyone turned to the place where he'd been sitting, as if I'd somehow overlooked our companion. It was kind of insulting. He wasn't that small…

"He's wandered off again," Wren sighed. "I'm sure he'll be back soon."

"So what do you plan to do next?" Ingol asked, returning the conversation to its previous course.

"We need to find the rest of the stones," Wren told him. "We know there is one in Kempt, which is where we're headed."

"I will come with you," Ingol told her.

"Don't you have to finish your mission and go back to your forge?" she asked.

"Yes, at some point," Ingol said with a shrug. "I actually have a bit of a confession to make."

I looked at the dwarf sharply, my hand still resting on the hilt of my sword.

"On our journey through The Diamond City, Shal'eth told me that there was a half-elf chosen to lead the fight against the rising darkness. He said that if I was ever given the opportunity, it would be very important that I aid her."

"That's basically what he told me too," I said to Ingol. "And, somehow, I ended up here."

Ingol nodded. "Then, Lady Wren, I vow to remain by your side, to defend and aid you, though it cost me my life. Until your quest is finished, I am at your humble service," Ingol proclaimed, rising to his feet only to drop to one knee in front of Wren.

"Oh, there's no need to–" Wren spluttered, appearing extremely uncomfortable. "But what about your forge and your people?" she added.

"If the world is lost, they will not be spared. I feel there is no better way to help my people than to serve you," Ingol assured her. "I am a dwarf of my word and do not give it unless I mean to keep it."

Wren smiled at him gently, emotion thick in her voice. "Thank you! I would never have gotten this far without the help of my friends. I am happy to add another."

I barely stopped myself from rolling my eyes. In my experience, words meant little and actions meant everything. Wren should let Ingol prove himself before getting all weepy-eyed over his flowery promises.

I took the first watch. About an hour in, I spotted Gnombie approaching from the north.

"Where have you been?" I asked softly.

"Just scouting ahead," he replied, coming to sit close by.

"See anything interesting?" I wondered.

"Not really," he told me. "Just more of this." He gestured to the barren ground where we'd camped.

"Next time, you might let us know before slipping off," I suggested. "If something bad had happened to you, we wouldn't even know where to start looking."

"Fair enough," the gnome replied, though I doubted he'd follow through.

We sat in silence for ten more minutes, then he turned in, leaving me alone with my thoughts. I dreaded arriving in Kempt, my old home. I was certain to be unwelcome even if my treachery hadn't reached the ears of the city guard.

Half-breeds in general were despised among polite company. Some considered our very existence an abomination against nature. As if that wasn't enough, I'd recently learned that my mother's family line was cursed, which tended to make people disdain me even more than other half-breeds.

That still wasn't even the worst of it. There was someone in Kempt I needed to see, my half-sister, Noral. I may not have felt any kinship for what remained of my family, but they had loved Kraster and deserved to know what had happened to him.

Once I'd finished my watch and laid down, it took me a long time to fall asleep as I tried to push away the dread of what was to come.

In the morning, we continued traveling. The landscape changed very little during the next five days. On the fifth, I started keeping watch for the familiar landmarks that would signal we were approaching the city of Kempt. However, we must have been farther south than I'd thought, because we still hadn't reached the outermost farms.

On the following day, I was sure we were getting close. There were numerous farmhouses, but the ground was barren and unplanted. We stopped to check a few of the dwellings but found them completely deserted.

Around midday, we started seeing other travelers. The first group was made up of about thirty humans all carrying large bundles on their backs as they trudged along in the same direction we were going.

The next was twice as large and included families with children of all ages. They told us they were seeking refuge in Kempt before begging us for food. We had next to nothing to spare, only our last loaf of bread, which was devoured the moment Wren offered it. After that, we avoided the groups and rode past without giving a greeting.

In the early evening, I brought Tempest to a sudden stop. Out of the corner of my eye, I saw Valor swerve to avoid bumping into the shadowy steed.

"What is it?" Wren asked.

"I know this place," I whispered.

In front of us was a tavern called The Spilt Milk. Several cats were resting on the doorstep, bathing in the sunlight-not that the sun was very warm today, despite it being the middle of summer.

Quickly, I glanced around to get my bearings.

This was indeed The Spilt Milk; however, something was very wrong. The tavern was only half a day's ride from Kempt and usually bustling with farmers this late in the evening. At the moment, it looked completely abandoned.

I dismounted, motioning for the others to stay put. Slowly, I walked to the entrance, terrified of what I would find within. The door creaked ominously on its hinges as I pushed it open. The tavern's main room was dimly lit. A dozen more cats were inside, lounging on tables and chairs.

"Hello?" I called.

There was a moment of stillness, then I heard movement from the backroom. The tavern owner popped out a second later, and I heaved a sigh of relief to see something normal. Except the expression on his face was wary, and he held a piece of wood like a club in his hand.

"What do you want?" he demanded.

"I'm sorry, are you closed?" I asked in confusion.

"Might as well be," muttered the man. He was short but solidly built. "You look familiar," he added after squinting at me for a moment.

"I'm part of the Kempt military," I told him. "Or, at least, I was."

He nodded slowly, lowering the wooden club.

"What happened here?" I asked.

"The plants didn't grow," he replied.

"I– I don't understand," I said. "What do you mean?"

"The farmers–they planted their fields, just like they do every year–but only a few seeds sprouted, and even those died quickly."

I remembered the fields of wheat and other crops that had always surrounded the tavern. The cats, which cluttered nearly every surface in the tavern, would hunt the mice by day and come here in the evenings for a bowl of milk paid for by the grateful farmers. Now the mice and the farmers were gone, along with the milk, most likely.

"Why?" I asked.

"I'm no farmer," the man told me. He'd moved a step closer to stroke the ears of a large tabby. Its rough purr filled the empty room.

"But, if I had to guess," the man continued, "I'd say it's because we've had such a cold summer, and the warmth of the sun never reached the seeds that didn't sprout and wasn't enough to sustain those that did."

The door opened behind me. I turned to see Wren, Ingol, and Gnombie enter. The tavern keeper fumbled for his wooden weapon.

"They're with me," I told him quickly.

Wren's eyes took in the room uncertainly before settling on a fluffy, white cat sprawled on the counter. With a squeal, she darted forward to scoop him up.

"What's his name?" she asked eagerly, as she cooed to the animal.

"Snowball," the man answered.

"Can we stay here for the night?" I asked. "We can pay."

The tavern keeper nodded. "I don't have any food, though. Ruffians came through earlier and cleared me out. I'm not even sure why I'm still here. Should probably join the others and head for Kempt. People are saying it's the only place within a hundred miles where there's food."

"That explains all the travelers on the road," Ingol said.

"Will Kempt be able to support them all?" Wren asked.

"I doubt it," I replied. "But we'll see tomorrow when we get there."

We went to bed hungry that night, and there wasn't anything for breakfast either. All we had in our packs were a few of the apricots preserved by Dimble's Legacy. I didn't offer them up, because I knew they wouldn't do much to fill our stomachs.

I also had a feeling that they were special and would be needed for something important later.

Chapter 9
The City

As we drew near Kempt, the number of travelers on the road steadily increased. Once the city was in sight, the crowd was so thick we couldn't even see the road. Thankfully, I was in the lead with Tempest. People tended to shrink away from the shadowy steed, so our progress was slowed but not halted.

There were several ragged camps outside the city where refugees were milling about. Others stood in a long line extending from the city's gate. Nearly all of them were denied entry.

When we finally reached the front of the line, the guard waved us off immediately. "Get lost. We don't even have enough space for our own people, much less beggars from other lands."

"Actually, I'm military," I said, dropping my voice low and glancing around. "I'm on special assignment for General Greyward."

Carefully, I slipped the guard an insignia of rank. It was Kraster's because his was way more impressive than mine, but I knew all the right words to say.

"You?" the guard asked skeptically.

"Yes," I replied. "That which is most vital often hides in plain sight, and when we return from lands afar to hearth and home, a warm welcome is all we look for."

I gave the guard a meaningful look. He nodded grudgingly and handed me back the insignia.

"I apologize," he said with a mock bow. "Welcome home."

Once we'd passed the gates, I could easily understand why they were turning people away. The city was packed. Nearly every street was full of refugees with nowhere to go and nothing to do.

"This way," I said to the others, dismounting and carefully pushing through the press of bodies.

"Where to?" Wren asked.

"The last place under the sun I want to go," I told her. "But we may be able to get some information and even a little help." That last part seemed doubtful. Noral had never been the helpful type, at least, not to me.

She'd been the one to take Kraster in after his accident, keeping him in the city to ensure he had access to the best healers while he recovered.

The streets weren't nearly as densely packed when we reached the merchant quarter. Twice more I had to show the military insignia before being allowed to move deeper into the city.

At last, we reached the home of my half-sister. I'd never been invited here, but Kraster had pointed it out several times. Whenever we were stationed in Kempt, Noral and her husband had made a point of inviting Kraster to dinner, because family was *so* important to them.

"What is this place?" Wren asked as I stowed Tempest in my shadow.

"Kraster's sister lives here," I murmured.

"Kraster's sister? So, your sister too?" Wren asked.

"She doesn't see it that way, but yes," I said with a shrug. "Maybe you guys should wait outside."

"Are you sure?" Wren pressed. "I feel like you could use the moral support."

I sighed, trying to figure out if Noral would be more or less likely to attack me with an audience. Not that she stood a chance of besting me physically, but this was sure to be emotionally scarring either way.

"I think you should stay here," I told her. "This is a– *family* matter."

"We'll wait with the horses," Ingol offered.

With a nod of thanks, I approached the door. I could feel Wren's worried gaze following me the whole way. After a few deep breaths, I began to knock. In the middle of the third one, the door opened, revealing Noral. Her expression soured as she took me in.

"What business do *you* have with *me*?" Noral asked contemptuously, her brown eyes suspicious.

"Nice to see you too, sis," I retorted. "Can I come in? It'll be quick."

Slowly, Noral backed up a step, allowing me to enter. "I am not your sister. Now, where is Kraster?" she demanded as soon as I crossed the threshold. While she was the shortest of my father's children, Noral's small frame was somehow still imposing.

I hesitated. Not sure where to start.

Noral's frown deepened. "The only reason I let you in is because I haven't heard from him in months. No one at the garrison will tell me anything. The general and nearly the entire army left at the start of summer. They haven't returned, and no word has been given as to their whereabouts. Now, we are suddenly overrun by refugees bearing tales of terrible attacks on their homelands, all while we face the possibility of famine, and still, no one will tell us anything.

"So I'll ask again, where is my brother?"

"Don't you mean *our* brother?" I couldn't keep from replying, bitterness filling my voice.

Noral curled her lip. "No, I mean *my* brother. The one born of *my* parents, who I all but raised after that terrible accident, which I'm sure you had a part in. You can tell me where he is, or you can get out," she snapped.

"He's dead," I said softly.

Noral stared at me hard for a long moment.

"No," she mouthed. "No, it isn't true."

"I'm sorry, but it is," I told her as gently as I could.

"When? How?" she demanded. "Was there a battle? Were you there? You don't seem injured."

Her eyes studied me judgmentally as I began to explain. "Kraster and I were on a– a special mission. Half the world is under siege by dark forces. That's why there are so many refugees in Kempt. They are the ones lucky enough to have escaped. We were actually headed this way when we came to a fortress."

My throat constricted slightly, but I forced myself to go on, knowing full well that my voice sounded strained. "We thought there were just a handful of goblins inside, but they surprised us."

Hot, angry tears filled Noral's eyes. "I don't believe you! Goblins could never have killed Kraster! He was too gifted."

I hesitated before continuing. "They had a– a hydra."

"A what?!" Noral gasped, wide-eyed.

"We didn't know it was there until it emerged from the river," I explained. "Kraster and I fought it while our companions escaped."

"You attempted to fight a hydra?" Noral's eyes narrowed to slits. "You let Kraster fight it?"

"I tried–" I started.

"You tried? You failed!" Noral cut me off. Her cheeks were red and her eyes puffy, but most of the tears had vanished. All I saw in her face was fury.

"It should have been you!" she shrieked at me. "You should have died, and he should be here instead! He was powerful and talented! He could use magic! You are nothing! Nothing compared to him! It should have been you!"

I hadn't thought Noral still held the power to truly hurt me, not after the years of abuse I'd endured at her hands both in the village where we'd grown up and here the few times we'd run into each other. However, my half-sister's words cut fresh wounds in my heart.

"If I could have given my life for his, I would have," I assured her.

We were silent for a moment, eyes locked.

The door opened. I glanced to my left, expecting to see Wren, but it was Tillen, Noral's husband. He stopped as he took in the tension between the two of us.

"What's going on here?" he asked cautiously, moving to Noral's side.

"This– *half-breed* showed up while the city is in the middle of a crisis to tell me that Kraster is dead!" Noral spat.

Tillen looked over at me sharply. He didn't know me very well, as we'd only seen each other in passing, but I was sure Noral had colored his perception of my character.

"Kraster's dead?" Tillen gasped. "Is it true?"

I nodded.

"I want his things!" Noral burst out. "Give me his things! They belong to me, not to you!"

"There wasn't much left," I tried to tell her, but she was already stalking toward me and reaching out to grab at Kraster's pouch, which hung on my belt.

"Thief!" she cried as I stepped back, forcing myself not to draw a weapon. "Murderer! Give me his things!"

Noral might have lunged forward and tackled me to the ground if Tillen hadn't caught her from behind. She fought him for a moment before turning and burying her face in his chest as great, racking sobs shook her body. Tillen rubbed her back slowly.

I remained frozen for a long moment, then turned for the door, but walked to the table instead. On it, I placed Kraster's military credentials, his watch, his comb, and the book of letters from his family.

I couldn't leave his journal, both because of the confidential information it contained and because it was filled with memories of the time we had spent together.

Tears blurred my vision as I headed for the door.

The others were waiting for me outside. All of them wore somber expressions, giving me the impression that they had heard every word I'd exchanged with my half-sister. Wren's face was sorrowful enough to break my heart afresh.

"Well," I announced, clearing my throat and choking back my emotions. "That went well."

Wren rushed forward to wrap me in a hug. I appreciated the thought, but it made me feel very self-conscious.

"We should be moving on," I said when the hug had lasted nearly half a minute, and Wren showed no sign of releasing me.

"Where are we going?" Ingol asked.

I tried to shrug, but Wren's grip impeded the motion, so I began working to disentangle myself.

"We should head for the bad part of town," Gnombie suggested. "I imagine it'll be easier for us to blend in there."

He was right. Although it hurt to know that, even though Kempt was the closest thing I had to a home, its people were just as likely to reject me as Noral had.

"Is there a place like that here?" Ingol asked.

"There's a place like that in every city," Gnombie told him.

"Not in dwarf cities," Ingol muttered under his breath.

"I'll take us to Unkempt," I said quietly.

"Unkempt? Seriously?" Gnombie asked.

I nodded.

Gnombie and Ingol exchanged a glance, and I could tell they were trying not to laugh.

"Yes, the unsavory part of Kempt is called Unkempt," I told them, rolling my eyes. "But *I* didn't name it."

"By all means, show us the way," Ingol said, doing his best to suppress the smile that turned up the corners of his mouth.

With a sigh, I started leading them farther into the city.

Chapter 10
The Search

I'd spent my fair share of time in Unkempt when I first joined the army as my unit often worked in tandem with the city guard. There were the usual rowdy taverns, brothels, black market shops, and rogues' guilds, which inevitably sprouted up wherever humans congregated. A blind eye was turned to certain of these operations, provided they kept their dealings quiet and out of Kempt proper.

Occasionally, a strong show of force would be required to remind the patrons and perpetrators alike that they were only allowed to remain so long as they stayed in the good graces of the city guard. Even still, there wasn't much hostility between the guard and those of Unkempt. I would be lying if I said I'd never stopped by during my off hours for some cheap drinks after a long day of work.

As a result, I confidently led the way to an inn that bordered Unkempt but was deemed safe enough to leave a few coins in your room without fear of them disappearing. When we arrived, the place was packed to the gills. I had a feeling there wasn't a room to be had anywhere in the city. When I went inside to speak with the innkeeper, my suspicions were confirmed. However, I was able to procure two stalls for Raspberry and Valor, which left us free to venture into Unkempt without worrying about our animals.

"Should we try to find somewhere else where we can rest?" Wren asked after the horses had been cared for.

"I doubt there's much point to that," Ingol announced. "Can't imagine every place isn't as full as this one. I think it was good luck just being able to find a pair of stalls at the same establishment."

I nodded, agreeing with the dwarf.

"Now, where do we start looking for that collar thing?" Gnombie asked.

"I'm honestly not sure," I admitted. "I've never searched Kempt or Unkempt for a magical relic before."

"Maybe if we just mention Baarthagon's Collar someone will point us in the right direction," Wren suggested.

I had a feeling it was going to be more complicated than that, but couldn't think of a better way to solve this problem. I'd been stationed in Kempt nearly half my life and had never so much as heard it mentioned... Or had I? I strained my memory for anything in reference to a collar. Something was tickling in the back of my brain, but it refused to surface.

"Baarthagon?" Ingol asked. "Wasn't he a fiend summoned by one of the human rulers?"

"You're right!" I gasped. "I remember now; I heard the tale told by a bard once."

"How did it go?" Wren asked.

"It all happened here, in Kempt," I recalled. "The governor of the city was Lord Jirus. He was immensely rich and lived in constant fear of someone stealing his wealth. Due to his obsession, he used one of the ancient artifacts he'd obtained to bind the fiend called Baarthagon, a powerful and malicious creature.

"At first, he kept Baarthagon in his vault. As time went on, his fear grew, and he began to have the fiend patrol his palace by night. However, nothing would soothe Jirus's paranoia. Before long, he unleashed Baarthagon on the city.

"Kempt would have been destroyed had the king of Aurum not ridden to its aid. He and his knights battled with Baarthagon for five days before the fiend was at last vanquished. When they finally breached the palace, they found Jirus dead. It is said that he chose to take his own life before someone could take it from him."

I trailed off, coming to the end of what I remembered.

"What about the stone?" Wren asked.

"That must have been the ancient relic that helped Jirus bind the monster," Ingol concluded.

I nodded. "Baarthagon's Collar."

"Then where is it?" Gnombie asked.

"I would have assumed the king took it back with him to The Great City, but Asteropaios told us it was here, so it must have been lost after Baarthagon's defeat," I said.

"You think no one ever found it?" Ingol wondered.

I shrugged. "Most of the other stones were being used, so why not this one too?"

Everyone nodded.

"Then how do we find it?" Wren pressed.

"Well, we know what it does," Gnombie pointed out. "Maybe we should start looking for someone with a fiend."

Everyone was quiet for a moment.

"Or not," Gnombie mumbled.

"It's the best idea we've had so far," I told him. "If there is a fiend in this city, it's sure to be in Unkempt."

"Then I guess we should start searching in the morning," Wren said, glancing at the setting sun.

"Nah," I shook my head. "There's no point going to Unkempt in the morning. All the action happens at night."

"Oh, that makes sense," Wren observed.

"Let's get something to eat while we wait for sundown," I suggested.

The prices in the city were astronomically high. We managed to sell a couple of the small treasures we'd taken from the goblins. The proceeds gave us enough to purchase two loaves of bread and a large wedge of cheese.

I really wanted a drink. It felt like I'd earned one after having to deal with Noral, but with so few coins to our name, there was no way we could swing it. Plus, I hadn't drunk anything in a long time, and I wasn't sure once I started I'd be able to stop.

The sun was beginning to set as we made our way to Unkempt. Just like in the rest of the city, the streets were extremely crowded.

"Watch your pockets," I muttered to my companions as we joined the throng. Those around us were mostly human, but there were enough other races that we didn't stick out as much as we had in Kempt proper.

"Should we try to find that bard?" Wren asked. "The one who told you the story about the collar. He might have more details."

I nodded and headed for The Floating Anchor. The tavern was splitting at the seams when we arrived, and a burly man by the door was turning people away. One look through the window, and I could see why. The barmaids were trying not to get crushed as they waded through the mass of standing patrons while carrying armloads of drinks toward tables.

I approached the bouncer anyway, motioning for the others to stay in the street. "We're full," he announced, hardly looking at me.

"I can see that," I replied. "Was going to ask you if Rybor Kems has been around lately?"

The big man finally looked at me when I named the bard who used to be a regular entertainer at the tavern.

"Haven't seen him since Morthon was declared King of Unkempt. Rumor has it Rybor owed him some money for gambling debts and never paid up," the bouncer told me.

"Morthon? The King of Unkempt?" I asked in surprise. "How did he manage to pull that off?"

I knew Morthon as a smuggler of small, exotic creatures. As long as those creatures ended up outside our walls, we didn't care where he got them or where he sold them. But to be named King of Unkempt meant that his faction had grown to become the most powerful of all the gangs in the city.

"It happened a month or so ago," the bouncer told me. "He opened that old amphitheater and turned it into a gambling den."

I blinked at the man, still not understanding how this explained Morthon's rise to power.

"It's more than a gambling den, really," the man went on. "They hold pit fights there. He never would have gotten away with it in the old days, but with most of the military gone, there was no one who could stop him."

I nodded slowly. With what was going on all over Planosia, it made sense that the export business was probably no longer a viable source of income. Apparently, Morthon had moved on to bigger and better things.

"Thanks for the information," I told the bouncer, slipping him a few silver coins. We didn't have many to spare, but I might have more questions later.

"The bard's gone," I reported to the others. "We'll have to look for a new lead."

"That's disappointing," Ingol said.

"I don't know that he would have been able to tell us much more," I replied. "I'm sure it's just a story he heard or read somewhere. Who knows how much of it is true?"

"Well, let's get to work," Wren announced. "If we search high and low, I'm sure we'll find something useful."

We did as she suggested. Ingol and Wren went off to look in the various shops. I advised them to keep their heads down and try to blend in.

I took Gnombie to see if I could connect with a few of the locals who were known to me as informants of the city guard. The gnome mostly stuck to the shadows and followed me from a distance.

I spotted one of my contacts, a not-so-blind beggar, on his usual street corner. He was strumming a small lute with a copper cup set in front of him, which was basically empty. I dropped a few coins in it as I crouched before the gangly man.

"Thank you kindly," he murmured when he heard the clink of the metal in his cup.

"Anything for a friend of the city," I replied, giving him the key phrase to signal my intent.

The beggar looked more than a little uncomfortable.

"Been a long time since I spoke to one of your kind," he responded quietly.

"I will try not to take much of your time," I told him. "I am simply looking for someone who may have acquired a large and dangerous guardian recently."

The beggar made no reply but seemed to be considering my words in confusion.

"Perhaps this guardian was acquired through a dark ritual of some kind," I prompted.

Still, the man made no answer.

I sighed. "Have you heard of anyone summoning a fiend or other creature lately?" I asked directly.

The beggar surprised me by laughing. "No! Of course not! If something like that happened, the entire city would know."

"Not if it was carefully controlled or contained," I countered.

"To what purpose?" the man asked. "It would be useless in such a state."

"Well, thank you for your help," I said, rising.

The beggar was still laughing as I walked away.

Gnombie caught my eye from his place crouched behind a barrel. I gave the smallest shake of my head, signaling that I hadn't learned anything useful.

I moved on, searching for a pickpocket who looked far younger than his thirty-four years. He usually ran with the street children of the district, but I couldn't spot him. My next contact had a small pushcart of fruit that he peddled up and down the major streets of Unkempt. He was also missing. I figured that with the food shortage, he probably didn't have any wares to sell.

Gnombie continued to shadow me as I tried to track down a fourth contact without success. Much had changed in a few short months. Morthon's crew had grown in size, spreading far and wide. They had almost completely pushed out Jornack, the former King of Unkempt, and his cronies.

The streets slowly began to empty as the night grew later and later. Instead of going home and to bed, it seemed most of the crowd was being sucked into the amphitheater. Every once in a while, a cheer or the thunder of applause emanated from within.

As Gnombie and I headed back to meet up with Wren and Ingol, the night's festivities came to an end. A stream of people flooded out of the amphitheater. The majority of the patrons were quite drunk. We carefully dodged through, keeping an eye out for our friends.

At last, I spotted them talking to a very large, very animated individual. He was a man who appeared to be in his late thirties. His shirt was open, revealing a fresh scar on his chest, which was wrapped in unnatural amounts of muscle. Across the man's back was a massive sword, nearly as tall as I was and probably weighing as much as me.

Even though their conversation seemed to be congenial, I approached with caution.

"Now, if I can just find Gertrude, I'll be on my way," the man bellowed joyfully.

From his flush, I surmised that he was decently deep in his cups.

Carefully, I slid into the space beside Wren. "Everything all right?" I breathed to her.

Wren nodded. "This gentleman was a little turned around and was asking us for directions when he realized he'd lost his traveling companion."

"Gentleman?" the man howled with laughter. "I'm no gentleman. I'm Rojer! Champion of the arena!" Rojer flung his hands out for dramatic effect and nearly fell over.

"And what does this Gertrude look like?" Ingol asked, eyes glancing at the rapidly dispersing crowd.

"She's beautiful!" Rojer swooned. "Long and lean! Dazzling! Gorgeous! She's my one in a million!"

I scanned the people around me, not seeing anyone who came close to that description. However, Rojer was drunk and clearly infatuated, neither condition helpful when making an accurate judgment of your lover's beauty.

"Maybe that lady there," Wren suggested, pointing at a tall woman with her back to us.

Rojer turned, looked at the woman, then burst into laughter.

"Not a woman!" he cried, voice filled with mirth. "My Gertrude is a sword! The best companion a man can have!"

Silently, I exchanged glances with my companions.

"Ummm…" I started, "you are aware that you have a very large sword on your back, aren't you?"

"On my back?" Rojer appeared shocked. "What would Gertrude be doing there?"

He reached a hand up to his shoulder, flexing a bulging bicep as he did so.

We all jumped back several steps to avoid decapitation as Rojer drew Gertrude from her sheath. He swung her around wildly for a moment, then gave her a hug, somehow managing not to slice himself open on her keen edge.

"Gertrude, my love, where have you been? I missed you so!" Rojer sang to his sword.

I was surprised to see that very few passersby had so much as glanced in our direction. Rojer and his antics must be well known in these parts.

A moment later, Rojer returned Gertrude to the sheath on his back and turned to us.

"Now that my love has been found," Rojer began, "is there any chance you could direct me to my room? It's at The Two-Horned Unicorn."

"I know where that is," I told him, pointing back over my shoulder. "You go down this street and take a left, then it's the second right, and you should find it, no problem."

"So go left, then right, and right again– and– and another left?" Rojer asked, giving me a blank stare.

"Maybe we could walk you there?" Wren offered kindly.

"Oh! Thank you ever so much!" Rojer exclaimed, gripping her tiny hand in his massive one and shaking it firmly. "I would be very much obliged, only–" He paused and glanced around uncertainly. "I seem to have lost my companion, Gertrude."

Chapter 11

The Champion

We finally managed to convince Rojer that Gertrude was planning to meet him at The Two-Horned Unicorn after he'd "found her" in her sheath for the third time. Following each discovery, he'd burst into a fresh song, after which, we would have to explain to him again that we were taking him to his lodging.

It was only his immense gratitude that kept me from giving up in frustration. I'd been drunk plenty of times, but there was no way I'd ever been this bad. Unless Kraster had just never told me. It would be the kind of thing he'd have done. Always trying to help me, despite the fact that it was a losing battle most days. I was suddenly very glad that in the last few months he'd been able to see me free of that particular vice. I hoped he'd sensed the changes in me that I'd felt.

Before I let myself wallow too deeply in the past, I forced my mind back to the present. Rojer was weaving to and fro across the street, greeting every stranger he saw as loudly as he could. At this rate, it would take hours to get him to his lodgings.

After our fourth delay, Wren told Rojer that Gertrude was waiting, and we needed to hurry lest she leave. This made him break into a jog. Despite his uneven gait, he remained upright, and we reached our destination in less than ten minutes.

"What is that on the sign?" Wren asked, looking up.

"I think it's a goat?" Ingol told her uncertainly.

"Why a goat?" Wren wondered.

I tried to hide my grin and keep from laughing as they puzzled over the meaning.

"At last, I am home!" Rojer declared. "Now if only Gertrude were here!"

"She will be soon," I assured him. "You should probably go to bed and get some rest. I'm sure she'll be there when you wake up."

Rojer nodded slowly, then shook his head. "I'm too hungry to sleep. Come! Join me for breakfast! It will be my thank you for all of your help tonight!"

Breakfast? I thought. *It's the middle of the night!*

"We couldn't possibly impose–" Wren started, but Rojer cut her off.

"Of course you can!" he said, pulling out an enormous bag of clinking coins. "The winnings tonight were fabulous, and there will be more tomorrow!"

"All right," I agreed, before the others could object. We were short on funds, and it had been days since we'd had enough to fill our bellies.

The tavern was still about half full despite the late–technically early–hour, but began clearing out a short time later. The barmaid, who hurried over to Rojer, was all smiles as she ushered us to a large table. She listened with wrapped attention as he ordered an enormous amount of food, more akin to a feast than a breakfast.

"Everyone here is so kind to me," Rojer sighed. "They know a champion when they see one!"

"Pardon me for asking," Ingol started. "But what kind of champion are you exactly?"

"Why, I'm the champion of the arena, of course!" Rojer told him. "Have you never come to watch me do battle against the monsters of the UnderEarth?"

Rojer looked from one to the other of us as Wren, Ingol, and I shook our heads. Gnombie, who was sitting with his back against the wall at the far end of the table, didn't appear to be listening to our conversation.

"We have only just come to the city," I explained to Rojer. "The last time I was here, the arena fights didn't exist."

"Oh, I see. Well, you must come and watch me sometime. I am most fearsome and never lose!"

78

Wren nodded, giving Rojer an enthusiastic smile.

Just then, the food arrived, and it was glorious. There were piles of bacon and sausage, a heaping platter of muffins, biscuits, and toast, all spread thick with jam, butter, and honey, along with two dozen scrambled eggs topped with cheese. I found myself feeling much the same about the breakfast as Rojer did about Gertrude.

While we ate, Rojer began to regale us with tales of his victories in the arena. Although his words never slowed, the enormous man managed to eat nearly as much as the rest of us put together.

Once most of the food had been devoured and his sentences were growing slurred and sloppy, Rojer rose on unsteady legs and headed to bed. He left a large pile of coins on the table, which the barmaid snatched up quickly.

"He's quite the character," I observed before she could walk away.

"That he is," she replied. "Lucky that he came to this place, or we would have had to close our doors, what with the astronomical price of goods these days. We don't normally let out rooms here. Rojer is actually taking the owner's quarters, but he's paying a prince's ransom for it, so no one minds.

"Don't know what we'll do if he ever leaves," she added before clearing away the empty plates from the table.

Now that we were alone, I motioned for Gnombie to move closer.

"None of my contacts turned up any clues," I admitted.

"It's not surprising," Ingol said with a shrug. "If anyone with a loose tongue knew about the stone, I'm sure the secret would have gotten out long ago."

Wren and Gnombie nodded in agreement.

"So you think it's never been found?" I asked.

"I didn't say that," Ingol replied. "I just think whoever found it hasn't been using it or hasn't told anyone they are using it."

"Then how do we find it?" Gnombie asked.

I hesitated, then turned to Wren. "It might be time," I murmured to her.

"What?!" Wren's eyes widened. "I– I don't think I should."

"Just this once?" I asked.

"But it won't be just this once," Wren said mournfully. "There are three more stones after this one, and we don't know where any of them are."

I gave Wren a helpless look. I hated trying to push her into doing anything she didn't want to, but we were at a dead end.

"Might I ask what you two are talking about?" Ingol interjected.

"I have a stone that can help us find the others," Wren admitted.

"Then why haven't we used it yet?" Ingol's brow furrowed in confusion.

"Because we were warned that we shouldn't," Wren explained.

"Not exactly," I corrected her. "We were told that there would be risks."

"What kind of risks?" Ingol asked.

"That was unclear," I admitted.

"I think you should try it," Gnombie piped up suddenly. The gnome had hardly spoken since we reached the city.

"But–" Wren started to protest. Gnombie held up a hand.

"We've used some of the other stones, haven't we? Like when we were engulfed in the poisonous spores that killed so many elves," the gnome pointed out.

"Yes, but that was more of an accident," I confessed.

"But if you had been able to do it consciously, you would have, right?" Gnombie pressed.

"Of course," I replied. "Otherwise, we would have all died."

Gnombie nodded slowly, then turned to Wren. "Char will consume this world unless we stop her, and to stop her, we need the stones."

Wren met his gaze miserably.

"Look, Wren, we don't want to force you to do something against your will, but I don't know what else we can do," I told her. "I used The Heart of Jong for nearly an entire day and night. I was exhausted afterward, but that was all. I don't think using The Scrying Stone one time will hurt you. The Oracle and Asteropaios just wanted us to be careful."

Wren didn't appear convinced. "Can't we try to find another way?" she begged. "We've managed thus far with very little direction. Surely, the answer is here. We just need to find it."

All of us were silent for a long moment.

"Fine," I conceded, reminding myself how young Wren was. "We'll give it one more day. After that, if you won't use the stone, I will."

Wren's eyes widened at the suggestion. "I couldn't let you do that! You already saved us once with a stone. Besides, I don't even know if you would be able to use it."

I let the conversation drop, and we headed back to the inn where we'd left the horses. Dawn was only a few hours away as we slipped into the stalls with Valor and Raspberry. While the others settled themselves among the hay, I sat with my back against the wooden wall, wondering if I could slip the stone from Wren's pocket without waking her. My watch ended before I decided whether or not to act.

I woke in the late morning, feeling sick from sleeping on such a full stomach. I don't think I would have been able to eat breakfast, even if we could have afforded it.

We spent the remaining daylight hours searching the nicer parts of Kempt for any sign of the stone. Our efforts were fruitless. When night began to fall, we returned to Unkempt and continued our mission with a similar result. The only positive was that we again ran into Rojer. He wasn't nearly as drunk this time and remembered us from the night before.

"My good friends!" he greeted us. "I must thank you for all your assistance yesterday."

"It was no trouble," Wren assured him.

"Oh, I'm never *no trouble*," he replied with a wink. "Please come and have breakfast with me again as a thank you."

I would have declined, despite my empty stomach, but something in Rojer's eyes appeared eager, giving me the feeling that he wasn't asking so much to be kind as because he was lonely.

Once again, our midnight breakfast was a feast. Rojer told us many stories, some of which we'd heard last night, but were infinitely more sensical the second time around.

"Have you ever heard of something called Baarthagon's Collar?" Wren asked when Rojer was forced to stop talking due to having shoved an entire muffin into his mouth.

"Nope. No idea what that is," he answered once his airway was clear. Before we could respond, he launched into a recount of his first fight in the arena, when he'd proved himself a true champion.

"I think it's time we try The Scrying Stone," I told the others as soon as Rojer had gone to bed.

An expression of terror crossed Wren's face.

"Give me the stone," I said, holding my hand out to her. "If the other one didn't hurt me, I doubt this one will either."

"This is a bad idea," Wren protested.

"Well, we are out of good ones," I countered.

Wren hesitated, glancing around at all of us.

"Shouldn't we wait and use it in the actual morning, when we're fresh?" she argued. "Then we can go straight there without needing to sleep."

I weighed her words carefully.

"She makes a good point," Ingol said. "It doesn't make much sense to locate the stone while we are all so worn out."

"Fine," I agreed, lowering my arm. "But in the morning, I am going to use the stone."

Wren nodded eagerly.

We left The Two-Horned Unicorn and returned to the horses, who nickered happily to see us. After so long on the road, I was glad they were getting a few days of well-earned rest.

The straw of the stable was no longer fresh, and the loft above was almost empty. I doubted it would be replenished in the near future. Soon, our sleeping situation would become downright unpleasant, another reason I'd rather not linger in the city.

I had eaten less at Rojer's breakfast this time, and, when Gnombie woke me for my watch, I didn't feel nearly as sick. The sun was well up before I gave Wren a shake, rousing her for the final shift. My internal clock was unsure of what was going on, but I was tired enough that I managed to drift off eventually.

A gasp from Wren woke me less than ten minutes later.

She was sitting cross-legged in the hay, one hand palm up in front of her, the other placed downward on top of it. Teal light was spilling from between her fingers.

"Wren! What are you doing?" I cried, getting up and racing to her side.

Wren's eyes, which were shut, opened, and I pulled up short. Instead of her usual brown irises, her eyes were a swirl of white and teal.

Gnombie and Ingol hurried over and knelt on either side of me.

"Don't touch her," I breathed, putting my hands out.

I sensed them nodding, but didn't take my eyes off the half-elf girl as tiny spasms moved through her body. Wren's eyes closed again a moment later. Slowly, her head bowed until it was almost touching the ground. All was completely still for a second, then she sat bolt upright, and her eyes snapped open. I was relieved to see that their normal coloring had returned.

Wren's voice was weak as she rasped out, "I know where the stone is, but I have no idea how we are going to get it."

Chapter 12

The Arena

"It's in the arena?" Gnombie gasped.

"Beneath it, to be exact," Wren replied.

"Where there's a gaping hole leading to the UnderEarth?" Ingol's astonishment was written all over his face.

"I'm such an idiot," I groaned, drawing the gaze of my companions. "It makes so much sense. Morthon was always able to get his hands on exotic creatures and their parts to sell. Now, he's using them to stock his arena."

"I don't follow," Ingol said.

"You think he has Baarthagon's Collar, and is using it to control the creatures," Gnombie guessed.

I nodded at the gnome. I'd figured out as much when Wren told us about her vision. She'd found herself somewhere below the arena, watching as the stone's power compelled a large monster out of a gaping tunnel swirling with dark mist.

"So, how do we get the stone?" Ingol asked.

"If you know who has it, we could jump them," Gnombie suggested.

Wren shook her head. "It was too dark for me to tell who was using the stone. All I saw was an orange glow, but I knew it came from Baarthagon's Collar, just like I knew I was seeing under the arena."

"I don't suppose you could use your influence with the city guard to help?" Ingol wondered, turning to look at me.

I shook my head. "There's no way. Even if I hadn't deserted, I doubt any of them would want to kick the hornet's nest. With Greyward's army gone and the city drowning in refugees, they are just trying to keep the peace."

"Maybe Rojer would help?" Wren suggested. "He seems to really like us."

"The arena is literally his bread and butter," I reminded her. "It's made him a big shot and lined his pockets with gold. Even in his most drunken stupor, I can't imagine he would ever want to ruin that."

The others nodded.

"He's not the only one," Ingol pointed out. "Unkempt is the only place in the city that is thriving, and it's all because of the arena."

"So everyone is going to be working against us?" Wren asked glumly.

"We'll just have to keep our mission covert," I replied. "What we need first is more information."

"Do you think we should go to the fights tonight?" Ingol wondered.

"I think some of us should," I told him. "The rest of us should be *in* the fights. That way we can infiltrate on two fronts."

"Who would fight?" Gnombie asked.

"Not you," I replied. "Something tells me you would be better at investigating the dark corners of the place."

The gnome gave me a slight smirk.

"I've been fighting half my life, so I have no problem stepping into the arena, either alone or with a partner," I continued.

"I'll go with you," Wren announced.

I nodded. She was the one I would have picked as her hand-to-hand skills were quite impressive. While Ingol boasted the stocky, muscular build of his people, I was yet to have seen him wield the gilt staff he carried, and I didn't think the arena would be a good place to find out it was all for show.

"I guess that means I'll be a patron tonight," the dwarf said.

"If you don't mind," Wren put in quickly.

"No, that will be fine," Ingol replied. "I can use the fact that I am from a different land to ask lots of questions without drawing suspicion."

"Then it's all agreed." I smiled, glad that we finally had a plan.

After shaking the hay from our clothing, Wren and I set out for Unkempt. When we stepped inside The Two-Horned Unicorn, the barmaid recognized us and scowled in our direction.

"If you're here to take advantage of Rojer's kindness again, you'd best be off," she told us.

I gave her a questioning look.

"What do you mean?" Wren asked.

"He brings people back with him all the time in the wee hours of the morning. I understand that it makes him feel happy to celebrate with others, but then they start turning up whenever they feel like it, trying to insist that they are Rojer's best friends and want to order food and drink to put on his tab. Well, I'm not having it! Make yourselves scarce, or I'll go and get Rojer and have him chase you off himself. It's a downright indecent thing to do! Taking advantage of that man's generosity in such a way!"

Finally, the woman ran out of breath. She was short and stout, cheeks flushed red from her tirade.

"Actually, we'd like to see Rojer. That's why we're here," Wren told the barmaid. "If you could get him for us, we'd appreciate it."

The woman gave us a hard look, then confusion crossed her face.

"You're really here to see him?" she asked.

Both of us nodded.

"Oh, my apologies. Usually the threat of bringing him down is enough to scare off most of the grifters who come looking for handouts."

"We are not looking for handouts," I assured her. "We wanted to talk with Rojer about becoming arena fighters."

"Well, that's very different," the barmaid said, embarrassment filling her voice.

"Glad that's cleared up," Wren beamed. "So, can we see Rojer?"

"He's actually still asleep," the woman admitted. "And he hates to be woken up." From the distressed look in her eyes, I imagined it was something that had occurred once and would never happen again as long as he was within the walls of this establishment.

"We'd be happy to get a drink while we wait," I said quickly, pulling out some coins before the woman started huffing and puffing at us again. She scurried off while Wren and I took a table close to the stairs.

"What if we can't get in even with Rojer's help?" Wren fretted.

"Then we go as spectators," I shrugged. "But I don't think it'll come to that."

"Why?" Wren wondered.

"Because that place thrives on bloodshed and will always be in need of arena fodder," I explained.

Wren nodded thoughtfully as the barmaid brought over a pair of tankers filled with amber liquid. Wren took a thoughtful sip of hers. I started to raise mine to my lips but hesitated and set it back down. Once, I would have drained the entire cup in one draft, but I didn't feel the urge today.

We waited another twenty minutes, then heard a series of loud thumps from above.

"If that's not Rojer, then they've got a troll up there," I muttered.

Wren giggled.

After more thumping, and what sounded like a few muffled curses, Rojer finally came down the stairs. He looked less haggard than I'd expected. The barmaid greeted him with a giant smile and directed him to our table. He glanced in our direction and, while he did seem to recognize us, he wasn't as delighted by our presence as I'd hoped.

Rojer and the barmaid exchanged a few more words, then he headed our way. Wren scooted over slightly to make room for his massive bulk as he sank onto a chair, which creaked loudly.

"Good morning, ladies," Rojer greeted us.

"Good morning!" Wren exclaimed.

"It's good to see you again. We were wondering if we could offer you a drink?" I asked, sliding my untouched tankard toward Rojer.

"I usually don't drink before fighting," Rojer said. Despite his words, he eyed the ale eagerly, and his fingers slowly closed around the handle.

"I suppose I could make an exception, just this once," he mumbled as he took a long drink.

"We've been very impressed by your stories the last few nights," I began. "My friend and I think we'd like to try our hand at an arena fight or two."

Rojer glanced between us. "I'm not sure you're cut out for the arena," he scoffed. "That place is dangerous, and I'd hate to see you get hurt."

"Well, can't we start small and see how it goes?" Wren implored. "We're tougher than we look."

"Sure you are," Rojer said patronizingly.

I managed to hold onto my temper and not do anything rash. Kraster would have been proud, or shocked. Honestly, probably both.

At last, Rojer let out a long sigh. "I suppose I could introduce you to Elkkin. He's the one who arranges the fights."

"We would really appreciate it," I told him.

The barmaid brought over a bowl of thick soup containing large chunks of meat and potatoes. At Rojer's bidding, two smaller bowls were produced for Wren and me.

"You can pay me back with your winnings," he told us with a wink.

An hour later, Wren and I were inside the arena standing in front of Elkkin while he explained to us that all participation was voluntary and any injuries we would probably sustain were no one's fault but our own.

The interior of the building was vast. My best guess was that it had once been a warehouse, built long ago, before this part of the city became so unsavory.

There was a large oval in the middle with a sandy floor. Around it were high walls of stone meant to contain the combatants and the beasts. The seats above the walls, which went up almost vertically, were arranged in several tiers. Behind the viewing areas, there was ample space filled with food and drink stands and, of course, betting booths. The lower tiers were more refined than those above. Refined was actually too polite a word. Nothing in Unkempt could truly be called refined, but the seats in the nicer sections had cushions at least, even if they were stained and ripped in some places.

Once Elkkin finished with us, Wren and I found ourselves in the combatant waiting area where we could watch other fights and prepare for our own. It was actually kind of nice. We were offered drinks and comfortable chairs. Rojer, a mug of ale in his hand, was there too, along with several more fighters, including another team.

At the far end of the oval arena stood a large set of wooden doors. They were at least four, maybe even five times the size of normal doors. Unfortunately, they were closed, which was disappointing. As fighters, I'd hope we would see more of the facility, especially the underground space where the creatures were kept. So far, I hadn't even spotted a staircase leading downward.

I continued to observe everything as the arena started to fill. There was no sign of Ingol or Gnombie, although I doubted I'd see the latter unless he wanted me to.

When it was time to begin, a young lad, thin as a rail, was chosen to go first. He seemed nervous, and I wondered what level of desperation had driven him to try his hand in the fights. Luckily, all he faced were a pair of giant, grub-like creatures, each the size of a fatted pig.

From the first thrust of the boy's spear, I could see that he was untrained and unprepared. When I glanced over my shoulder at the betting boards, I saw that he wasn't favored.

The monstrous grubs were faster than expected and moved forward quickly to engage. While the boy stabbed at one of them, the other sprang forward with astounding speed and agility, latching itself onto the boy's shoulder and clinging there.

The boy yelped, falling to the ground as he writhed, struggling to free himself. He wasn't successful, and the second grub bit into his side, producing an even louder scream from the thrashing boy.

I had to grab Wren's arm to keep her from going to his aid. He was shouting for help, and a moment later, a high-pitched sound filled the arena. Both grubs released their hold and began scuttling back to the massive wooden doors, which opened to admit them.

"That probably leads to the lower levels," I whispered to Wren.

She nodded, but her concerned eyes were still fastened on the boy. Several people had hurried to his side and were helping him out of the fighting ring.

The second match was between an old, battle-scarred man and a nightmare of a bear that towered twelve feet in the air when it stood on its hind paws. The man won but had to be carried out of the arena on a stretcher and did not return.

Wren and I were called next. There was a mixed response from the crowd. Most were far enough away that any hint of our elvish features would be impossible to detect.

The doors across from us opened. I strained my eyes to see inside, but all was shadowy darkness until three scorpions came charging out, each the size of a pony. The crowd gasped at their appearance. I glanced to my left and saw that we were not favored to win on the betting board.

Much as I knew this was a mission to gain information, I felt the desire to prove everyone wrong rise in me. I drew my swords and took up a fighting stance.

The first creature was nearly on top of me before I moved, rolling to the left beneath its massive claw. As I ducked under, one of my swords shot skyward, and I severed the limb. The creature loudly clicked its displeasure.

I sprang lightly to my feet, then had to dodge several attacks from the stinger, which arched over the beast's back, dripping with poison.

The second scorpion was right next to me. I darted through its legs to hide beneath the beast's carapaced body as stinger attacks continued to rain down. The wounded scorpion didn't appear to care that its ally was between us. The monster I was hiding under lurched as a venomous barb sank deep into its back.

As the now-poisoned creature stiffened and started to fall, I scrambled out from under it on the opposite side, giving myself some distance from the one I'd maimed earlier.

Out of the corner of my eye, I saw Wren facing down the third scorpion. She darted in and kicked several of the beast's legs in rapid succession, a sickening crunch following each blow.

The first scorpion charged me again. This time, it was ready for my dodge and managed to catch my leg with its one remaining pincher. Before it could crush my bones, I slashed at the claw with both swords. One glanced off, but the other found purchase, slicing through the carapace and into the flesh underneath.

The scorpion whipped around. Its grip was loose enough that I was hurled across the arena and came crashing down on the dirt. Winded, I struggled to rise as the beast bore down on my position.

I feigned another dodge. The creature skidded to a halt and turned to intercept. Carefully, I leapt onto its broad back. My landing was a little clumsy. I dropped one of my swords but managed to stay on, straddling it like a horse. The beast was still for a moment, then began to buck wildly. After tightening my leg muscles to hold me in place, I took my remaining sword in both hands and raised it high before plunging it into the creature's back. The scorpion went still, and I pulled my blade free. Scrambling along its back, I made my way to the monster's head, then repeated the process, driving my weapon into where I hoped the brain was located. I'm not sure if I hit it, but the giant animal spasmed and reared up before crashing violently to the ground.

Again, I was thrown halfway across the ring. I got up faster this time, looking around quickly for more enemies. There were none. Wren had dispatched her scorpion and finished off the one that was poisoned.

All was quiet for a long moment. I expected the silence to be followed by deafening applause, a sound that I had never imagined would ever be directed at me. Instead, a chorus of boos filled the air. I sighed, knowing I should never have raised my expectations.

Chapter 13
The Underground

A moment later, it was over. Wren and I moved back into the holding area for fighters. Rojer gleefully thumped both of us on the back. "I knews' you'd be graat!" he slurred. "I'ms' gonna asks' Elkkins for a fin'er's fee."

Rojer was called to a fight a moment later. Despite being drunk, he attacked his foe, a razor-spined lizard, with great gusto. It was incredible to watch as he basically defeated the creature purely by enthusiasm. I couldn't help but notice that the crowd cheered wildly for him.

There were a few more rounds, then Wren and I were up again. Our next battle was easier than the first, because there was only one foe. The monster was a slimy creature, the size and shape of a troll, who reeked of putrid meat and sewer waste.

Again, the betting odds were against us, but only slightly this time. It took less than two minutes for Wren and me to bring the monster to its knees, where I lopped off its head.

Our final fight of the night was against five hyenaish creatures. The battle started out poorly. The beasts worked well together and managed to separate me from Wren. They also stayed far enough away to avoid my swords and Wren's fists. Only when I pretended to stumble to my knees did one come within range. I instantly clipped the side of its head with a blade.

As soon as its blood hit the dirt, the rest of the creatures rushed in to rip their packmate to pieces in a manner that almost made me gag. Wren and I took the opportunity to move together and put our backs against a wall. I edged us around the arena, trying to get closer to the doors the monsters had come through. I'd been too far away every time one entered to see anything. My hope was that, once we finished off the hyena mutants, I'd be able to get a quick glance at what lay beyond when they came to retrieve the bodies.

A moment later, our foes' attention was on us again. They came in a rush but broke off at the last second. I darted forward, taking the nearest one by surprise as it turned. The creature impaled itself on my weapon, then jerked away with a screech of pain. The same scene as before played out, with the mutants turning on their own packmate in a fit of bloodlust.

Wren and I edged away from the sickening display, again moving nearer to the doors. The crowd was cheering like crazy, apparently loving the gory spectacle.

With only three left, the creatures no longer had the advantage. I picked the next one off with a throwing dagger. The last two got into a savage fight over its body. After their brawl, only one beast remained, but he was badly injured and easy to dispatch. I hated to think what would have happened if Wren or I had been the first to bleed.

Pretending to be tired and trying to catch my breath, I remained on the far side of the arena while we were announced victorious. The odds had been against us again, but I doubted they would be any more.

Finally, the large, wooden doors swung open, and several workers brought a cart out to retrieve the bodies. Past the threshold, I saw an iron portcullis a dozen yards back, then it looked like the floor sloped down, turning into a ramp. That was all I could glean from my quick glance as I headed back across the fighting ring.

The night ended with Rojer taking on a gigantic cyclops. Several times I feared he would lose. Rojer got hit hard enough in the head that I was sure he had a concussion. Finally, he used Gertrude to smash the cyclops's head flat.

The crowd went wild as Rojer, who was struggling to stand, raised Gertrude above his head before toppling over. A few of the ringside medics, several with magical healing abilities, rushed forward and began treating the champion.

A moment later, they had Rojer back on his feet. He tipped each of them generously for their assistance.

As the crowds began to leave, Elkkin appeared, bringing each of us our winnings. The bag he gave to Wren and me was smaller than the one he gave to Rojer, but it was still considerably more money than we'd had in a long time.

"Come and celebrate with me!" Rojer demanded of us. The healing spells that had been performed on him seemed to have fixed most of his intoxication as well.

"Of course!" I agreed.

A short time later, we found ourselves back in The Two-Horned Unicorn.

I spent the meal trying to milk Rojer for any information he might have about how the arena was run and where the creatures came from. Either Rojer was wonderful at keeping secrets, or he truly knew absolutely nothing. An hour later, Wren and I left with no additional insight.

"Hopefully, Ingol and Gnombie learned more than we did tonight," I muttered to Wren on our way to the stable.

She nodded her agreement.

"Sorry we're late," I said, as Wren followed me into the stall where we'd been sleeping. "We were–"

I stopped short, realizing our friends weren't there.

"They said they'd meet us here, right?" Wren asked, glancing around.

Valor was the only one in the stall. He whinnied happily, and Wren moved to pet his velvety nose. Lazily, the horse's eyes drifted shut under her stroking.

"That was the plan," I recalled.

"I hope they didn't run into trouble," worried Wren.

"We should probably go look for them," I sighed. Weariness weighed heavily on me now that the adrenaline of battle was wearing off.

"What if they are out there looking for us?" Wren wondered.

"Ummm…" My brain was too tired to process all the different possibilities.

"Maybe we should wait here," Wren continued. "Oh, but if they are in trouble, we need to find them immediately!"

"Let's wait until it's light," I suggested. "We're both dead on our feet. If the others are looking for us, they'll be back by then. If not, we'll be in better shape to deal with searching for them. You can rest first."

Wren nodded and settled down. I remained standing, knowing that I would fall asleep if I didn't. During my time as a soldier, I'd gone many nights without rest. However, I'd never been on a mission that lasted this long. It was exhausting.

Luckily, even when I did sleep, some part of my brain remained alert. Probably the elf part. Full-elves didn't have to sleep much, and when they did, it was more of a trance. However, the human half of my brain was pretty sure I needed ten hours a night, a luxury I rarely got.

Just as dawn was rising over the nearby rooftops, I recognized the squat form of Ingol heading toward the stable. I heaved a sigh of relief and moved to greet him at the entrance to the stall.

"What happened?" I demanded softly. "And where is Gnombie?"

"He's hiding in the arena latrine," Ingol told me. He seemed rather pleased by the idea.

"He's what?" I gasped. "What in the blazes is he doing there?"

"We'd better wake up Wren," Ingol said. "She's going to need to hear this, and we don't have much time before we have to leave."

"Leave and go where?" I asked, already moving to shake Wren.

Once she'd blinked the sleep from her eyes, Ingol started relaying the tale of what he and Gnombie had been up to last night.

"When we arrived, we were given vouchers for a free drink, which I immediately made use of. The ale wasn't very good, nothing like what we craft inside the mountains, but I digress. I got in line for a second and turned to see if Gnombie planned on using his voucher. However, he was nowhere to be seen.

"So I had another drink, found my seat, and decided to see what there was to see. I watched the lad fight, then the old man, then the two of you."

Ingol's voice sounded grim when he spoke of the boy who had lost almost immediately to the giant grubs, but he brightened at the mention of Wren and me.

"You were both spectacular, as I imagined you would be," Ingol went on. "In fact, I believed in you so much, I bet on you."

"Really?" Wren asked in delight.

Ingol nodded. "Of course! Although it wasn't all that much in the first round, as I didn't have the coins to spare. After you defeated the scorpions, that changed, and I continued to profit from your victories all night!"

"You're welcome," I laughed. "But what did you and Gnombie learn about getting under the arena?"

"Well, I didn't learn very much," Ingol admitted. "Just about the time you finished your third match, I finished my seventh ale; that one tasted much better, so they must have tapped a better keg.

"Anyway, that was when Gnombie found me. He said he'd discovered a hidden passage that led down to the pens where they keep the monsters."

"Did he see the stone?" Wren asked eagerly.

"I'm not sure," Ingol answered.

"We know it's down there somewhere, which is good enough for me," I replied. "So, what's the plan?"

"Well, it took us a while to work that part out," explained Ingol. "That's why I wasn't here to meet you, which I do apologize for.

"Gnombie said during the fights they were constantly moving the beasts into position, then bringing back their carcasses to be harvested. We both agreed that it would be better to return during the day when the place is quiet."

"Harvested?" Wren wondered.

"Of course," I answered. "Those animals provide a lot of resources Unkempt and Kempt are both running short on right now."

"What sort of resources?" Wren furrowed her brow.

"Meat for one," I told her, watching as her eyes got wider. "And the poison from the scorpions we killed is sure to have medicinal properties. Plus the hides of those–"

"You mean we've been eating monster meat every morning for breakfast?" Wren gasped in shock.

"Most likely," I shrugged before turning to Ingol. "Please continue."

"Both of us lingered after the fights had finished until they started pushing people out and the cleaning crew arrived. That was when Gnombie told me to head back here while he hid. He said that a little before noon he'd open one of the side doors to let us in. From there, we can take the hidden passage to the underground."

"That's actually a really good plan," I told him.

"You don't have to sound so surprised," he muttered.

"Noon, huh? That should give me time for a nap," I announced sleepily.

Wren kept watch so I could get a few hours of rest before it was time to go. We packed our belongings and paid the landlord in case a hasty getaway was needed, which I felt sure it would be.

The streets of Unkempt were all but deserted when we arrived. We tried to appear nonchalant, slowly wandering up to the arena and pausing for a moment with our backs to its walls.

Ingol reached behind him and knocked gently on the door. We all held our breath for a long minute, then the door swung open, and we darted inside.

It took a moment for my eyes to adjust to the gloom of the windowless interior.

"Good to see you," I greeted Gnombie with a nod. "Did you have any trouble hiding?"

"Not at all," he replied quietly. "But we should refrain from speaking as sound carries quite well in here."

No one said anything more as we followed Gnombie through the maze of passages. I was lost after the fourth hallway, or was it the fifth? It was impressive that the gnome had learned them all so quickly in only a single night.

Less than ten minutes later, we arrived at what appeared to be a flat wall. Carefully, Gnombie slid the tip of his dagger between two of the panels and gave it a little twist. The panels separated to reveal another hallway, this one sloping downward.

"Great work!" Wren whispered to the gnome. He nodded curtly to her, and we hurried down the passage. A moment later, the entrance closed behind us.

There was even less light in this part of the arena. Fortunately, my eyesight was pretty good, and I could see light coming from the end of the corridor ahead.

Gnombie motioned for us to stop, which we did while he crept up to peek around the corner. Without glancing back, he waved us forward until we could all see into the large chamber beyond. The room felt like a cellar, with dirt walls and stone pillars supporting the roof high above.

The chamber appeared to be empty of people, but several torches had been left burning. These illuminated a collection of empty metal crates, which stood in rows. They were of all sizes, some terrifyingly large.

"It's just like my vision," Wren breathed. She pointed to the opposite end of the room, which was blocked from our view. "That's where the opening to the UnderEarth is."

"We should stay far away from it," Ingol advised.

Everyone nodded.

"Any idea where the stone is?" I asked both Wren and Gnombie.

Quickly, Wren pointed at a door to our right. It was set in the far wall of the chamber. Carefully, I stepped into the light. My hand was resting on the hilt of one of my swords, but nothing happened as I moved to the door. The others were close on my heels.

"Any idea what's in there?" I breathed.

"It's the room where the wielder stays," Wren replied.

"The wielder?" Ingol asked.

"The one who controls the beasts and commands them into their cages," Wren explained.

I nodded without looking at her, my eyes fixed on the door. After listening carefully, I reached for the knob. I tried to turn it, but nothing happened.

"Locked," I whispered.

Gnombie was beside me in a second, a set of lock picks in his hand. A moment later, he slowly turned the knob, and the door opened a few inches.

Within, a lamp was burning, and I could make out a sleeping form on a bed. Carefully, Gnombie eased the door farther open. It squeaked once, but the figure didn't stir.

The room had earthen walls and a low ceiling. Besides the bed, there was a desk in the corner, a table with three stools, and a wooden wardrobe.

Advancing on the bed, I drew my sword.

"You aren't going to kill him, are you?" Wren mouthed, eyes wide.

I shook my head. It would be so much easier if I could, but it hadn't been my intention. Wren's shoulders relaxed visibly, and we approached the sleeper together. A sour smell hit me when we were within a few feet. For the first time, I noticed the collection of bottles and tankards under the bed. They reeked of sour beer.

Did I used to smell like this? I thought.

The figure moved then, and I stiffened, but he was just rolling over in his sleep. Once he settled into the new position, he started snoring soundly.

Gnombie and Ingol were already searching the desk. They came away shaking their heads. Wren knelt to look beneath the bed, as the gnome and the dwarf moved on to the rest of the room.

"Well, this is very interesting," a high-pitched voice said as Ingol swung open the doors of the wardrobe.

Chapter 14
The Fae

All four of us jumped and then stared at what was inside the wardrobe. On one side hung normal clothing. The other side was divided into shelves. On the top one sat a wire cage similar to the kind that held birds.

"Don't just stand there gawking! Let me out of here!" the voice spoke up again from inside the cage. This time I was able to see the speaker. The creature was small enough that it could have fit in the palm of my hand. It had skin the same color and texture as tree bark, along with long arms and legs connected to a body that wasn't quite human.

"Nobody touch it!" Ingol ordered rather loudly.

I cringed and glanced at the sleeping man, but he continued to snore.

"Drat," the creature said. "I was hoping that would work." It let out a dramatic sigh. "It was worth a try at least."

"What are you?" Wren asked, coming closer.

"That's not important," it told her. "What is important is that I'm stuck in this cage and can't get out." Its voice turned mournful. "I'm trapped here all the time, and they won't let me go back to my family."

"The fae don't care about family," Ingol spat.

"Fae?" Wren's voice took on a delighted note, which the trapped creature instantly picked up on.

"Yes! I'm a magical fae and can maybe offer you a wish if you let me out of this cage," the creature piped up.

Wren was about to speak, but I cut her off. "We might be willing to make a deal, but first, lower your voice. If your master wakes up, the chances of you getting released go to zero."

"Oh, he won't wake up," the fae assured me. "He drinks himself to sleep pretty much every night now and never stirs, no matter how much racket I make."

To prove its point, the fae burst out singing, its voice rather shrill and quite unpleasant.

"Stop that," Ingol snapped, and the fae did.

"Only because you asked *so* nicely," it told Ingol, sticking out its tongue at him.

While we had been speaking, Gnombie had been searching the wardrobe.

"It's not here," he told us.

"What's not here?" the fae demanded. "Are you looking for something?"

None of us replied.

"Something like this?" it went on, producing an orange stone out of thin air. The rune for guidance was etched onto its glowing surface.

All four of us gasped.

The fae chuckled. "I thought so. Now, how about a deal? Otherwise, this stone is mine! Mine! Mine!"

"What kind of deal do you want to make?" I inquired guardedly.

The stone vanished again, and the fae creature rubbed its grubby little hands together in delight. Most people think of the fae as being elegant and beautiful. This one looked more like a little gremlin. However, the fae were well known for their deceptive appearances.

"First, I want you to let me out of this cage," the fae said. "Then I want you to kill him." The creature pointed a slender finger at the man snoring in the bed. I could see his face from this angle. He looked younger than I'd expected. Not that I assumed Morthon was doing his own dirty work down here, but learning to wield magic took time.

"Candra–" Wren started.

"Candra?" the fae asked, pulling itself up on the thin bars to look at me. "Is that her name?"

"It's actually Bankimcandra," Wren told it. "But she goes by–"

"No!" This time it was Ingol who cut her off. "No names around that creature."

I felt the blood drain from my face as I realized what Wren had just done.

"Bankimcandra!" the fae exclaimed. Come to me, Bankimcandra! Do my bidding! Open my cage, and free me!"

I expected to feel the irresistible urge to obey. That was how it was described in all the stories when the fae learned your name and commanded you by it. Instead, I felt nothing.

"No, thank you," I replied to the creature.

"That's strange," it muttered. "I can tell it really is your name, but there's nothing connected to it, no soul tether, if you know what I mean."

I kind of did. I'd been told once that my soul wasn't attached to my body the way everyone else's was. It had to do with some curse that had been laid on my bloodline long before I'd been born. According to The Oracle, the only way to get rid of it was to die.

"Well, she seems to be broken, but I'd love to get to know the rest of you," the fae said with a winning smile.

"Hey! I'm not broken!" I snapped.

"How stupid do you think we are?" Ingol demanded.

The creature sighed and dropped back down to the bottom of the cage. "I have to find *some* way to amuse myself. I've been stuck in here for ages!"

"Why?" Wren asked. "Why are you here? And why do you have that stone?"

The fae gave her a hard look, like it suspected she was trying to use a trick to get information. However, her open countenance betrayed only curiosity and compassion.

"I was captured by the original master of this place, some mortal who's dead now. He tricked me into revealing myself. How was I to know that he would have a dragon's gift?"

"A dragon's gift?" Gnombie asked.

"Yeah, the stone, stupid," the fae spat. "It's supposed to be used for 'guidance' but, wouldn't you know it, a human discovered a way to use it to enslave other creatures. Color me surprised.

"With it, he took my name and locked me in this magical prison. Now I have to do whatever the bossman and the boy say."

"Who is the lad, exactly?" Ingol asked.

The fae shrugged. "I don't know, some lacky. Every few years, the bossman gets a new one. They are the only two who know my name. Invoking it, they force me to use the stone for them."

"They make you do it because it wasn't meant for mortals to wield," I realized aloud.

"Exactly," the fae confirmed. "The bossman is afraid to even be near it too long. He makes sure my handler gets switched out fairly often because he worries that one of them will try to use me against him and take things over. So far, none of them have been that smart."

"So you're the one who uses Baarthagon's Collar on all the beasts from the UnderEarth?" Wren asked.

"That's right, sweetheart," the fae told her with a wink. "Glad you're keeping up."

"For how long?" Gnombie asked.

"I don't know, five centuries or so," the fae answered. "Pretty much ever since the opening to the UnderEarth was discovered here."

My jaw dropped open. "I thought that was a relatively new development."

"Nooooooo," the fae said. "It's gotten bigger over time, especially lately, but the first crack opened long ago. Every night, the monsters come, and I use the stone to get them all into their cages snug as little bugs. Then they fight and usually die, or they are just straight up killed. Either way, it's nothing but work, work, work, and I'm tired of it. So please get me out of here!"

We all hesitated.

"You know fae can't lie, so trust me when I say it's the only way you're getting this stone." The fae flashed Baarthagon's

Collar at us again. With a mighty spring, it leapt up and stood on the underside of the cage's top as easily as if it was the bottom.

"So what do you say? Want to make a deal?" it asked, looking at us upside down.

I considered for a long moment. Making deals with fae was a terrible idea, but we needed that stone.

"All right," I conceded.

The fae chortled in delight.

"Wait," Ingol warned. "I've met the fae a few times, and it has never gone well."

"I don't see what other option we have," I told him. "We just need to be really specific about what we agree to."

The dwarf sighed but didn't argue further.

"We do want the stone," I admitted to the fae. "But we aren't going to be murdering anyone in their beds for it."

"Maybe you could roll him onto the floor first?" the fae suggested. It laughed at its own joke, while I folded my arms across my chest.

"Fine," it said. "But he knows my name and so does the bossman. That's a big problem for me."

"Can't you go back to the king or queen of the fae and get a new name?" Ingol asked.

"I mean, yes, but I like my name," the little creature whined.

Ingol and I both glared at the fae.

"As you wish, no murders," the fae conceded. "Man, I have been in this cage way too long if I'm willing to give up on my list of demands so easily."

"It can't be helped," I told it. "Here are the terms I am willing to offer. I will take you in your cage out of the city, and once I am a day's ride away, I will release you. At that time, you will give me the stone called Baarthagon's Collar."

"Sure!" the fae agreed.

"I'm not done yet," I warned. "Before we leave this room, you will promise to never return to Kempt, to seek no revenge on any who held you captive or on their friends and family. This also means you cannot coax or bargain or otherwise engage someone else to do it for you. Upon your release and relinquishment of Baarthagon's Collar, you will immediately return to the fae lands without harming any creature along the way. Once there, you will remain with your people for the next two hundred years."

"That's harsh," the fae grumbled. "I do *not* get along with my siblings."

"Too bad," I said. "That's the deal, take it or leave it."

"Fine," sighed the fae. "I'll take it. I agree to all your terms. Now get me out of here!" The creature's voice rose to a piercing octave.

"And no more of that," I snapped.

"Wasn't part of the agreement," giggled the fae.

"True, but if we get caught, none of us are going to make it out," I warned.

The fae rolled its eyes but didn't say anything.

I reached forward and seized the cage.

"Careful," Ingol cautioned, but it was too late.

Thankfully, nothing happened when I touched the wire sides of the cage.

"Hey! I can't see!" the fae complained as I tucked the cage under my cloak. "What's the point of getting rescued if you can't see?"

"You actually *get* rescued," I snapped.

"Fine." The fae's voice was sulky, and I could easily imagine it pouting.

The torches were burning low when we emerged into the large chamber.

"We've lingered too long," Gnombie breathed.

In the distance, I could hear voices coming from somewhere close at hand. Quickly, we raced for the secret passage. It felt much longer going this direction, but, at last, we reached the end. Quickly, Gnombie opened the panels so we could get out.

The sounds of the arena coming to life filled the air. My heart was pounding in my chest. I felt certain we'd stumble across a group of workers at any moment. Once, we did have to duck

106

down a side passage as several men walked by carrying hammers and long boards. Another group came along a moment later, rolling several kegs on their sides.

We waited until the coast was clear, then raced for the exit. Thankfully, the fae made no noise, and we reached the outer door in less than five minutes.

There were still many hours of daylight left as we fled from Unkempt to Kempt. While Ingol mounted Raspberry and Wren swung onto Valor, I summoned Tempest in the privacy of the stable for Gnombie and myself.

The roads of Kempt seemed incredibly long as we headed for the nearest city gate. The closer we got, the tighter the press of refugees. At last, we reached the exit.

"You're the first people to leave all week," the guard told us in wonder. "Doubt you'll be able to get back in."

"We're on official business," I announced, flashing him my credentials.

I breathed easier after we were through the gate. Once free of the crowd camped around the city, I pushed Tempest into a canter, aiming to put as much distance between my old home and myself as possible.

"What's going to happen now that the stone is no longer in the city?" Wren wondered.

It was a question I hadn't stopped to ask myself.

"The army of Kempt will have to fight the creatures," Ingol answered.

"They don't have an army anymore," I told them. "And the guard is stretched pretty thin."

"Then what are they going to do?" Wren asked in a small voice.

"The people will have to step up or– or–" I couldn't bring myself to admit that I feared the city might fall. It seemed that no matter where we went, destruction followed. Now I had even brought it to a place I once called home.

We rode in silence until just before sunset.

"We must be out of the city by now!" A voice screeched.

I jumped, having nearly forgotten about the fae concealed in my saddlebags.

"I can't wait any longer!" it shouted. "It's musty in here, and I have been knocked around for hours!

I stopped Tempest and dismounted, gauging that we'd ridden for at least seven hours. That seemed far enough. Reaching into the saddlebags, my fingers groped for the cage and lifted it out.

The fae glanced around.

"Oh, we've been out for a long time," the creature observed.

I nodded.

"I fell asleep," the fae admitted. "Otherwise, I would have started talking a while ago."

"Then luck has favored us," grumbled Ingol.

"Well, aren't you just a special little dumpling?" the fae snapped at him, then turned back to me. "So, now you have to let me go, right?"

I nodded.

"Yes, and you have to give me the stone," I reminded the creature.

"That was the agreement," the fae confirmed. He was grinning wickedly, and I didn't like it, but I had no choice. I'd made the agreement, I needed the stone, which meant I had to release the fae.

Carefully, I tried to open the cage door, but it was rusted shut. Pulling as hard as I could, I ended up ripping it off completely. I put out my hand, and the fae hopped onto it, clutching the stone to its chest.

"Freedom!" it trilled.

"The stone," I commanded, holding out my other hand.

"Here you go," the fae said, dropping the orange stone into my palm. A tingle went through my body. It was the same sensation I had felt the first time I held each of the stones.

Like a grasshopper, the fae jumped to the ground. Slowly, its shape began to change and morph until it was twice my size and looked rather like an enormous snake with six eyes.

"Now, I'm going to kill you all!" the creature announced cheerfully in the same shrill voice despite its vast change in size.

Chapter 15
The Return

"Filthy, murderous, back-stabbing creature!" bellowed Ingol, holding his staff in a defensive stance.

"Calm down," I said. "It can't actually hurt us."

"Excuse me?!" huffed the fae. "Of course, I can hurt you. And I plan to. I plan to hurt you very badly, in fact."

"Our agreement was that you wouldn't," I reminded it.

A wicked smile flashed across the fae's lips. "I only agreed not to hurt those who had held me captive. You don't know my name, nor were any of you the ones who put me in the cage."

"Yes, but whose saddlebags have you been stuck in for the last seven hours?" I asked.

The fae blinked and tilted its head slightly.

"I'm not sure that counts…" the creature said.

"She's right," Wren put in. "All afternoon we've had the ability to let you go, but we got to decide the where and the when. Doesn't that mean we held you captive?"

The fae blinked uncertainly.

"But if you really want to risk breaking your word, we can see what happens," I added.

The fae let out a long, arduous sigh. "I've been locked away far too long," it muttered. "I'm quite out of practice in the deals department."

"Also, weren't you supposed to *immediately* go back to your homeland?" Gnombie wondered. "Without harming any other creatures, if I recall correctly."

"There is that too…" the fae conceded.

"Then you really should get a move on," I encouraged.

"This is going to be such an embarrassing story," the fae moaned.

As it turned toward the northeast, the creature sprouted massive wings from its back and lifted into the air, soaring away with unnatural speed.

"Well, this is the first time I've ever heard of anyone coming out ahead on a deal with a fae," Ingol told us.

"It was pretty desperate. I'm sure that helped, " Wren commented.

I nodded and started unsaddling Tempest. It was a chilly evening, so I pitched my tent. It was large enough for Wren to share. Ingol put up the second tent for himself and Gnombie.

"We should have bought more food before leaving," Ingol observed.

"What food?" I asked grimly. "Anything they have left will be gone in a few days, especially if the supplies from the arena are cut off."

Ingol nodded and said no more. Another surge of guilt washed over me. There had already been a food shortage; now even more would starve. Plus, those living in Kempt were all but defenseless against the monsters of the UnderEarth.

You couldn't have done anything to help them. I tried to comfort myself, though I knew it wasn't quite true. I couldn't have done much, but I could have done *something*. The only thing that kept the guilt from consuming me completely was the pinch in my empty belly as I settled down to sleep.

In the morning, when the sun crested the horizon, I thought I could just make out the small rise of Kempt against its red backdrop.

I slipped my hand into the pouch on my belt, feeling the three stones I kept there and trying to assure myself that all of this was actually for the good of the world.

Five minutes later, I heard someone stirring inside one of the tents. Gnombie stepped out and came to sit beside me. We were silent until the sun had cleared the horizon.

"You did really good back there, in the city. We couldn't have gotten the stone without you," I told him.

"Thanks," Gnombie replied. "You weren't so bad yourself."

"I mean, I killed some stuff, but you're the one who found the stone," I said.

"Only three more to go," he replied.

"And we have no idea where to start looking for them," I sighed.

"What were their names again?" he asked.

"The Gem of Aero, Azazoth's Wand, and the last one, which The Oracle said was hidden in shadow," I recalled.

Something flashed in Gnombie's eyes for just a moment as I listed the stones.

"And Wren can't use the Scrying Stone to find them?" he wondered.

"She could," I conceded. "But using the stone endangers her. It's the same reason a fae was forced to wield Baarthagon's Collar for so many years. The stones are filled with the powers of the great dragons; they aren't meant for lesser beings."

"But she can find them if she has to, right?" Gnombie pressed.

"Maybe," I told him. "In Kempt, we knew we were close to Baarthagon's Collar, but the other three could be anywhere. I don't know whether that makes a difference or not."

"So what's next?" the gnome asked.

"When everyone wakes up, we'll figure it out together," I decided.

It didn't take long for Ingol and Wren to join us.

"We need supplies," was Ingol's immediate response when I put the question to the group. "Most of the big cities are sure to be just like Kempt, overcrowded and drained of resources. What we want is a small town, tucked away from the main roads.

"You're from around these parts, aren't you?" the dwarf asked, turning to me. "Is there anywhere like that close to here?"

"There is," I said with a sigh. "I know just the place."

"Then we should head there without delay," Ingol suggested. "Even if the food costs a pretty penny, I've got lots of winning from betting on your fights."

The dwarf grinned at me.

"What is the town called?" Wren asked.

"Owen's Falls," I told her. "I was born there and– and so was Kraster." Everyone grew quiet at the mention of my brother's name. "His family– my family– most of them are still there."

The memory of my meeting with Noral began replaying in my head. I was going to have to tell my father and my other half-siblings that Kraster was dead. I didn't know how I would get through it again. However, Ingol was right. We were desperate for supplies, and Owen's Falls was the perfect place to get them.

After mounting the horses, we turned north. It was only a day and a half journey to reach Owen's Falls, but it was the longest day and a half of my life. With each step that Tempest took, the dread inside of me grew.

Why don't you send the others into town and remain behind? part of my brain asked.

Because your father and siblings deserve to know what happened to Kraster, I argued back. *He would have wanted you to tell them, and you owe him that much. You owe him much more, in fact.*

Late in the afternoon, we started seeing trees and were soon in a full forest. This wasn't the perfectly manicured grove of the high elves, but an untouched woodland, sculpted by nothing but nature. The wood elf blood in my veins rejoiced at its very existence.

The following morning, the path took us upward, winding through glades and over small streams. I was nervous of the latter, but none were deep enough to require me to touch the water.

As we climbed, I felt the temperature drop and wondered if the crops here had sprouted.

Most of the human villagers in Owen's Falls kept small gardens or orchards to feed their families, but it was through exporting lumber that they made their living. The wood elves who

113

dwelt among the humans foraged rather than planted. Their mere presence helped the forest thrive, and so there was peace between them and their human neighbors.

Finally, we passed the first house on the outskirts of the town. It belonged to a widow who had hired Kraster to weed her flowerbed many a summer. When he'd left to live with Noral in Kempt, I'd offered to take the job, but the woman's cats had hissed at me, and she'd chased me away with a broom.

Next, we came to the livery and blacksmith run by two brothers, their children, and their grandchildren. While most of the local kids had learned to ride here, I'd never been welcome. Instead, I'd watched their lessons hidden in a tree overlooking the paddock.

"Should we leave the horses here, or is there an inn?" Ingol asked.

"There's a tavern, but it doesn't have a stable," I replied.

"Here it is, then," Ingol declared, sliding to the ground. It was a long way for him.

I remained a dozen yards away as Ingol and Wren acquired stalls for Raspberry and Valor.

"Such nice gentlemen," Wren was saying to Ingol as they returned to where Gnombie and I waited. I fought to keep from rolling my eyes as I put Tempest in my shadow.

We made our way further into the town, and I pointed them toward the dairy, the baker, and the butcher. Three places that had only grudgingly done business with my mother and me.

"You should be able to get provisions there. Just don't mention my name," I told them.

"Got caught stealing when you were a lass?" Ingol asked, with an amused twinkle in his eye. "Surely, they have forgiven you by now."

I shook my head. "That's not what happened, and they'll never forgive me."

"For what?" Wren asked.

114

"For being born," I replied, before turning toward the western side of the village. "I'll be back in a bit," I called over my shoulder.

The path I took led me to a row of cozy cottages. A few had milk cows grazing in the front yards. One lifted its head lazily to watch me pass. The last house on the right was where Kraster had grown up.

I paused. My chest suddenly seemed too small for my heart and lungs. This was the last place in the world I wanted to be. I had never been welcome here, and I never would be. People often claimed that blood was thicker than water, but where I was concerned, blood meant nothing.

Taking a deep breath, I began moving forward again. It would be better to just get the whole thing over with. I still hadn't made up my mind about whether or not to see my mother, another ordeal that was sure to be unpleasant, but I decided to worry about that later.

After today, I could leave and never come back. Kraster was the only thing that had tied me to this place, and that thread had been severed.

Chapter 16
The Discovery

Knocking on my father's door wasn't easy. I'd tried it a few times before, but it had never ended well, especially when Elmira, Kraster's mother, was home.

It was strange how I could battle a hydra and yet still fear that woman, she who had made my life miserable from the moment I was born.

Thankfully, she was not the one to answer. Hector, Kraster's youngest brother, opened the door and peered at me uncertainly. The last time I'd seen him, he'd been barely more than a toddler, so I doubted he knew who I was.

"Is Reagir around?" I asked, naming our father.

"He's out back," the boy answered, closing the door to a slit.

I nodded. "Thank you, I know the way."

Suspiciously, the boy watched me walk away with eyes nearly identical to the brother we had both lost.

I followed the stone path around the dwelling to where the barn stood. It was much like the cottage-humble, but well cared for. Reagir was there with his oldest son, Haskell. The pair were mending the fence of the sheep corral. If the coming winter was as unusually cold as this summer had been, they would make a fortune on wool come shearing season.

Haskell noticed my approach first. A sneer rose automatically to his lips.

"What do you want?" he spat, drawing our father's attention.

"That's enough," Reagir told his son. "Why don't you go inside?"

Haskell shot our father an unhappy look. "You're only doing this because Mother is away," he muttered as he stalked past me toward the house.

"Hello, Candra," Reagir said to me. "Shall we sit?"

He gestured to a wooden table with bench seats. I remembered Kraster telling me that his family had eaten many meals out here when the weather was nice, since the smaller table inside their dwelling couldn't accommodate the whole family.

I took a seat on one of the benches. The table had seen better days but was still sturdy. My father sat across from me. He was nearly a decade older than the last time I'd seen him. His already portly frame had added another fifteen pounds. His hair, which had always been curly and thick, was nearly completely silver instead of black.

"What brings you here?" Reagir asked. His voice was much friendlier than I'd imagined it would be. We'd spoken only a few times over the years of my childhood. He was never venomous like his wife but always distant, making sure to keep me at arm's length.

"I came to tell you that Kraster is dead," I managed to say with a steady voice. "We were in combat, and he was killed. I– I couldn't save him."

Sorrow crossed my father's face, and he turned to look out at the forest, which stood less than a dozen yards from the barn.

"Greyward sent word not long ago that he was missing and asked us to contact him if Kraster came this way. His mother will be–" My father cut off with a small sob.

"My– my poor boy. I thought I'd lost him once before," Reagir murmured softly. "Ever since, I wondered if he was only living on borrowed time."

"What do you mean?" I asked.

"The day he– fell." Reagir turned back to meet my gaze. "You remember it?"

I nodded. How could I ever forget? I had been there, watching from the woods as dozens of children, my siblings

117

among them, swam in the pool under the waterfall of Owen's Falls.

The longing to join them pushed me to climb one of the cliffs. Only the most daring were brave enough to jump from the top into the water below. My child's mind convinced itself that if I conquered my fear and proved my courage, I would be accepted by the other children. It was foolishness, of course. As soon as I looked down at the dark water, doubt flared up in my chest.

While I was hesitating, Kraster joined me. He wasn't aware of the curse but had saved me from drowning a few times, including earlier that day, and knew what would happen if I entered the water. Back then, I'd still thought it was all in my head, a challenge that needed to be overcome.

When my brother had tried to pull me away from the edge of the cliff, I fought to free myself from his grasp. During our struggle, he fell, striking his head on the way down.

I fled, slipping back into the forest unseen, as the other children cried out in horror. We'd been the only two on top of the cliff, the only two that knew the part I had played.

I hid among the trees and watched with bated breath, praying my brother was all right, but Kraster never resurfaced. His older siblings searched for him in the water, while the younger ones ran to the town to raise the alarm.

There was nothing I could do to help, but I couldn't bring myself to leave either. I remained hidden by the pool day and night while the search went on. It had taken two days before Kraster was found and pulled from the water. Somehow, his heart was still beating.

He was taken home to recover. A short time later, he left Owen's Falls and went to Kempt to live with Noral. I'd never expected to see him again and might not have if we hadn't ended up in the same regiment under Greyward.

"While he was unconscious, Kraster said many things," my father continued, cutting into my memories. "He talked about eyes filled with darkness and hatred and malice. And— and there was someone with him."

I cocked my head. Kraster had never told me this part of the story.

"Who?" I asked, the hairs on the back of my neck rising.

"I'm not sure, but he called her 'my lady'," Reagir answered. "At midnight on the day before he woke, I was sitting with him by myself. His eyes never opened, but I heard him thank her for sparing his life, then tell her he couldn't accept the gift that she offered?" My father's words came out as a question, and I felt sure he didn't understand what Kraster had been saying any more than I did.

"In the morning, he was conscious but babbling and out of his mind. I sent the others away so they wouldn't be frightened. He kept telling me about the eyes and how looking into them was like looking into the void and knowing it was going to swallow him whole, but then the lady came and saved him. I– I don't remember the name he called her. Charm, maybe?"

"Char?" I breathed.

Reagir's eyes widened. "Yes! That was it. Char."

My blood turned cold, and I surged to my feet, ready to defend myself despite the lack of enemies. Could it have really been Char? How? Why? What could this mean?

"Did he say anything else?" My voice came out hoarse and raspy.

"Not that I recall," my father answered, taking in my reaction with confusion. "He wasn't in his right mind. His eyes were completely black. I feared he might be blind, but the darkness faded, and he seemed normal again.

"Well, maybe not normal. It was clear that something happened to him in the water, which left a lasting impression. Whatever took place preserved his life, and it was no surprise to me when he found he could use magic."

My mind was racing a mile a minute. Could Kraster have really seen Char? Had she saved his life? But how? Why? Unless…

119

Char was one of the great dragons of old, just like Shal'eth and Asteropaios. Was it possible that the stone containing her gift was in the pool? Had it been right under my nose this whole time?

"Has– has anything else like that ever happened at the falls either before or since?" I asked.

My father shook his head. "No, although many parents were reluctant to let their children swim there for some time after. However, things are back to normal now. Kraster even took your commander, General Greyward, up there to see the falls."

"What?" I blinked at him. I did remember Kraster excitedly telling me Greyward wanted to visit Owen's Falls and meet his family. My brother had even invited me to join, despite knowing I would decline.

"It's true. I guess after hearing Kraster's story, Greyward wanted to see where it happened.

"He paid his respects to us first. I think it was wonderful how Greyward took Kraster under his wing and made him his prodigy," Reagir beamed.

"I– I need to go," I breathed, moving away from the table.

"Wait a moment," my father said, rising from his seat and coming to face me. "Candra, I'm– I'm sorry."

I looked at him in surprise.

"I'm sorry for a lot of things. I should have been a father to you. Regardless of who your mother is, you are my daughter. It wasn't fair that Elmira blamed you and forgave me. I shouldn't have allowed it, but I did because of my own guilt. If there's ever anything you need, I will do all I can to help you."

"Thank you," I murmured before walking away.

In my heart, I knew that my world was so much bigger than this tiny town and this humble man that the thought behind his offer was all I would ever need from my father.

I still felt dazed by his unexpected gesture when I met up with the others. Quickly, I motioned for them to follow. As we began hiking through the woods toward the falls, I explained everything Reagir had told me.

"You think there's a stone *here*?" Wren gasped.

"I don't know," I replied.

"The event you speak of does seem like more than mere coincidence," Ingol wondered. "But did Char ever possess a stone? The legends of my people name her only as a monster of the UnderEarth."

"She was one of the great dragons first," I said, recalling the story I'd heard in the garden at The Hall of Asteropaios. "Her gift was light, but she used it to explore all the dark places of the world where she let herself become corrupted. Once that happened, she convinced most of the other great dragons to turn traitor with her."

"That's when their gifts stopped working, and they started losing their power," Wren added.

"Before she could conquer the world, Shal'eth locked Char away with the power of the elemental spirits," I continued. "Sif said her prison was fracturing, allowing some of her essence to escape. I'm betting the pool by the falls is one of those places."

Wren, who was beside me, nodded. "The Oracle of the Three Sisters did tell us that one of the stones had 'passed into shadow'. I should have guessed that it was Char's. The– The Shadow Stone, I suppose we could call–"

"No, it is The Void Stone. Void is Char's gift now," Gnombie cut Wren off. A shudder passed through me at his words.

"That's probably a more accurate name," Wren agreed.

We reached the falls half an hour later. There were a few children throwing rocks into the water, but none were swimming since the day was too cold.

"Of all the places for a stone to be hiding," mused Ingol. "Unbelievable."

I nodded as I guided our group around the edge of the pool to the base of the waterfall. It was the closest point to where Kraster had landed after his fall from the cliff.

"Is anyone a good swimmer?" I asked, only half joking.

The others exchanged hesitant glances.

"I'm okay at it," Wren said, beginning to remove her pack.

"Wait! This isn't wise," Ingol warned. "We must exercise caution. It could be dangerous to touch something tainted by Char or even get too close to it. If all you have said is accurate, then she is one of the strongest dragons ever born and has been consumed by her own corruption. Who knows what effect such a malignant power source would have on a mortal?"

"Maybe we can get a magical box or something to hold it in?" Wren suggested.

"If I had access to a forge and the right materials, I could make such a device," the dwarf told her.

"That won't help us today," I said to Ingol, before turning to Wren, "and you'll never be able to search all of that water by yourself."

"But what else can we do? If it's here, we have to find it!" Wren protested. She looked at the small lake, and her shoulders slumped.

"What about using The Scrying Stone?" I asked cautiously.

Wren hesitated.

"Otherwise, we could waste many days looking for something that isn't even here," Ingol put in.

"All right, I'll do it," Wren decided. "It shouldn't be too hard, since I'm only searching a small area."

Wren sat down cross-legged on a nearby rock with a flat top. She took out The Scrying Stone, laid it flat in one palm, and held it in front of her stomach. Carefully, she placed her other hand on top. The rest of us grouped around her and waited in silence.

Closing her eyes, Wren inhaled deeply. She remained like that for a long moment before her head snapped up, and her eyes opened. They had again transformed into orbs of swirling white and teal. A few tremors went through Wren's body. Suddenly, her head dropped onto her chest, and she took several gasping breaths.

"It's not here," she panted. "The Void Stone isn't in the water."

I let out a sigh, trying to hide my disappointment.

"Did you see where it was?" Ingol inquired.

Wren shook her head. "I widened my search to the village but didn't find it there either."

"And you couldn't widen it anymore?" the dwarf pressed.

"It– it would have been much harder," Wren told him, worry seeping into her voice.

"There's no point in trying," I announced, much to the surprise of the others. "If it's not here, then I think we should assume that Greyward has The Void Stone.

"I'm not sure if he knew what he was looking for, but I think Greyward heard about what happened to Kraster and figured out something of great power was hidden here. So, he came to look for it and discovered the stone.

"He wasn't close to me like he was to Kraster, but I do remember things started changing shortly after his visit to Owen's Falls."

"You believe Char is controlling him through the stone?" Wren wondered, concern puckering her forehead.

"Maybe," I answered.

"What changes did you see in him?" Ingol asked.

"We had a lot more drills and practice missions," I explained. "It was almost like Greyward was preparing us to capture other cities instead of merely defending our own."

I glanced at Wren and added, "This all happened in the time leading up to him ordering the attack on your village. He was looking for something there. At first, we thought it was the teapot, but it was really The Scrying Stone. In the last message he sent to Kraster, Greyward was asking about the stones we'd gathered, wanting Kraster to bring them to him."

Ingol nodded slowly. "With or without Char's direct influence, it seems that the general has been corrupted as well."

"You are correct," I murmured. "He must have known about the stones before we did, and I believe he is searching for them."

"That's going to make it very hard to get The Void Stone," Wren commented. "And any others he's found."

I paused for a moment. *Any others?* I thought. *Has he found any others?*

"Actually, it might make our job easier," I said. "Knowing who has it is half the battle. Also, I am familiar with both Greyward and the Kempt army, which will give us a leg up."

"That certainly is an advantage," Wren concurred.

"I agree," Ingol added.

I glanced at Gnombie. He was standing a little back from the rest of us. "You've been awfully quiet," I observed. "What do you think?"

"I think it makes sense," he answered softly before looking away.

"Then it seems we are going west," I announced.

Chapter 17
The Curse

As we followed the trail back to the village, a weight seemed to settle on my shoulders. We had agreed to leave straight away, but I knew I couldn't do that.

"Why don't you guys get a drink at the tavern?" I suggested. "There's one more person I need to see before leaving town."

"Your mother?" Wren asked.

I nodded.

"Should we procure lodgings for the night?" Ingol inquired.

I shook my head. "This won't take long."

"The tavern it is," Ingol said, leading the others away. Wren glanced at me over her shoulder several times as though wondering if she should offer to come along.

Once they were out of sight, I turned my feet to the eastern side of the village, the place where the wood elves lived. There was no path to follow, but that didn't bother me. I knew these woods.

After breaking with their high elf kin in the south, thousands of wood elves had journeyed north. Instead of building a city or anything of the like, they had spread out, living in small communities. Some of these had gone completely feral, even going so far as to live in Fae Forest.

As I entered the domain of my mother's people, I could feel their eyes watching me from among the trees. No one came forward with a greeting. I was just as much of a shame to them as I was to my parents.

The dwelling I had grown up in was built in the lower boughs of an ancient oak tree. A nine-foot-tall ladder reached from the ground to the porch, which wrapped all the way around the one-room house.

I scaled the ladder easily and knocked on the door. There was no answer even after I knocked a second time. I turned the door knob anyway. Wood elves didn't believe in locks.

The interior was dim, and it took a moment for my eyes to adjust to the gloom. The place was much as I had left it. Everything was meticulously clean and put away with not so much as a speck of dust anywhere to be found.

Callisto, my mother, was sitting at the beautifully carved table, which stood beside an open window overlooking the forest to the north. Unlike my father, she hadn't changed at all since the last time I'd seen her.

"Hello, Mother," I said, as her empty gaze slowly turned in my direction. Her face had always been gaunt beyond her years, as if the long youth of the elves did not bless her blood.

"Go away." My mother's voice came out weak and watery.

"I'm not staying," I told her. "I just wanted to come by and– and see how you are."

"I'm fine. Now, leave," she ordered. My mother looked anything but fine.

I took a step forward. "Listen, I–"

"No," she snapped, scrambling to her feet and moving away. "Don't come any closer to me with that– that *thing*."

I halted. "What thing?" I wondered.

"That curse," my mother all but wailed. "I carried it for so many years. The agony of it grew and grew, hollowing me out until I could no longer bear it."

Her eyes studied me for a moment, and the words of The Oracle came back to me as whispers in the air.

You were cursed long ago.

You are disliked and distrusted, hated and scorned.

You will be cursed for the rest of your life, until you take your final breath.

"You know about the curse?" I gasped.

She nodded. "It belonged to me before it was passed to you, as it has ever been in our line, from mother to daughter."

126

"Why did you never speak of it?" I asked. "I don't understand why you wouldn't tell me."

"You don't have to understand," she murmured. "You just have to leave, and take it with you. I can't bear to look at it anymore. I had to be rid of it, so I bore you, to end the curse."

"What?!" I choked out.

"You're too close!" she shrieked. "Take it away! I don't want– I don't want to feel anything anymore!"

"You– you seduced my father because he was human," I realized aloud. "You wanted a child you knew would die before you, a half-breed, who would likely not be able to bear a child."

"You are my path to freedom," my mother whispered.

My mouth fell open, but I couldn't speak. All I could do was stare at her.

"Please go," she begged. "The pain is too great."

Her legs gave out, and she slid to the floor, covering her face with her hands.

"How can you be so evil?" I snarled at her.

"I'm not evil," she replied without looking up. "Evil would have been to smother you in your cradle. I considered it but decided to allow you the few years that your human blood would permit. I thought I could be that patient, at least."

You– you don't have a soul!" I screamed.

"I don't want one," she wailed.

I didn't know what to say, so I turned and left the dwelling, slamming the door as hard as I could on my way out. I paused on the porch. My mother had spoken of outliving me, but she seemed so weak and lifeless, nothing but an empty shell. How much longer could she go on like that? In my heart, I doubted she would last another moon.

Not bothering with the ladder, I jumped down from the porch, pulling Tempest from my shadow and landing on his back. He was galloping for the tavern a moment later. I felt like I should have been crying, but no tears filled my eyes even as I heard again in my mind all of the things my mother had said.

The tavern was just growing busy as I arrived. A few men lingered outside chatting as another passed through the doors. I tied Tempest up outside, hoping no one would notice the unusual, shadowy horse.

I'd never been allowed inside the tavern before. As soon as I crossed the threshold, I had to duck away from the gruff man who owned the place. He was Kraster's uncle, the brother of my father's wife.

Ingol was seated with some of the local woodsmen and appeared to be in the middle of a solemn conversation. Instead of interrupting, I went to join Wren at a table in the back corner of the room. I managed to reach her without anyone glancing my way or recognizing me.

"How did it go?" Wren asked as I sank into the chair beside her.

"About as poorly as it could have," I told her.

Wren's brow knit together with concern.

Thankfully, Ingol returned at that moment, giving me the chance to change the subject.

"What's the news?" I asked.

"Nothing good," Ingol reported with a shake of his head.

"Really?" I wondered.

"They said the forest is dying, something about the sap not running right," Ingol recalled. "I don't know much about trees, but they think it's because of the weather, and even the elves can't do anything to stop it."

"That's bad," Wren murmured.

"Aye, it will be if it doesn't warm up soon," Ingol replied. "They estimate they'll lose a tenth of the forest this winter along with all of the saplings."

"I don't remember anything like that ever happening before," I told them.

Suddenly, I glanced around the room.

"Where's Gnombie?" I asked, lowering my voice.

"He said he had an errand to run," Ingol answered. His tone seemed skeptical, and I glanced at the dwarf questioningly.

"I know I only joined you a short time ago, but there's something about that gnomish fella I don't really trust," he admitted.

Wren and I exchanged a quick glance. We'd shared similar concerns in the past.

"Why?" asked Wren.

"He's got an– an aura about him," Ingol answered. "And today he was acting so strange when we were talking about the stone. How well do you know him?"

"Not that well," I admitted. "He kind of hopped onto our mission out of the blue."

"Gnombie has been helpful, though," Wren pointed out, coming to his defense. "He's fought beside us many times, found a way to get to Baarthagon's Collar, and even got your horse back for you, Candra."

"Your horse?" Ingol mused. "He did that?"

"Yes," I told him.

"Do you know how?" the dwarf inquired.

"He kind of wouldn't say," Wren admitted.

"I thought as much," Ingol muttered.

"What are you getting at?" I asked.

"Well, I don't mean to drive a wedge between you all," Ingol went on. "However, as a Flame Keeper of my people, part of my training is to watch for those who might have hidden enmity or malicious intent. I don't just observe actions but was trained to see on a deeper level. It's difficult to explain, but to me, Gnombie looks tainted, as does that horse of yours."

Slowly, I nodded, wondering if Kraster would have looked tainted too. He'd been secretly helping Greyward. Had that been his choice, or did Char hold some sort of power over him? I would probably never know.

"How can we tell if he's working against us?" Wren asked.

"Well, I do have a way to test the magic behind enchanted objects," Ingol told her.

"Does Gnombie really count as an object?" I wondered.

"Of course not, but your horse does," Ingol corrected me. "Learning about the beast's origin might help us determine Gnombie's intentions. And it would probably be best for me to perform the test before he returns."

"Let's do it," I decided, rising to my feet.

Ingol and Wren followed me out to where Tempest was tethered. From a distance, he simply looked like a very black horse, but as we approached, I noticed for the first time in a long time his depthless eyes and unnatural stillness. Plus, in the full light of the sun, he was slightly translucent.

Ingol took a ring from his pocket and placed it on his right hand, then chanted a few words I didn't understand. A glow came from the ring, spreading from his fingers to the rest of his body. It made his silver armor glitter, all traces of dirt and imperfection gone as the plates of metal shone with brilliant light.

The dwarf appeared different to me now. His countenance was noble and pure. I'd known that he held a place of honor among his people as a Flame Keeper, but that title held new meaning after seeing him like this. For the first time, I realized the dwarf was significantly more powerful than he appeared.

Reaching out a glowing hand, Ingol placed it on Tempest. At first, the horse shrank back from the touch, then he stiffened and went still. After a long moment, Ingol drew his hand away.

"This creature is a shade," he said grimly.

"What does that mean?" Wren asked.

"It's a monster of ill-creation, crafted by one powerful in dark magic," the dwarf explained. "Shades bind themselves closely to a target and, when that person dies, devour their soul."

Wren's mouth opened, but she didn't say anything.

"Shall I dispatch it?" Ingol directed the question at me. His eyes met mine, and there was a hardness to them that reminded me of stone.

I nodded once, and the dwarf removed his staff from his back. Its silver ends blazed with pure light. Ingol again murmured an incantation, then swung his staff with all his might. It struck the shade on the shoulder. The weapon passed right through the beast as if it were made of smoke. In a few heartbeats, the rest of the body dissipated into nothingness, the bridle, saddle, and bags all falling to the ground.

Sorrow filled me as I thought about the animal whose form the shade had taken.

"Tempest *was* my horse," I told Ingol. "A real horse at one point. He deserved a better fate."

"Aye," the dwarf nodded. "Shades often take the likeness of things their victims are familiar with. Our *friend* Gnombie knew you'd want the beast back, so he returned the shade to you in a form he knew you'd keep close. I've seen you put the beast in your shadow and that's– well, it isn't natural."

I nodded slowly.

"But how did Gnombie do it?" Wren wondered. "Does he have magical powers? Is he a mage?"

Ingol shook his head. "Nay, I have sensed no such gift in him."

"He did leave us for quite a long time before returning with Tempe– the shade," I reminded Wren.

"He disappears quite often," she observed. "Do you think he's been contacting someone?"

"It seems likely," I admitted.

"Probably the same someone who crafted the shade," Ingol added.

"He's been lying to us this whole time?" Wren asked sadly.

"It would seem so," I told her.

Wren's shoulders drooped. "I was just starting to trust him."

"So was I," I said. "But there is still something that doesn't make sense. I've used the shade several times to escape mortal danger. If it wanted me dead, why did it help me?"

"Who said it wanted you dead?" Ingol asked. "Shades don't care when their prey dies; they simply steal the soul after it happens."

"And as for whoever sent the shade, they may not want to kill you, at least, not until your death is most useful to them."

"Lovely," I muttered. "That means whoever it was probably wants us to continue collecting stones so Gnombie can steal them from us."

Wren was suddenly patting her pockets. A moment later, she sighed in relief.

"I still have both of mine," she reported.

I double-checked and nodded to her. "He hasn't taken any yet, but we will need to keep a close eye on him. It may be time for our union to come to an end."

Chapter 18

The Message

Gnombie found us an hour later down by the livery where we'd left Valor and Raspberry. Ingol had just finished haggling for a stocky pony that was the perfect size for him to ride. We were in the process of adjusting Tempest's tack so it would fit the small steed, when the gnome popped up, practically out of thin air.

"Who's this?" he asked, gesturing to the pony.

"My new mount," Ingol informed the gnome cheerfully. "I'm going to call him Nettle. That enormous horse was just too big for me. I'll be far more comfortable on this fellow since I'll be so much closer to the ground."

Gnombie nodded slowly and turned his gaze in my direction.

"And you'll be riding...?" he trailed off, leaving the question hanging in the air.

"I'm going to ride Raspberry," I answered. "Kraster loved him so much that I can't bear the thought of selling him."

The gnome nodded slowly, eyes studying me. I knew he wanted to ask if Tempest was hidden in my shadow, but he didn't quite dare. It wouldn't take long for him to figure out that the shade was gone. However, a town full of witnesses might not be the best place for that topic to come up.

Finally, we finished equipping the pony and set out. I was glad we weren't spending the night in Owen's Falls. By morning, I would have been the talk of the town, which was something I'd rather avoid. There might be some rumors, but I wouldn't be around to hear them.

Gnombie rode behind me as we departed. He remained silent most of the day. It felt unnerving to have him there, and I half expected to receive a knife in one of my kidneys. Despite my concerns, the gnome hardly moved as we descended from the forested hills around Owen's Falls.

We made camp shortly before sunset. When Gnombie volunteered to take the first watch, an uneasy feeling swept through me. As a precaution, Wren and I slept close together, the stones safely stowed between us.

I woke before dawn, shivering with cold in the gray light. I tried to go back to sleep but soon gave up. It had been a clear evening, so we hadn't pitched the tents. However, the night was chillier than expected.

Wren was on watch, seated with her back to me. In front of her, the remains of our fire were little more than embers. Dread lanced through my heart at Wren's stillness. Why hadn't she built up the fire? I twisted free of my blanket and rushed across the open space to reach her. Wren's head was slumped on her chest. I grabbed her shoulders, praying she'd just fallen asleep.

Her eyes opened. They were filled with swirls of teal and white. I reared back as though stung. Only then did I notice how she was holding her hands in front of her, palms together, teal light escaping from between them.

"Wren! What are you doing?" I gasped.

She made no reply, and there wasn't anything I could do except wait for her to come out of the trance. It took far longer than usual, or maybe it was just my terror that made the seconds stretch on for what felt like hours. While waiting, I added more fuel to the waning fire. Absent-mindedly, I threw a handful of leaves into the flames, enjoying the blistering heat as they flared and turned to ash.

It took me a moment to realize what I'd done. The leaves I'd added had been dead. *But it's summer*, I thought. *There shouldn't be any dead leaves right now.*

Clouds covered the horizon, making it hard to gauge the passage of time. However, I was certain the sun would be rising soon. Ingol and Gnombie still had not awoken. I saw no point in rousing them until Wren's trance ended.

If it goes on much longer, maybe I should have Ingol summon Sif, I thought. The earth genie knew more about the stones than we did. Maybe he could tell us how to free her.

At last, Wren took a long breath of air, and her eyes cleared. I heaved a sigh of relief, then had to leap forward and catch her before she fell headfirst into the fire.

"What were you doing?" I snapped, keeping my voice low enough not to disturb the others. Carefully, I helped Wren back into a sitting position.

"I– I was looking for The– The Void Stone," she whimpered. "I wanted to make sure we hadn't made a mistake about it not being in the pool. Otherwise, we'd be traveling all this way for no reason."

The pain in her voice caught me off guard. I studied her face for a moment as blood began to trickle out of her nose.

"Wren?" I asked in concern.

"You were right," she choked out. "The general had the stone, but once I found it, I couldn't let go, and– I saw– I saw–"

Wren's eyes were wild and haunted, not looking at me so much as through me.

"He was on the western coast with his army," she continued.

"At The Coral City?" I asked.

"No, a little north of it," she told me. "They were waiting for The Isle of Tranquility to fall."

"What?!" I gasped. "Waiting for it to fall?"

Wren nodded weakly. More blood was coming from her nose now.

"I think you should rest," I told her.

Suddenly, both of her hands shot out as she latched onto the front of my shirt.

"It was pulled to earth by Greyward using The Void Stone." Her words came out with a blazing intensity I'd never imagined she possessed.

"At first light, it fell from the sky and crashed onto the beach. Many men perished in the aftermath of the impact, but

Greyward ordered the rest forward to subdue the inhabitants and search for what he called a 'stolen treasure'."

"Do you have any idea when this is going to happen?" I asked.

"Now," she whispered, still holding onto me. "It's happening right now." Wren turned her head to the east. The clouds had parted just enough to allow the first glimmer of dawn to be seen over the horizon.

"Are you certain?" I gasped.

Wren nodded.

I opened my mouth to say something, but she began speaking again.

"After the isle fell, I saw another army arrive. It was led by a young man with golden hair, the one I keep dreaming of. He was mounted on his flaming lion and arrayed in immaculate golden armor. He's a king. I'm not sure how, but I know he is!"

"By his side was a paladin of light, a mighty wizard wielding a staff topped with fire, and a gnomish war golem. Their army flung itself at Greyward and his troops.

"The battle was terrible. Blood was everywhere, blood red like the sun."

"Who won?" I breathed.

Wren's eyes cleared a little, and she looked at me and seemed to see me this time.

"Greyward was killing men by the dozens with The Void Stone. Its power distorted him, and he didn't look human anymore.

"He headed for the king. I was afraid Greyward would kill him too, but the wizard came to his aid. Together, they drove Greyward back and– and the golden king– he cut off Greyward's head."

My jaw dropped open. Greyward was dead. It was almost impossible to believe.

"The fight continued," she went on, words growing faint. "There was more blood, so much blood."

Wren swayed unevenly, and I realized she was also bleeding from her ears. As I moved to help her lie down, her eyes rolled up into her head, and she went limp.

"Ingol!" I called desperately, counting the heartbeats until the dwarf was at my side.

"She used the stone and had a vision, but then she passed out," I rushed to explain. "Get Sif! He might know how to help her!"

Ingol nodded and hurried to retrieve the hourglass.

I sensed Gnombie standing behind me and looking over my shoulder. Shifting to the other side of Wren, I was able to watch them both.

Ingol returned a moment later, the hourglass holding Sif's essence in hand. He performed the summoning ritual, and the craggy body of the earth elemental slowly formed.

"I am Sif of the Sand," he announced with a bow. "What does mast–"

"Do you know what's happening to her?" I interrupted.

Sif turned his attention to Wren. "She appears to be unconscious and leaking," he observed.

"I know that!" I snapped. "She used The Scrying Stone and had a vision."

"I see," Sif replied. "It seems she over-exerted herself. There is nothing we can do. She will, most likely, recover in time."

"But it's never affected her this strongly before," I protested. "Wren said she couldn't end the vision. Is that why she passed out?"

"I cannot say for sure, but if she was unable to stop the stone from draining her, then yes, that could be the cause. As she becomes more attuned to using the stone, her ability will grow stronger, and she will be able to avoid losing control," Sif informed me.

"Eventually, will it be safe for her to use The Scrying Stone?" Ingol wondered.

"No," Sif replied. "It will always take a toll on her."

Sif turned back to Wren. His eyes, two small holes in his rocky head, skimmed over her still form for a moment. "She doesn't look too bad. I believe she will wake within the hour and be just fine. However, she should not use the stone for a couple of days."

"Can I heal her with The Heart of Jong?" I wondered.

"I would not attempt it," the genie answered. "Mixing magic from the stones can have very bad side effects. It would be safer to let her recover on her own."

"That's good to know," I said with a nod of thanks.

"Is there anything else I might assist you with?" Sif asked, pivoting to look at Ingol and Gnombie in turn.

"Not for now," Ingol replied. "You may return to your vessel."

"Of course." Sif bowed his head and dissipated back into the hourglass.

Wren opened her eyes half an hour later. Aside from having a terrible headache, she said she felt all right.

We held a discussion and decided to remain where we were for another night so Wren could rest. The following day, we planned to continue west and seek the two stones we knew lay in that direction. The first was the one Greyward possessed, and the second was the one he'd been seeking. That only left one more to find. The end of our quest was finally in sight.

"What do you think happened to The Void Stone?" Wren whispered to me after Ingol and Gnombie had gone to pitch the tents and gather firewood.

"There's no way to know," I answered. "Someone could have picked it up, or it might still be on Greyward's corpse. We'll have to search carefully once we reach the battlefield."

"I hope the golden king didn't find it," she fretted. "Ingol said it wasn't safe to touch, and he seemed–" Wren hesitated while searching for the right word. "He seemed *good* to me. I'm not sure why, but I felt like he was going to do great things and rule the people wisely and fairly."

"We'll have to solve that problem when we get there. Even if he has touched it, I'm sure we can find a way to help him," I assured her.

"I've been wondering if that was part of the reason Kraster was still communicating with Greyward," Wren went on slowly. "Maybe his exposure to the stone when he was in the water made him subject to Char and those who embraced her power."

Relief flooded through me. I'd thought of that as a possible explanation for my brother's actions but couldn't help questioning if I was being too partial. It would ease my mind immensely to believe he hadn't willingly betrayed me.

"Wait a minute," I gasped, then ran to grab my pack. "We can warn them!"

"Candra?" Wren asked, wincing as she tried to sit up.

I was back by her side a moment later. Quickly, I pulled out Kraster's communication charm. "Greyward has a charm just like this one," I told Wren. "I can send a message to whoever holds it next, and they will be able to answer."

"That's wonderful!" she exclaimed. "It might not be too late!"

"I need a minute to think about what to say," I replied. I dared not give away too much information, but I needed to make my message alluring enough to evoke a response.

When I was ready, I closed my eyes and cupped the charm in my hands, projecting the words through it with my mind.

I know General Greyward has been slain. I wish to know who has acquired his possessions as there is something on his person that is very dangerous and should not be handled. Please respond so that I may help you protect yourself and your companions. I will contact you again tomorrow at dawn.

I knew I was pushing the limits of the charm's abilities with such a long communication, but I hoped none of my words would be lost.

"The message has been sent," I told Wren, who nodded eagerly, then winced, gritting her teeth in pain.

All afternoon and evening, I caught myself checking the communication charm constantly, wondering if I would get a response or if the matching charm had been lost.

Wren fell asleep early, and the rest of us were a quiet bunch around the fire that night. Gnombie seemed to sense that the group's opinion of him had shifted. He sat just outside the light of the fire ring, his hood pulled up to conceal his face.

As I was lying down, the charm clutched in my hand, I felt a tingle in my palm. Someone had responded to my message.

As soon as I felt the sensation, the words of the response flooded into my mind.

I am Apricot, defender of the land. If you were a friend of the general, then you are no friend of mine. How can I trust your words when I know nothing of who you are?

"Apricot?" I breathed. "Surely, not."

My mind took me back to a morning near the start of this journey. Kraster and I had run into a golden-haired young man, only little more than a boy. My brother persuaded him to follow his heart and seek adventure while he was still in the flower of his youth. It seemed Apricot had done just that. In fact, he'd taken it farther than either of us could have imagined since he was now leading armies and riding a flaming lion. Wren had even described him as a king.

A golden king, a flaming lion, and– I mused, then sat bolt upright.

The words of the ancient prophecy came to me then:

The flame shall be lit
The lion shall waken
The lost returned
The crown retaken

A brilliant dawn
A triumph roared
A golden king
A line restored

Could Apricot be the one foretold? A simple boy on the surface, but maybe he was more. If his touch had lit the lamp at Lion's Hill and awakened the beast, did that mean he was of the lost line of the ancient kings? I fell asleep pondering these things and trying to craft a response that would make him trust me.

My eyes opened as soon as the first traces of dawn colored the sky. Gnombie was sitting by the fire, keeping watch with his hood still drawn over his head.

"You're up early," he commented as I joined him.

"I received a message from the one who killed Greyward," I told him.

"Did he find the stone?" The gnome's dark eyes were unreadable.

"He didn't say," I replied, glad I was able to give him an honest answer. In my opinion, the less Gnombie knew about the location of the stones, the better.

"But he found the communication charm," Gnombie pointed out.

"Or he was given it," I countered.

"What are you going to say to him?" the gnome asked.

"I'm still working on that," I answered.

We lapsed into silence. After a moment, Gnombie rose and headed for the tent he shared with Ingol. It was easier to think without his dark eyes on me.

When Kraster and I had encountered Apricot, he'd been happy and carefree. In truth, my brother had spoken to him far more than I had. Maybe I could use that to my advantage.

I do not know if you remember me, but I remember you. We met at a tavern far in the north. My brother was the one who set you on your path. At that time, we were deserting Greyward's army and on a mission for one of the great dragons. We are trying to save the world, not from a man, but from darkness. Will you meet with us so that we might aid each other?

"It's sent," I murmured to myself once finished. "Now, we shall see what the king says."

Chapter 19
The Betrayal

After receiving my second message, Apricot agreed to meet us. We spent the next ten days traveling west toward The Coral City.

From my continued correspondence with Apricot, I got the impression he had already surmised that there was something bigger happening than just Greyward going on a murderous rampage. I promised Apricot a full explanation when we spoke in person. He replied with the location of a small hamlet, a score of miles from The Coral City, where we could meet.

For the first time, I felt optimistic. Apricot had an army filled with skilled warriors, not to mention his elite crew of fighters, which Wren had described.

Our days of travel were fairly uneventful until the morning of the third day, when we woke to find Gnombie gone, along with all of his possessions.

It seemed doubtful that we would see the gnome again. I was surprised he hadn't tried to take our stones either by stealing them or by slitting our throats. Gnombie was a puzzle I couldn't figure out. What had his purpose been? Why had he helped us, yet given me a soul-devouring shade? Was he on our side or our enemy's?

The mood was undoubtedly lighter with him gone. We felt free to talk and joke as we traveled. Ingol even sang for us in his rich, dwarfish voice.

The night before our meeting with Apricot, we camped a few miles from the designated location. The sea was still a day's journey to the west, but the cold breeze coming from that direction carried a hint of salt.

"Are we going to show Apricot the stones?" Wren wondered.

"I think we should," I told her. "Unless we see anything to indicate that he has been tainted by Char."

"How will we know?" Wren pressed.

I glanced at Ingol, who gave me a nod.

"I will attempt to sense his aura when we arrive," he told us. "If anything feels ill, I will signal."

"Then what?" Wren demanded unhappily. "We murder him?"

I hesitated, the answer coming slowly to my lips. "We must protect the world, and to do that, we need the stones. We cannot let anything stand in our way, not even Apricot."

A scowl darkened Wren's face. I understood how she felt. The last thing I wanted to do was kill the golden-haired youth Kraster had convinced to forsake farming and seek his destiny.

When we reached the meeting spot the next morning, I saw that a lavish pavilion had been raised. The cedar poles and white, silken sheets of fabric looked fit for a king.

Leaving the horses, Wren, Ingol, and I entered. Inside was a long, polished table. Seated on the side opposite were several faces I recognized and a couple I didn't.

The first was Apricot. He looked much older than when we'd met at the beginning of summer. The traces of boyhood had vanished, leaving behind the noble visage of a young knight. He was dressed in his armor, which was as I had imagined from Wren's description: golden and glorious.

To his left was a man who was clearly a wizard. From his pointed hat, muted robes, and white beard, there could be no doubt in my mind. According to Wren's vision, he had been the one to help Apricot defeat Greyward. Even seated at the table, he had a staff gripped in one hand. The top of it wasn't on fire, as in Wren's vision, but glowed brightly with red light.

Sitting on its haunches behind Apricot was a lion with wings of flame. Those wings seemed familiar to me, as though I'd seen something similar before but couldn't recall where or when. The lion watched us with the bored expression of disdain that I had observed many times on cats a hundredth of this one's size. Even still, there was something very human about its great, orange eyes.

On Apricot's right was someone I had never expected to see again. It was Lucille, the high elf woman whom I had met in Thea. She was wearing armor similar to Apricot's, but hers was a silver metal tinged with orange the same shade as her eyes. On her shoulder was an orange and brown emblem of a tree.

Beside Lucille was an even more unlikely individual. A gnome named Gnomex who we'd encountered in Gnomania while retrieving Dimble's Legacy from the golem factory. He didn't sit on a chair like the rest, but on a mechanical golem of sorts. The construct rested on the ground with the top dome of the head pulled back to reveal a small seat and a control panel.

"You!" he squeaked, the first to speak. "You're the ones who massacred my people!"

I paused just inside the pavilion's opening, Wren and Ingol right behind me. All eyes turned to the gnome who had surged to his feet.

"They are our enemies!" he shrieked, then he squinted hard at Ingol. I think he was trying to figure out if the dwarf was Kraster. In all fairness, when he'd met us it had been night, and Wren was holding him in a headlock. Plus, he was so small that I'm sure dwarves and humans just seemed large to him.

Apricot's eyes turned on me. "Is this true?" he asked.

"We were not responsible for the massacre," I replied. "We had no more idea what was happening beneath the gnomes' plateau than any of you did."

"Yet, you showed up on the day of the assault to take the one thing that might have been our salvation," Gnomex spat.

I looked him directly in the eye. "As I told you then, we were trying to stop a great evil."

"Well, you failed, and my people paid the price," he replied with a shake of his head. "Myself and several others piloted the completed golems, but we weren't enough. Thousands of gnomes died, and the rest had to flee. We are scattered and homeless now, all thanks to you!"

144

"Our actions changed nothing. Your people were out of time. If we had not taken Dimble's Legacy, it would have ended up in the hands of the enemy," I snapped back.

Gnomex curled his lip in disgust. "I will never trust you nor do I wish to sit at the same table. I have sworn vengeance on all those who have wronged my people. That is why I have joined the human army. They will help me seek justice."

"I am very sorry for what happened in Gnomania," I told the gnome. "But I have not come to speak with you. Leave if you must."

I turned my attention back to Apricot as I purposefully stepped forward and took the seat across from him. Ingol and Wren followed my lead, sitting on either side of me.

Apricot appraised me with cool eyes. "Tell me, where is your brother?" he asked.

"My brother is dead," I answered without so much as a tremble in my voice.

"I am sorry to hear that," Apricot told me, and I believed him. "Please, explain what has brought you here. You said you were on a mission from a great dragon, but it seems my friend believes you to have caused death and destruction among his people."

"That is because evil forces are hunting us," Wren spoke up. "We have only just managed to stay ahead of them."

"Evil forces?" the wizard asked with one raised eyebrow. "I know of no evil forces."

"Have you not been paying attention?" Ingol blurted out. "Your gnome companion just spoke of the invasion of his homeland, reports of an attack on The Hall of Asteropaios are widespread in my people's domain, and my friends are witnesses of the devastation of the high elf forest in the south."

I noticed Lucille shift uncomfortably at his words.

"I could go on," the dwarf stated. "There are evil forces all around us. We're practically drowning in them. If you do not see, it is because you have chosen not to."

As the wizard began to reply, Apricot held up a hand. The wizard looked none too pleased at being silenced. Reluctantly, he shut his mouth.

"You have told us that there are many bad things happening in the world right now," Apricot said. "We already knew that. What we are yet to hear is this plan of yours that will save the world."

"We don't know it," I admitted hesitantly, earning a snort from the wizard and a sneer from Gnomex.

"Shal'eth, one of the great dragons of old, gave us the task of gathering eight stones, each a gift given to a dragon long ago," I explained.

"And then what?" Apricot asked. "What happens after you have them all?"

"I am not sure," I replied slowly. "What I do know is that it's very important who uses the stones once they have been collected."

"And, pray tell, who would that be?" the wizard inquired. "You?"

"Certainly not," I snapped, then turned to glance at Ingol and Wren. "Among my companions, I am the least. Ingol is a Flame Keeper, trained to serve the eternal light. Wren was raised at the shrine of Shal'eth and appointed by him for this mission. Both are far more qualified than I."

A shadow of doubt crossed Ingol's face, and Wren hunched down in her chair.

"You believe *they* could be more suitable than the king?" boomed the wizard. "Than King James Trenton Bartholomew Apricot, eighth of his name, long lost heir of the slain King Ardit, lawful ruler of The Great City, The Land of Golden Fruit, and all the kingdoms of men?"

It was Apricot's turn to look slightly embarrassed. "I'm just Apricot for now," he mumbled.

"Maybe you are correct," I told the wizard. "As I said, I do not know. I am trusting that once our task is complete, The Great Shal'eth shall return and offer us the knowledge of the ages to save our land. If the stones are meant for Apricot, then so be it. I will not stand in his way."

The wizard and I glared at each other for a long moment.

"I believe they speak the truth," Lucille cut into the silence smoothly. Apricot glanced at her eagerly. I could tell her opinion meant more to him than that of the others.

"I know of these stones," the high elf went on. "Our friend, Axel, wields one in his staff."

All attention turned to the wizard, who narrowed his eyes darkly at Lucille. "I wasn't aware you were educated in anything beyond the use of swords and shields," he said to her through gritted teeth.

"I am educated in many things," the elf shot back. "I knew that you had Azazoth's Wand the moment we met."

Axel's lip curled. "It is Azazoth's no longer. I took the stone from the wand, and it is mine now." There was a dangerous edge to his words.

"It will remain Azazoth's Wand for a very long time," Lucille countered. "Despite the fact that he has passed on, he was the greatest wizard to ever live. Long will it be before his name is forgotten."

"This is wonderful news!" Ingol broke in, ignoring the clear tension between Axel and Lucille. "We didn't know where that stone was, but now we do. That just leaves two more."

"If you think I am going to hand my staff over to you, you are gravely mistaken," the wizard snarled at Ingol.

"No one's suggesting that," I told him hastily. "I don't see any reason why we shouldn't all work together to find the rest of the stones. We know Greyward had one of them, but it is tainted and seems to have the ability to corrupt anyone who touches it. We feared one of you might have done so unknowingly."

I looked at those sitting across from me.

Slowly, the lion rose to his feet and turned to Axel. "You insisted on being the one to search the general's body," the beast said aloud. "Yet you brought us no stone when you showed us the rest of his belongings."

147

The lion had a much more human voice than I'd expected. It was soft at the moment, but I imagined there could be power behind it if needed.

"You have also been using magic to shield your aura ever since," Lucille said. "If you have touched The Void Stone, there is still time to help you."

"This is preposterous!" spluttered the wizard. "Are you all really accusing me of treachery?"

Did she just call it The Void Stone? I wondered to myself. *That's the same name Gnombie used. That can't be a coincidence.*

"I will not listen to this anymore!" Axel cried, rising from his seat and marching out of the pavilion.

I watched him go with great concern since he was taking at least one of the stones with him.

The lion coiled himself and reared up, placing his front two legs on the table so he could peer down at me and my companions. His flowing mane wasn't fiery like his wings, but each hair glowed like an ember.

"I am Lamasku of the Lamp. I sense that two of my kind are with you," he said. "I would very much like to hear what they have to say."

I stared at the beast blankly for a moment.

"Do you mean Puvva and Sif?" Wren asked.

The lion dipped his shaggy head to her. "Indeed, I do."

"I'm confused," Apricot said, looking between us and Lamasku.

"I told you that there were three others like me," the lion explained. "Two of them are here with us in their own vessels."

Wren brought out the teapot, and Ingol did the same with the hourglass. As both began the summoning process, I heard a strange sound. I rose from my chair and hastened to the entrance of the pavilion. Lucille did the same, her movements unnaturally fast. Apricot followed a second later. Just as I stepped outside, a gigantic blast of fire struck the pavilion, collapsing it and engulfing it in flames.

I whipped around. An enormous portal hung in the air just behind a fire-breathing, fifty-foot-tall goose.

The Hawnkenquack! my brain screamed at me.

The monster opened its mouth, and I could see a red glow building within. I dodged out of the way as another stream of fire engulfed the remains of the pavilion.

"Wren! Ingol!" I cried.

Out of the corner of my eye, I saw Axel standing inside a circle of runes. The wizard's face was twisted into a vicious smile. Apricot rushed toward him with the flaming lion by his side. Lucille was on their heels.

However, I only cared about my trapped friends. Ignoring the heat, I carefully wove through the mounds of burning cloth, attempting to reach the place where Wren and Ingol had been sitting. The outline of the table was mostly visible beneath the blackened fabric of the pavilion. I kicked a flaming pole out of the way and drew one of my knives, then started to cut away what was left of the charred cloth.

"Wren! Ingol!" I called again, eyes filling with tears.

Something moved under the remains of the pavilion a few feet away. I ripped the fabric open to create an escape route.

Puvva was the first to emerge. In her hands, she held her teapot. Close behind her was Sif, carrying his hourglass. When no one followed them, I started tearing away as much of the cloth as I could.

"My master has perished," Puvva told me flatly. "I must return to my previous master and learn who my new master will be, as one was not arranged for me prior."

"Wait!" I choked out as the genie started to walk away. "Wren is dead?"

"That is correct," she stated, not even slowing her gait.

"I'm so sorry," Sif told me.

I gave him a questioning look, unable to form words.

"Ingol too," he confirmed. "And a gnome I did not recognize."

Everything inside of me went numb. Wren was dead. Ingol was dead. I was alone.

Sif put a hand on my shoulder. It was hard and warm.

"I have to go to Shal'eth too," he told me. "I'm sorry to leave you like this, but I have no choice."

With a regretful look, Sif hurried after Puvva.

Not knowing exactly how I got there, I found myself on my knees among the charred ruins of the pavilion. Smoke and ash clogged my eyes from the areas that were still burning, but I didn't care.

This was the end. My mission had failed. How could I possibly be expected to go on alone?

A screech, like a metal blade on a granite wall, brought me back to the present. The Hawnkenquack had turned and was torching a row of trees.

I staggered to my feet.

To my right, Apricot, Lamasku, and Lucille had reached Axel.

"What have you done?" Apricot yelled, coming to a halt just outside the ring of runes.

Axel made no reply, only pulled out a knife, whispered a spell, and sent the blade flying through the air. It stabbed Apricot in the chest, embedding itself deeply in his heart.

Lamasku let out a bellow of pain and recoiled.

"No!" Lucille screamed, kneeling to catch Apricot's body. She looked up at the wizard in horror. "How could you do this?" she breathed. "We needed him. The world needed him."

"*Your* world, maybe," the wizard replied.

Fumbling in my pouch for The Heart of Jong, I sprinted toward Apricot. I didn't know much about how the stones worked, but if anything could save him, it could.

"Why, Axel? Why?" I heard the tears in Lucille's voice. "You took The Void Stone, didn't you? There's still time for you to be cleansed before its evil consumes you!"

Grinning, the wizard held up a purple stone. The rune for void had been scraped shallowly over the surface, defacing another rune underneath. The very sight of it made me shudder.

I dropped to one knee on the ground beside Apricot, The Heart of Jong clutched in my hand. I was too late. His eyes were open, but glazed, and his skin was already growing cold.

"You will not stop me," Axel told Lucille. "I've been planning this for a very long time. My master, Rakus, taught me many things, but as the years went by, I saw that he never aged while I grew older and older. I found books a millennium old, written in his hand.

"He never shared the gift of eternal life with me, but I have found my own way! I learned of Azazoth's Wand and the other stones. Once I have them all, I will reign over this world for all of eternity!"

"If that's what you think, you are a fool!" Lucille spat. So quickly that I couldn't even follow her movements, she had her broadsword in her hand and was attacking the wizard.

Suddenly, the Hawnkenquack's head snapped in our direction. Its eyes focused on me.

I charged.

It was stupid, but I didn't care. All I wanted was to destroy the monstrosity that had killed my friends. Running with all my might, I gathered myself and leapt straight at the beast's head, swords pointed at the nearest eye. The creature opened its mouth. I saw fire building within, the flames that would be my death.

Chapter 20
The Meeting

With a battle cry on my lips, I leapt violently to my feet, bringing down the tent around me.

"What?" Wren cried groggily.

At the sound of her voice, I wrenched the fallen fabric out of the way.

There she was, still lying in her bedroll, looking up at me with wide eyes.

"I– I had a dream," I said, even though it felt so much more real than any dream I'd ever experienced.

"I did too," Wren whispered hoarsely. "I died, and so did Ingol."

"What?" I gasped, dropping to the ground beside her. "This is very important," I said, "how did you die?"

"We'd gone to our meeting with Apricot," Wren started. "While we were talking, one of his people, a wizard named Axel, stormed out. The flaming lion from Lion's Hill was there too. He asked Ingol and me to summon Sif and Puvva. Just as we did, you, Apricot, and a high elf paladin ran for the door, then a wave of fire struck us. Ingol and I were pinned down by the wreckage. He worked so hard to free me, but the flames reached him first."

Horror filled my friend's eyes. "I watched him burn to death and could do nothing to help," she whimpered. "Everything was on fire, and it was too hot to breathe."

Large tears were rolling down Wren's cheeks. "I was in a lot of pain, and the world was dark. I felt like I was floating, then I heard you screaming and opened my eyes. You were here, and there was no fire…"

Wren ran out of breath.

"That's exactly what I dreamed," I told her.

"I don't underst–" Wren started.

"Is everything all right?" Ingol's voice interrupted.

"Ingol!" Wren shrieked in joy. She started scrambling toward where the opening for our tent had once been.

I followed her out into the cool night air. Wren launched herself at Ingol, all but strangling the poor dwarf as she hugged him.

"I'm so glad you're alive!" she said, somehow managing to weep and laugh at the same time.

"I am too," Ingol told her. "But I'm very confused. What is going on? Why would I not be alive?"

"You don't remember?" I asked him.

"Remember what?" he wondered.

"Our meeting with Apricot," I answered.

"We haven't had it yet," the dwarf replied.

"Yes, we did!" Wren announced. "You died, and I died; it was terrible." She was crying again.

"What are you on about?" Ingol asked, trying to free himself from Wren. She gave him one last squeeze and a kiss on the cheek before letting him go.

"Wren and I seemed to have shared a dream or maybe a vision of some sort," I explained.

Ingol's eyes widened. "You dreamed of our meeting tomorrow?" he asked.

I nodded.

"And we died?" he questioned.

I nodded again.

"What are we going to do?" Wren gasped. "We can't walk into that trap."

"We need to warn Apricot," I said.

"You're sure he's not the one who wants us dead?" Ingol asked.

"No." I shook my head. "Axel killed him too."

"I hate to ask, but isn't it possible that you both just dreamed this?" Ingol wondered.

"We both dreamed exactly the same thing?" I raised an eyebrow at the dwarf.

"Or, maybe, one of you woke up and told the other, and suddenly you both thought you'd dreamed it," Ingol clarified. "I want to see if there's another explanation before we start throwing around accusations. I know you both quite well, and I'm not even sure what's going on here."

I considered for a moment, certain I hadn't made anything up based on what Wren had said.

"Summon Puvva and Sif," I commanded.

"Why?" Wren asked in confusion.

"Because they were both there," I explained. "And if they remember it too, then that means something really did happen."

Both of my friends went to retrieve their vessels. A moment later, Puvva and Sif stood before us.

"This is very strange," Puvva said, cocking her head to one side. It was unusual for her to be summoned and not instantly launch into her customary greeting.

"How do you mean?" asked Sif after he'd given his address.

Puvva looked very hard at Wren, especially studying the two bracelets that appeared on her arm whenever the genie was present. These indicated the number of wishes she had left. I'd tried to see if something similar happened to Ingol, but the dwarf wore a lot of armor, so I'd been left to speculate.

"Were you not dead a moment ago, or had I slipped into a delicious fantasy?" Puvva inquired of Wren.

"Delicious fantasy?" I growled at the genie. "You want Wren to die?"

"Yes," Puvva answered bluntly.

"Is it so you can be free?" Wren asked sadly.

"No, I simply want all mortals dead, drowned beneath the cleansing waters of the sea," Puvva clarified.

"That's enough of that," Sif snorted. "I apologize on her behalf–"

"You shall not," Puvva cut him off. "Because I am not sorry and have only spoken the truth."

"Enough!" I all but shouted at the bickering pair. "Puvva, what you saw, Wren and I saw too. It was some kind of dream."

"I see," Puvva mused, looking at Wren. "You used The Scrying Stone for a group vision of the future."

"Group vision?" Ingol, Wren, and I all asked at the same time.

"Yes," Puvva answered.

"And?" I pressed.

Puvva rolled her eyes at me. "It is as it sounds, you foolish mortal. She used The Scrying Stone to see a vision of the future. You and I were pulled into it." The genie sighed as though she'd just explained the most rudimentary thing in the world.

"The stone can do that?" Wren squeaked.

"Indeed," Puvva told her. "The Scrying Stone's primary function is to guard the future. That is the gift that was given to Shal'eth."

"The Great Shal'eth could see the future?" Wren asked.

"Of course," Puvva replied. "At least, before he lost the ability to wield his gift. Once that happened, he could only join in group visions when someone else held The Scrying Stone. What else do you think he's been doing all these years?"

"I never thought about it," Wren admitted.

"Obviously," Puvva mumbled under her breath.

"How did Wren create a group vision while she was asleep?" Ingol wondered, then glanced at Wren. "Unless you were actually trying to use the stone."

"I wasn't!" Wren assured him.

"It seems your connection to The Scrying Stone is very strong," Puvva reflected. "Your subconscious must have activated its power."

"It's happened before," Wren admitted. "I've seen lots of things, but sometimes they don't seem very important. One night, I dreamed I was in a wheat field. I stood there for hours and hours, watching the wind move through the stalks, but nothing else happened."

"It appears that the stone is using *you*," Puvva pointed out.

"What does that mean, exactly?" I asked the genie.

She rolled her eyes at me, but at least I got an answer. "It means the stone is showing her things on its own. While her subconscious is probably directing the visions slightly, she is not choosing them."

"Is that why my nighttime visions have never hurt me?" Wren wondered.

"Yes," Puvva replied. "It's the difference between struggling against the current and floating along with it."

"Then what you three saw, it was real?" Ingol asked, looking between us.

"It is a possible future. One I am sure you all will choose not to fulfill," Puvva answered.

"Definitely," I muttered.

"Then we need to decide how best to avoid it," Ingol said.

In the end, I convinced the others that I should send a message warning Apricot of a possible trap and asking him for a private meeting between the two of us. Neither Wren nor Ingol liked the idea. While they both offered to go in my stead, it had to be me, since I was the only one Apricot had met before. Also, there was no way I would let either of my friends endanger themselves after I'd witnessed their deaths last night.

Four hours later, I mounted Raspberry and rode to the new location that Apricot's answering message had described. It was a field with a single oak tree.

I'd left my stones with Wren and Ingol. When I'd taken them from my pack, my hand had touched something else, something I had been saving for a long time. As my fingers closed around the circular object, I finally knew what I was going to do with it.

I arrived at the meeting place before Apricot. Dismounting, I left Raspberry to crop the scraggly grass while I moved closer to the tree. As I approached, I saw that the leaves had started to change color even though fall was far away.

"It's dying," a voice said behind me.

I spun around. Apricot stood there. I was surprised I hadn't heard his horse's hooves, then I noticed Lamasku a dozen feet behind him.

"Everything is dying," I murmured, then extended my hand to Apricot, offering a golden piece of fruit. It was one of the few apricots I had left, preserved in its prime by the power of Dimble's Legacy. Apricot looked at it in wonder as he received the beautiful fruit.

"Greetings, King James Trenton Bartholomew Apricot, eighth of his name, long lost heir of the slain King Ardit, lawful ruler of The Great City, The Land of Golden Fruit, and all the kingdoms of men," I said with a bow.

Embarrassment colored his cheeks. "I'm just Apricot for now," he mumbled.

"As you wish," I replied with a deep nod.

"You requested we meet alone due to a possible ambush?" Apricot asked.

I nodded. "It's true, and I am sorry to be the one to tell you this, but your life is in danger from one whom you trust."

"If you are speaking of Lucille, you are wrong," Apricot announced quickly. "I know what some have said of her, but she is trustworthy, and you won't be able to convince me otherwise. She was the one who sought me out and revealed my lineage. I didn't believe her at first, but she told me the prophecy and took me to Lion's Hill, where I touched the lamp and woke the lion of flame."

"No, not her," I replied. "Lucille is loyal to you."

"I'm glad to hear you say it," Apricot told me. "I've had many advise me that trusting an elf is foolishness."

I gave him a curious look, then reached up to brush my hair back, revealing a pointed ear. "Didn't you know that I am a half-elf?"

"No," Apricot shook his head with a little laugh. "I guess I didn't. Is your brother a half-elf too?"

"No," I answered solemnly. "He was human, through and through, but he is dead now."

"Oh, I'm so sorry to hear that," Apricot told me. "He seemed very kind and brave."

"He was," I murmured. We both fell silent for a moment, then I looked the young king in the eye.

"It's Axel," I told him softly. "He's going to betray you."

"Axel?" Apricot tilted his head slightly. "He's saved my life many times. Why would he turn on me now?"

"Because he was using you and your army. You have seen the stone in his staff?" I wondered.

Apricot nodded.

"It is an ancient relic, one of eight gifted to the great dragons long ago. One of them, The Void Stone, is corrupted. It came from a fallen dragon named Char. Those who touch it become tainted too. Axel took this stone from the body of General Greyward. I do not know if his intentions were pure before that, but I have reason to suspect they were not.

"Now he possesses two of these stones and is seeking the others in order to subjugate the land to his rule."

"How do you know all of this?" Apricot breathed.

"My companions and I are also gathering the stones," I admitted. Apricot gave me a sharp look as I continued. "We've been told that they are the only way to save the world."

"How many do you have?" Apricot asked. There was a suspicious edge to his voice.

I hesitated but decided it was better to lay all my cards on the table. "Five."

Apricot nodded slowly. "So you were the ones who took the stone from Gnomania, leaving them helpless against the invasion from the UnderEarth?"

Maybe I had been too honest. I'd hoped that this particular subject wouldn't come up since Gnomex hadn't been invited to this meeting.

"It's not as simple as that," I started.

"I think it is," Apricot cut in.

I pursed my lips and answered with care. "We had no way of knowing that an attack was coming, and I truly do not believe that the stone would have been enough to save them. Had it fallen into the wrong hands, even worse things could have happened."

"Worse things?" Apricot asked skeptically. "Such as?"

"I don't know," I said. "I did not foresee that, but what I did foresee was that if we met with you tomorrow, as we had originally intended, you, Gnomex, both of my friends, and maybe even Lucille and I would have been murdered by Axel."

"And how did you foresee this?" Apricot wondered.

"One of the stones we've collected is called The Scrying Stone," I told him. "With it, we were able to glimpse the future. A possible future, at least."

"And did you steal that stone too?" he asked, voice touched by anger.

"No," I whispered. A wave of sorrow washed over me, not because he was wrong but because he was right. Maybe we had messed everything up, and the world was falling apart as a result of our actions.

Apricot must have seen the misery on my face, because his expression relented.

"Listen," he began, "I think you have been trying to do the right thing. I'm just not sure what you've been doing *is* the right thing. Put yourself in my place for a moment. I hardly know you, and now you're asking me to question the loyalty of a friend. Plus, I feel like you would have just taken Axel's stone, or stones, if you could have. How am I supposed to trust you?"

I swallowed, trying to think of anything I could say, any way I could prove not only my intent, but the truth of my mission.

"Lamasku," I said loudly. The lion glanced at me, but didn't say anything and turned his head away quickly.

"He is simply my mount," Apricot told me.

"Do not try to deceive me," I replied. "I know exactly what he is. You see, my two companions each carry a vessel of their own."

Lamasku looked at me again and came several steps forward.

159

I addressed my next words to him. "I believe you are familiar with Puvva of the Pot and Sif of the Sand."

"I know them," the lion confirmed.

"And do you know Shal'eth?" I continued.

"Intimately," Lamasku answered.

"He was the one who sent us on our quest. He gave us Puvva and The Scrying Stone. What do you make of that?"

Lamasku hesitated. He and Apricot exchanged a long look before his eyes found mine again.

"Shal'eth is a dragon, and dragons do not think in the terms of mortals. Whatever Shal'eth is planning, he may consider a hundred thousand lives a small price to pay in order to achieve the bigger picture. Not to mention, he has been deceived before and committed unspeakable acts. Having blind faith in him would be a mistake."

I contemplated the lion's words in silence. When I had spoken to Shal'eth, I was so convinced by the things he said that the conviction had driven me all across Planosia. Now I was starting to question if it was merely the power of his dragon's tongue that persuaded me, not the truth of his words and the nobility of his spirit.

"What about Asteropaios?" I asked, almost desperately. "We told her of our mission, and she aided us on our path. She even recreated her gift for us."

"Asteropaios you should trust with your life," Lamasku replied. "She alone remained faithful when the others were turned. If she has bid you to continue your quest, then do so."

A great deal of the weight on my heart lifted at his words.

"Then you think I should give them my aid?" Apricot asked Lamasku.

The lion nodded solemnly. "The dragons broke this world. It seems now they are trying to fix it. Although I fear it is too late."

"I will return to our camp and speak with Axel," Apricot told me. He raised his hand to stop the objection that rose to my lips. "I will take precautions in case he attempts anything."

"He is very powerful," I couldn't help saying. "He was trained by another great wizard. Plus, he has two stones of immense power."

"I will speak to Lucille of all that you have told me, and we will make a plan," Apricot promised. "What will you and your people do?"

"There is one stone left whose location is a mystery," I explained. "It is called The Gem of Aero. Greyward was looking for it when he attacked The Isle of Tranquility. We will search among the rubble and attempt to recover it."

"There's not much left," Apricot said grimly. "When the isle was brought down, it shattered on the beach, then rolled into the sea, vanishing from sight."

I shuddered at the thought of how deep that water must be.

"Were there any survivors?" I asked. "Someone we might be able to ask about the stone?"

"Before the isle fell, we saw a cloud of creatures take flight," Apricot began. "They headed to the south but never came close enough to the ground for us to make out what they were. No bodies were found in the water or washed up on the shore."

"Then south my companions and I shall head in the hopes that we might find them and that they will have the final stone," I said.

"And if they won't give up the stone?" Apricot wondered. It didn't come out as an accusation but a question.

"We will find a way," I told him. "Once all eight stones are brought together, I believe whatever is going to happen will happen very quickly."

"That seems likely," Apricot said with a nod. "I will send you a message when I can."

He walked to Lamasku and mounted. The beast leapt into the air and soared away on wings of flame.

Chapter 21
The Letter

As soon as I returned to the others, I could see that something was wrong.

Ingol was sitting hunched on the ground, staring at a piece of parchment. I had to blink a couple of times before I could convince myself that I really was seeing tears in the dwarf's large, round eyes.

Wren crouched beside him, one hand placed lightly on his arm. On his opposite shoulder perched what appeared to be a bird. As I drew closer, I saw that it was mechanical in nature, with a small, yellow gem set in the center of its chest.

"Is everyone all right?" I demanded, sliding off Raspberry before the horse had come to a full stop.

Ingol looked up at me, face full of despair.

"What's happened?" I gasped, a horrible fear crushing the air from my lungs.

"It's my forge," Ingol started in a choked voice. "The King's Forge, which has been lit for a thousand years. It's gone out."

"Gone out?" I asked uncertainly.

"They were attacked, and the fires of the forge were smothered," the dwarf explained. "By the time my people were able to press the enemy back, it was too late."

"I'm so sorry," I told him.

"I should have been there," he growled, making a fist and crumpling the parchment.

"You're a valiant warrior, Ingol," Wren said gently. "But it sounds like there were too many of them."

"I am a Flame Keeper!" he protested. "It was my duty to die before allowing the fire to go cold."

"Then I'm glad you're here," I told him. "Forges can be relit, but the world would be a worse place without you in it."

"I appreciate your kind words," Ingol said, looking between Wren and me. "But the forge cannot be relit."

"Why not?" Wren asked.

"At its core is a piece of what we call magmos metal, the only one ever found," Ingol explained. "It burns hotter and slower than any other element and would have continued to do so for countless millennia."

"Was it taken?" I wondered.

"No." The dwarf shook his head. "But a breath from Morazz the Fire Drake himself was required to ignite it the first time, and that great dragon hasn't been seen in the land for centuries."

"Maybe there's another way," Wren suggested.

Sadly, Ingol looked down at the crumpled letter in his hand. "There's no hope of that. Even if there was, I wouldn't be around to see it. I have abandoned my post, failed my people, and shamed my family. I will never return to the mountains now."

"You came on this journey to help not just your people but all the people of Planosia," I reminded him.

"It does not matter," Ingol sighed. "Even if they will not pass judgment on me, I shall pass it on myself and remain in exile forever."

Wren and I exchanged a glance over the dwarf's head.

"Once we have gathered the stones and saved the world, our new mission will be to find a way to relight your forge," she vowed. "We will make sure you can go home, just like the rest of us."

I cringed slightly. There certainly wasn't a home waiting for me at the end of this quest. I hadn't even considered what I would do once it was done. However, her words had a good effect on Ingol.

"Really?" the dwarf asked. "You would aid me?"

"Of course!" Wren cried. "Especially after all you've done for us!"

"Then I will accept your help and attempt to redeem myself." Ingol's tears had dried up. He clambered to his feet and turned to look at me. "Now, tell us how your meeting went."

I spent the next twenty minutes relaying my conversation with Apricot.

"Sounds like it didn't go so badly," Ingol commented after I'd finished.

"It didn't go that well either," I muttered. "But it was definitely better than the alternative."

"That stuff he said, about all the damage we've done, he's right, isn't he?" Wren asked forlornly.

"In a way," I told her.

"If the world is falling apart as quickly as Shal'eth seems to believe, then all of these things would have happened anyway," Ingol assured us. "Just maybe not as soon in certain locations."

"That's not comforting," Wren told him. "That means wherever we choose to go next is certain to be attacked. How can we knowingly lead the enemy to those from The Isle of Tranquility? Especially when they have already lost their home?"

"We do it because we must," I said. "If they have the last stone or know of its location, then we have to risk it."

"I agree," Ingol added. "It is too late to stop now."

Both of us looked hesitantly at Wren, hoping she was convinced.

"At least they should be the last innocents we have to endanger," Wren mumbled glumly, which I took as her agreement.

Even though the day was half gone, we set out, intending to cover as many miles as possible. The inhabitants of the isle had a decent head start, so speed was of great importance. We cut across the land, traveling south and west.

Wren offered to use The Scrying Stone, but I reasoned that it wasn't necessary, as such a large group of refugees would have trouble hiding their trail. Plus, if Wren searched for them now, while they were still several days away, she might have to do it again. Each use would require long stretches of time for Wren to recover. I was determined only to ask her to use the stone as a last resort.

Our path took us almost directly toward The Coral City. I had been there once, when Greyward dispatched Kraster and me to deal with a gang boss trying to expand his operation into Unkempt. It was our very first covert assignment and the first time we'd worked as a solo pair instead of part of a larger unit.

Things had not gone smoothly. Our cover was blown twice, at least a dozen times we found ourselves running for our lives, and I still had a scar on my ribs that showed how close I'd come to dying. In the end, my brother and I did manage to assassinate the gang boss and several of his subordinates. Both of us had been badly injured in the process and left behind quite a mess.

Still, it was one of my favorite memories because that was the mission where I finally learned to trust Kraster. He couldn't say the same since, apparently, he'd always trusted me, which really made no sense, but was true nonetheless.

Looking back, those were the best days of my life. What I wouldn't give for one more daring mission with my cheerful brother by my side, watching my back while I watched his.

Would you really give the world for that? I asked myself. As much as I wanted to say yes, I knew I wouldn't. I only wished the price had been my life, not Kraster's.

At twilight, as we were making camp, I heard the sound of hoofbeats from the direction we had come. I drew my blades, calling for the others to stand ready.

In the distance, we saw a lone rider bearing down on our position at a canter. The insignia he wore was a blazing, golden lion. When I saw it, I lowered my swords and walked a few steps forward. The rider pulled the horse to a stop in front of me.

"Are you Candra?" he asked.

"Yes," I replied.

"What was your brother's name?" he questioned me.

"Kraster," I told him.

The man nodded and held out a wrapped package.

I sheathed my swords and accepted it from the solemn messenger. Without another word, he turned his horse and departed.

"What is it?" Wren asked, coming to peer over my shoulder.

I started to unwrap the bundle and stopped as something fell out.

Wren squeaked and jumped back. I knelt and picked up the top of Axel's staff. The stone from Azazoth's Wand was still in it, glowing red as the sun, with the rune for fire carved into one of its smooth sides. This stone burned slightly instead of tingling when my fingers brushed its surface.

"I can't believe it," Ingol breathed. "He actually sent us Azazoth's Wand."

"What about The Void Stone?" Wren wondered.

I shook out the cloth wrapping carefully. There was no second stone, only a note, which fluttered to the ground.

Picking it up, I read aloud. "Candra, I hope my trust in you is not misplaced. The price to obtain this stone was very high. Lucille was gravely injured. She is not expected to survive the night. Axel has fled with The Void Stone. I do not know where he has gone, but I will hunt him to the ends of the earth. Apricot."

Carefully, I plucked Azazoth's Wand from the end of the staff head and handed it to Ingol. After considering for a moment, I also took Baarthagon's Collar from my pouch and gave it to the dwarf as well.

"Now we each have two," I told the others.

"Thank you for your trust," Ingol said with a solemn nod of his head.

He held both stones close to his eyes and inspected them.

"This one feels like fire," he murmured, looking at Azazoth's Wand. "Reminds me of the forge." His voice was sad, and I knew he was thinking of the home he might never see again.

A moment later, he'd tucked both stones into his breast pocket, close to his heart.

166

I slept very little that night. At dawn, I sent a message to Apricot.

We have received the stone. I am sorry to hear about Lucille. She was a noble warrior. Soon, we too will be hunting Axel.

Apricot made no reply, and I resolved to leave him in whatever peace he could find.

Halfway through the next day, we discovered a large patch of ground that had been torn and trampled by many creatures. They left a clear path in their wake, leading south toward Moshtia. There were footprints of many different sizes and shapes, along with the remains of fires and campsites, but we didn't see a single soul.

Before long, the trail turned east. We followed it for another six and a half days before it ended as suddenly as it had begun.

"They're just gone," Wren whispered, looking around in every direction.

"Apricot did tell me that they had fled the isle with wings," I recalled.

"They must have decided to fly again and shake off anyone following them," Ingol surmised.

"That's my guess," I replied.

"Then it might be time to use The Scrying Stone," Ingol said hesitantly. Both he and I turned to look at Wren, but she wasn't listening to us. Her eyes were locked on the eastern horizon.

"I'm home," she whispered.

"What do you mean?" Ingol asked.

I squinted into the distance and realized that she was right. Several hundred feet away, I could make out the edges of the vineyard that grew around Thea, where Wren had been born and raised.

Without a word to either of us, Wren leapt atop Valor and set off at a steady trot to the east. Ingol and I mounted and followed.

Our journey had led us back to the beginning.

Chapter 22
The Shrine

Even before we reached the first field, I could see that the vines were dead and the grapes shriveled. Wren had stopped her horse and was staring across the desolation. I brought Raspberry to Valor's side.

About half the fields were burned, the others were like this one, completely withered.

"I didn't– I didn't think it would be this bad," Wren whispered. "I've only been away a few months."

I thought back over the days. When Kraster and I had arrived, summer was just beginning, and the land was covered in green foliage.

"It hasn't rained since I left home," Ingol told us as he stopped Nettle on Wren's other side. "And it's been cold. Plants don't like those things."

"Why hasn't it rained?" Wren asked.

"I don't know," Ingol answered. "The weather has been peculiar of late. I thought Asteropaios helped you surface dwellers when there were droughts, her being The Queen of Storms and all."

"She does in some places, but she's never come here," Wren told him.

"She and Shal'eth were once mates," I said. "But they had a falling out."

"That would explain it," Ingol murmured.

Wren remained silent as we started forward again, heading for the little town in the center of the fields. Most of the buildings had been burned too. What remained of them were forlorn, white plaster walls marked with smoke. The shrine itself appeared untouched.

"He's here," Wren breathed.

"What?" I asked, turning to look at her.

"The Great Shal'eth. He's here. I can feel it." Wren dismounted and started walking toward the shrine entrance in an almost trance-like state.

I slid off Raspberry and hurried after her.

Inside, the shrine was a mess. The curtain that divided the room was slashed to ribbons, and the pedestal for Puvva's teapot was toppled and broken in half. The chairs, where I'd sat with Shal'eth at our first meeting, were all in one piece. I didn't know if that was because they had gone untouched or been repaired since. Five of them were grouped together in the back corner of the shrine. In the one that faced the door sat Shal'eth.

He was as I remembered him, having the body of a muscular human man and the head of a dragon with white scales and bright teal eyes.

"I've been expecting you. Won't you sit down?" Shal'eth asked, motioning to the extra chairs. Wren and I sat just as Ingol stepped inside the shrine. The dwarf drew in a sharp breath, then hurried to join us, taking the next to last seat.

"Ingol," the dragon greeted the dwarf. "Good to see you again. I am glad you were able to find Wren and Candra."

"More like they found me," Ingol mumbled.

"You knew we were coming?" Wren asked hesitantly.

"I knew it was likely," Shal'eth answered.

"How?" I wondered. I didn't feel afraid of the dragon anymore. He presented a mystery, but not really a danger, even though I was certain he could have killed any of us had he wanted to.

"I have seen many futures unfold, and, in nearly all of them, at least you two returned to me here," the dragon said, glancing between Wren and me. "Sometimes there were other companions with you and sometimes not."

My mouth suddenly went dry, but I managed to gasp out a single name. "Kraster?"

Shal'eth nodded slowly. "Often."

That one word broke my heart.

Often.

Kraster hadn't needed to die. He could have lived.

Often.

It had been more than possible; it had been probable. I could have saved him. I *should* have saved him, but I hadn't.

Often.

My eyes drifted to the empty chair.

I missed what was said next, too busy trying not to let grief and guilt consume me. When I did start listening again, Wren was telling Shal'eth of our journey. Ingol interjected a few times after the part where he joined us, but I remained completely silent.

"So now you have six stones," the dragon mused at the conclusion.

"And we think we are close to another," Wren told him excitedly.

"That is good to hear," Shal'eth said. "Time is running short, and it may be necessary for you to use The Scrying Stone to locate the exact posit–"

"Wait a minute," I interrupted.

Wren had been nodding along eagerly to the dragon's words. I knew she revered and respected him, but in that moment, something about the situation felt wrong.

Shal'eth and the others turned to me. My gaze hardened.

"How did you know we were coming here?" I asked the dragon.

"As I said, I have seen it in many different versions of the future," Shal'eth explained.

"But you can't see the future anymore," I replied. "All of the betrayers lost the ability to use their gifts."

Shal'eth stiffened ever so slightly when I called him a "betrayer". I hadn't meant to say it, but the word had come out unbidden. Wren was looking at me with a mortified expression, but I set my jaw.

"You are correct," Shal'eth conceded. "I have not been able to use The Scrying Stone for a very long time."

"So you had mortals use it for you," I guessed.

He nodded. "That is correct. Some mortals have the ability to wield the gifts of the dragons. Not to their full power, but enough."

"And Wren's mother was one such mortal?" I pressed.

"She was," Shal'eth replied.

While Wren and Ingol appeared confused by my line of questioning, Shal'eth seemed to understand where the conversation was going. He'd probably seen it before in one of the possible futures.

I didn't ask any more questions. I just looked the dragon full in the face, not nearly as easy a feat as it sounds, and it does not sound easy.

"Elise was very gifted with The Scrying Stone," Shal'eth began. "She trained with me for many years, learning to use the stone to see the future. Her ability allowed her to bring me into the visions. Together, we watched the future and attempted to craft a plan to save the world.

"For seven years we worked, trying to find the best path forward."

"Seven years?" I demanded. "Only seven years?"

Shal'eth hesitated before answering. "In the seventh year, Elise began to grow ill."

"Because she used the stone so much," Wren realized aloud.

Shal'eth dipped his head. "She knew the risks and the most likely outcome but chose to help me anyway. Soon, she could no longer use The Scrying Stone without excruciating pain. I suggested she take a break, but we both knew there was no time.

"None of the other shrine maidens or acolytes had her ability, so she decided to pass her gift along."

There was a sharp intake of breath from Wren.

"She thought that the blood of a high elf would make her child stronger and more powerful, able to help me find the answers when she could not," Shal'eth went on.

The dragon's words made the blood in my veins run cold. Wren's mother had borne her to pass on a blessing. Mine had

171

decided to have me to pass on a curse. Were we all to be pawns in the games of others?

Shal'eth turned to look at Wren, speaking to her as if the rest of us didn't exist. "Elise stopped using the stone for a time. Once you were born, she began again. The visions changed greatly after that, for we saw that this quest would be your destiny.

"It made Elise proud to watch you and everything you might accomplish. I am very sorry that you only knew her for a short time. There was so much she could have taught you."

The dragon fell silent, eyes still watching Wren, who looked back at him with an expression of utter shock. She took a few, shuddering breaths before speaking.

"You could have stopped her! You could have saved her! How could you do that to her? How could you do it to *me*?" The pain was raw in Wren's voice.

"You lied to me my whole life!" she screamed, rising to her feet. "You brought me up to be one of your shrine maidens. I was supposed to revere you like a king! All the while, you planned to sacrifice me the same way you did my mother! That was why I had special lessons. You were preparing me to use the stone!"

"It's all true," Shal'eth admitted calmly.

Wren was rendered speechless by the admission. Her chest was rising and falling rapidly as she stared at the dragon.

"I know you are upset," Shal'eth said coaxingly. "But there are few who can use The Scrying Stone. Its power is delicate, shaped by the mind of the user and the choices they intend to make. Only those well-trained and willing can wield it properly. Without gifted individuals, like you and your mother, all would be lost.

"I wish I had the ability to shoulder this burden, but I don't. For centuries, I've sat in this building, contemplating the evils I have done and how to fix them. The end is coming, and I barely have any power left at all. Less and less with each day."

"Good," Wren snapped. She turned and walked out of the room, pausing by the doorway to look back at Shal'eth. "I hope I never see you again."

Then Wren was gone, walking away into the late afternoon light. Shal'eth looked after her, the expression on his scaly face unreadable. I wondered how many times he'd seen this conversation end with those very words.

Fury filled me. He was sitting here, playing games with our lives, acting like he knew everything to come and was oh so wise.

"Are you working for Char?" I asked.

His head snapped in my direction.

"No," he answered, sounding surprised. Maybe I had finally done something he hadn't seen in a possible future.

"Are you sure?" I wondered. "You're both after the stones and seem willing to do whatever it takes to get them. I mean, what does it matter if a few of us mortals suffer horribly and die?

"I know you've already had two of the vessels release their hold on Char, and I haven't the faintest clue why."

"I assure you, I have the best interests of all at heart," Shal'eth told me. His voice, his eyes, everything about his being made me think he was being earnest, which is why I no longer trusted him.

"You know," I said, rising to my feet, "I never understood why you wanted *me* to go with Wren. It didn't make sense. By all accounts, I was your enemy. But for some reason, you convinced me that I was important and needed.

"I think I know why now; it's because I can use the stones too.

"Just like Wren was her mother's replacement, I'm supposed to be Wren's replacement. Once she's broken and of no more use to you, am I next? Was Kraster on the list too? How about Ingol? Did you plan to go through us one after the other? Weak, disposable, pathetic creatures that we are."

Shal'eth contemplated me silently for a long moment. "You were never my enemy," he whispered so softly I barely heard it. "And I am very, very sorry."

"An apology? Now?" I practically laughed. "I was right when I called you a betrayer earlier, because that's what you are. That's *who* you are. It doesn't matter if you're working for Char or just for yourself, you have betrayed Wren and her mother, you betrayed Asteropaios, and you've betrayed me."

For the first time, Shal'eth appeared shaken. Maybe using his once-mate's name had triggered something, but he lowered his head and made no reply.

"Come on, Ingol," I said. "Let's go find Wren."

The dwarf got to his feet and followed me to the door.

I half expected Shal'eth to try to stop us, or take our stones, or kill us, but he never moved from his seat, and I didn't look back.

Wren was standing beside Valor, face pressed against the horse's soft neck as she sobbed.

I gently patted her on the shoulder, not knowing what to say. Maybe I shouldn't have been so brash. Perhaps I could have found a better way for the secrets of Wren's past to come out, but I didn't do subtle very well.

"It'll be okay, lassie," Ingol told Wren. "I know you heard some terrible things in there, but the truth is always best, no matter how hard it is to hear."

"My own mother," Wren managed to choke out. "My own mother had me just so I could die for– for *him*!"

"She wanted to give you the best chance possible," Ingol assured her. "That's why you're half elf."

"Oh yes, and that was such an easy thing to live with," Wren scoffed.

"I know it wasn't," Ingol replied. "But your mother, she really must have believed in Shal'eth and his cause."

Wren gave the dwarf an accusatory glance.

"I'm not saying I do," he added quickly. "But she did. She thought she was helping the world, and maybe she was. Maybe Shal'eth is trying to do what's best."

"He should have found a better way," Wren protested.

"Sometimes there is no better way," Ingol said softly.

"So you trust him?" I asked.

The dwarf hesitated before answering. "Not entirely, but he isn't tainted like that gnome companion of yours. However, dragons are a different kind. Could be he's playing a game all his own."

"That's the sense I got too," I replied.

"Then what do we do?" Wren wondered, wiping the tears from her eyes.

"We keep going," I answered. "The world is tearing itself apart; Shal'eth was right about that much at least. And everybody who's anybody is trying to get their hands on the stones."

"I agree," Ingol said.

"But we don't even know where the last two are," Wren sighed. "And I am never using the Scrying Stone again!"

"That's all right," I told her. "Axel is a wizard, and I don't think he'll stay hidden for long. The other stone seems to have flown away, but I have an idea about that."

"What is it?" Ingol inquired.

"Now that they feel they've lost any pursuers, what would a large company who had to flee their home quickly need most?" I asked. "Especially in a land where it hasn't rained in ages."

"Water," Wren guessed.

I nodded. "The few streams we've passed recently wouldn't have been enough for such a vast company, so I'm sure they'll be looking for a larger source of water."

"Is there one close by?" Ingol wondered.

I nodded. "There's a river not far from here. I'd bet every stone we have that we will find those from The Isle of Tranquility there."

Chapter 23
The Infiltration

"It's not much farther," I told the others as the sun began to set on the day after we'd left the shrine. "Should be just over that rise." I pointed to a rocky outcrop ahead of us. Our horses reached the bottom of the slope a minute later and started the short climb to the top.

"What if they've already moved on?" Wren fretted.

I shrugged.

"I just hope we can–" Ingol started, then cut off as we crested the hill.

All three of us pulled up sharply on our reins.

"Get down!" I hissed, leaping from my saddle and hurriedly leading Raspberry back the way we had come.

I glanced over my shoulder when I reached the bottom of the ridge. The others were right behind me. I closed my eyes, listening for sounds that would indicate we'd been seen by the vast host camped beside the river below.

"Those were orcs!" Wren gasped.

I nodded.

"I thought they were extinct," she continued.

"So did I," I told her.

Wren furrowed her forehead. "They're the ones that have been living on The Isle of Tranquility this whole time?"

"They must be," Ingol answered.

"I'm going to have another look," I decided, handing Raspberry's reins to Wren.

Carefully, I scrambled back up to the top of the slope and peeked out at the landscape below. Hundreds of tents had been pitched along the riverbank. About the same number of fires burned throughout the camp, each with several large greenish-gray orcs assembled around it.

Besides the orcs, there were thousands of griffins. The enormous creatures seemed to be as docile as horses while their orc handlers fed and cleaned them. All in all, it was one of the most incredible things I'd ever witnessed, and I'd stood in the presence of more than one dragon.

If they had a stone, where would it be? I asked myself, eyes roving through the camp. There was only one tent that stood out from the others. It was made of a yellow cloth and was set quite close to the water's edge. The yellow tent was easily three or four times the size of the others, which were made of brown leather.

I watched the entrance for a few minutes and saw a couple of the largest orcs in the entire company walk inside. It was hard to tell in the fading light, but it looked like someone much smaller and lighter on their feet accompanied them.

Careful not to cause a rockslide, I maneuvered back down the hill to where my companions were waiting.

"If they have a stone, I think it's most likely to be in the big tent," I said, concluding my report.

"It's not a bad guess," Ingol replied. "But there is a way to be certain–" He cut off with a glance at Wren.

She was purposefully looking in the other direction. Maybe she would have been willing to at least have a discussion on the matter if it had been more than two days since we'd learned how the stone had led her mother to an early grave. Right now, however, the answer was no.

"I can't believe we're doing this," Ingol muttered two hours later as we squatted behind a rock. We were positioned on the top of the ridge. It was dark, but my elf blood allowed me to clearly see the hulking orcs as they moved between campfires.

"Courage," I whispered to him.

"There's a difference between courage and stupidity," he countered.

We'd spent the past two hours arguing about what to do. Once again, I found myself missing Kraster and his abilities. If he were with us, we could have easily put one of the sentries to sleep.

After taking them far from the river, it would have been easy to question them about the stone and its whereabouts.

Instead, we were going in blind to search for something we weren't even sure was there. If we found nothing tonight, I might need to put some pressure on Wren. If she wouldn't use the stone, then I would. At this point, I didn't feel like I had anything left to lose.

"If we are going to do this, we should get it over with," Wren said sulkily. She had been in a bad mood ever since Ingol brought up The Scrying Stone.

I nodded and drew the hood of my cloak over my head. Wren and Ingol did the same. They followed me as I began creeping down the hill to the camp below.

Having never expected to meet one, I knew almost nothing about orcs except that they were insanely strong and prone to violence. Hopefully, their eyesight was more like that of a human, and the shadows of the night would hide us. Most of the company had retired to their tents, but a few silhouettes lingered, keeping watch by firelight.

Before we had known that the refugees were orcs, our plan had been to speak with whoever we found so we could determine if they had the stone and how best to get it. We'd quickly put all ideas of talking behind us when we saw the horde camped along the river.

The tents were laid out in a sprawling fashion, which I used to my advantage as I tried to avoid the patches of light cast by flickering flames. Several times, I stopped and dropped back to take cover as an orc lumbered past. They were even larger up close, at least a head and shoulders taller than me. I couldn't imagine how they would appear to Ingol.

Despite the height difference, the dwarf had the greatest chance of passing as one of them. Concealed in his cloak, he was the right shape to be mistaken for an orc child.

When the yellow tent was just ahead, a fight broke out to my right. I pressed myself back into the shadows as two large, male orcs began to grapple. More of the creatures began pouring out of the tents close by. They formed a ring around the pair. The two males separated and stood snarling at each other before one lunged for the other's throat.

Thankful for the distraction, I backtracked several yards, then took a new slant toward the yellow tent. The cheers and boos of the crowd rose and fell behind us as we hurried forward.

Finally, we reached the side of the yellow tent. There was a dim glow of light coming from the gap where the cloth ended and the ground began. I took out a dagger and cut a small slit in the fabric. Putting my eye to the hole, I looked inside and saw that there was a fire pit in the center of the tent. It only held embers now, and the low stools around it were empty. The rest of the space was filled with crates, chests, and other pieces of baggage.

Carefully, I widened the slit until I could slip through. Wren followed as I looked around to make sure we were alone. Ingol joined us a moment later, after summoning Sif to keep watch for us. Wren had suggested we summon Puvva too, but I had nixed the idea. The pair seemed unable to do anything but bicker when they were together. Since Sif was by far the more helpful of the two, he'd been chosen for guard duty.

"Start searching," I whispered to the others as I walked to the closest chest. The lid opened with a creak, and I froze. After a moment, I carefully began examining the contents.

I was surprised to find that the chest held a collection of old books. They were so ancient I was afraid to touch them lest they crumble to dust. The titles written on the spines were all in a language I didn't know.

Holding my breath, I slowly lowered the lid, pleased that the creak was barely audible this time. Surprisingly, the next chest was also full of books, but these didn't seem half so old. I'd thought of orcs as brutish and uneducated, but clearly, the tomes were something they prized.

I checked the progress of the others. Wren was shifting through a trunk full of fabric, and Ingol was examining what appeared to be a case of rings. The latter were large enough to be used as napkin holders at the fancy dinners Greyward had never invited me to.

After a few more minutes of searching, I hadn't turned up anything useful. There were several crates of iron tankards, a padded box of glass goblets, and a few chests of different sizes, each containing pieces of an elegant suit of armor. The metal work was ornate and inlaid with yellow gems.

The only thing all of the items had in common was that they were old and well-used. Maybe the orcs considered them relics. I could see no other reason for them to have been brought along. Everything about this tent and its trappings seemed out of place compared to the rest of the camp.

A small box caught my eye. It was tucked into a corner between a leather griffin saddle and a rolled-up tapestry. I reached into the gap and pulled out the chest. It was locked. I sat down cross-legged on the floor and tried to jimmy it with my smallest dagger.

I wasn't very good at lock picking, but the lock was pretty old. On my fourth try, I heard a click. Lifting the lid, I was disappointed to find that inside was only a small journal. I would have put it back immediately, but I was interested to learn why this chest was locked when none of the others had been, even though their contents were far more valuable.

Curiously, I opened the journal. The top page was actually the last, since I'd opened the book upside down. I drew in a sharp breath as I caught sight of what was written on the paper in the common tongue. It was a list of names, but not just any names, they were dragon names. There were also comments beside each, which I read with fascination.

Asteropaios – The Queen of the Dragons – Still of sound mind, but not reining in all her glory. For an unknown reason, her power seems to have diminished, as have all of ours.

Shal'eth – Lost in mourning and self-imposed exile to the shrine in the west. He seeks desperately to repair what he has destroyed.

Morazz – The Fire Drake – Driven insane by the part he played. He is bound by magic and trapped in a prison of flesh that is not his own.

Camroc – The male twin remains in contact from the plateau. He has accepted his place but is willing to consider how to build a better future.

Zaydia – The female twin also serves her people from the plateau. She attempts to make penance for her wrongs in small ways, one kindness at a time.

Karradin – The Wise – My old friend searches for the heir to the lost line of kings. Should she find him, she will take him to Lion's Hill. I do not know what she can even hope to achieve. It is far too late to rebuild the kingdom of men. Even should she succeed, it will only rise to fall again.

Lathaan – Great Wing – Grounded once more but for the wings of others, present and accounted for, living in exile due to the prejudice of the world.

Char – The Corrupter – Bound by the elements. She still holds more power than any of the rest of us. Her future is rapidly approaching, and there is nothing we can do but accept our doom.

I hastily turned to the first page of the journal. After reading a few sentences, I realized it was a firsthand account of what had happened to each of the great dragons after they fell from power.

"Wren," I whispered, rising and turning to look for her. As I did, my foot caught the edge of the tapestry, knocking it over. It fell to the ground with a soft thud and began to unroll.

Hastily, I knelt to pick it up, but my fingers stopped moving just before they touched the fabric. The tapestry was of The Constellation of the Great Dragons, showing each of them in full color, and there, at their center, was another creature, one with wings of fire.

Before I could tell what I was looking at, part of the far wall of the tent pulled back to reveal a sleeping space. Wren gave a cry of terror as she locked eyes with the eight-foot-tall orc who had been inside.

It was hard to tell which of them was more surprised, but the orc recovered more quickly than she did. Faster than seemed possible for a creature of his size, he sprang at Wren and latched onto her arm. Ingol drew his staff, but before he could come to her aid, half a dozen orcs poured inside through the tent's entrance.

I drew my swords and leapt forward, facing down two foes. Each of them was armed with an axe as large as a horse's head.

The first orc roared something I couldn't understand as the tent erupted in battle. I spotted Ingol swinging his staff, then my view was cut off. I charged at the nearest foe, but never reached him, because someone seized me from behind.

Chapter 24
The Refugees

The orc that had grabbed me got an elbow in the gut for his trouble. My hope was that the blow would stun him long enough for me to escape his clutches. It didn't work. Even though there was a grunt of surprise, the arm around my waist only tightened.

I could sense the orc's other hand reaching for my shoulder, so I twisted violently to the left and managed to slip away, but only for a moment. A second set of hands caught my wrist, bending it back and making me drop one of my swords.

I swung my other weapon at him, only for it to be intercepted by the edge of an axe.

As quickly as I could, I pulled back, ready to strike again, but there were too many of them. Both of my arms were seized, and the hilt of my second sword was plucked from my grasp. They started dragging me toward the orc who had been sleeping in the tent. He had strange, yellow eyes that glowed in the dim light.

I fought the entire way, twisting and writhing, knowing that if I did not get free and save my friends, we would all be killed.

It can't end like this, I thought. *Our quest can't fail here, then my brother will have died for nothing!*

Gritting my teeth, I pulled with all my might, desperate to escape the hands of my captors. However, they were orcs, and I was a half-elf. There was no chance. They didn't even slacken their pace until I was lined up beside my friends, who were likewise restrained.

I locked my gaze with that of the yellow-eyed orc.

Something about his face was different from the others. Their skin was weathered and pocked, while his was smooth, without a single scar. Also, the shape of his jaw was longer and more narrow.

A strange look filled his eyes as I was brought to stand before him.

"Let her go," he said perfectly in the common tongue.

"Why would we let them go?" demanded a burly, grayish orc to my left. He stumbled over the words, and I could tell he wasn't used to the common language.

"Just her." The yellow-eyed orc pointed at me.

"She's the most dangerous one," protested the much smaller male who was holding my left wrist.

A glare from the yellow-eyed orc was enough to make them release me. As soon as their hands slipped from my body, I drew my largest set of daggers and readied myself to attack the green, female orc who was holding Wren's arms behind her back.

"Wait." The command came not from the yellow-eyed orc, but from a figure who stepped out of the shadows to stand beside him. She was definitely not an orc. Neither was she a human, nor an elf, nor a dwarf, nor a gnome, nor any species I'd seen before. Her face was more that of a fox than of a girl, but there was a strong resemblance to both. She stood on two legs, but a pair of vulpine ears peeked through her long, midnight hair. A robe covered in a deep blue design swirled around her body in a breeze that wasn't there.

"It would be rude to attack again without even hearing my master out," the fox creature told me. Her eyes were a hard gray, like the metal of a blade.

I relaxed my stance. Slightly.

"Thank you, Faleous," the yellow-eyed orc told her before turning back to me.

"There is no reason for us to be enemies," he continued. "I know who you are and why you have come."

"I'm nobody," I growled at him savagely, tightening the grip on my daggers. "You know nothing of me, and if you did, you wouldn't want to be my friend."

To my utmost surprise, the orc reached into a leather pouch hanging from his belt and pulled out a yellow stone the same color as his eyes. He tossed it to me. I caught it out of reflex, dropping one of my daggers in the process.

The stone was warm, and a familiar tingle rippled through my body as I clutched it. Even before I saw the rune for flight engraved on its surface, there was no doubt in my mind that this was The Gem of Aero, the seventh of the eight stones we were seeking.

The yellow-eyed orc motioned to those holding Wren and Ingol. My friends were released immediately.

"Why are you giving this to me?" I demanded, holding up the stone.

"It is what you came for, is it not?" he countered.

"But how did you know?" I pressed.

"The one you call Rakus told me," answered the orc.

"You know Rakus?" Wren gasped.

"I do," the orc said, nodding to her.

"Who are you?" I asked after a moment of silence.

He tipped his head to the side in a very unorc-like fashion, and a bemused expression spread across his face.

"You're like Shal'eth," I breathed. "You're one of the great dragons of old."

"Indeed, I am," he admitted, then spoke several words in a deep, guttural tongue. The orcs in the room quickly filed to the door and out into the night. Several of them looked over their shoulders at us, eyes ranging from hostile to curious.

"I was once called Lathaan Great Wing," the yellow-eyed orc went on. "But, as you can see, I have wings no more and am grounded once again."

"But if you're a dragon, what are you doing here?" Wren wondered.

"Why should I not be here?" Lathaan asked, spreading his arms to encompass the room and the items in it. "Because those I live with are orcs?"

"Well, yes," Wren started, then realized what she'd said and quickly backtracked. "No, that's not what I meant. It's just that you're a dragon! Shouldn't you be like– like–" Her voice cut off.

"Like Asteropaios and Shal'eth?" Faleous finished for her, a sneer in her voice. "Off being worshiped by foolish mortals?"

Wren made a sour face but nodded.

Just then, Sif came fumbling through the hole I'd cut in the back of the tent.

"Master! I saw a bunch of orcs leaving, and I–" the earth elemental cut off as he took in the scene.

"You?!" he cried in surprise, looking at Faleous.

"Me!" She grinned back at him, revealing pointed canines.

"I take it you two know each other," Ingol guessed.

"Indeed, we do," Sif answered stiffly. "The thief!"

"What did she steal?" Wren asked.

"The Isle of Tranquility," Faleous smirked.

"It was mine!" Sif growled. "The peak of my tallest and most beautiful mountain!"

Faleous sighed and rolled her eyes. "That mountain was useless. When I liberated the top, I made a home for orcs, griffins, and gnomes. You should be thanking me."

"But you ruined it!" cried Sif, almost tearfully.

"Wait," I cut in. "Do you mean The Gnome Plateau? It was once a mountain?"

"The most beautiful mountain ever to exist," Sif lamented.

"Hardly," scoffed Faleous. "It was much nicer as an isle."

"Was?!" Sif asked in horror.

"The isle fell from the sky quite a few days ago," Wren told him softly.

I never would have imagined an elemental could look heartbroken, but an expression of intense sorrow crossed Sif's face.

"I told you I'd give it back someday," the fox girl chortled. "Although I think it ended up in Puvva's domain. My bad." The way she grinned made it clear she wasn't sorry at all.

"That's enough for now, Faleous," Lathaan said, taking out a long flute of gray metal.

Closing her eyes, the genie dissolved into smoke and trickled into the flute. Without asking to be dismissed, Sif did the same with the hourglass. Clearly, he wanted to be alone.

"I am sorry about her," Lathaan apologized to us. "She enjoys provoking others more than she should."

"We have another one like that," I muttered.

"Once I was no longer able to use my gift, I returned to my true form," the dragon picked up where he'd left off. "You see, while I am a dragon, I hatched without wings. Much as I longed to fly, I could not. At least, not until I was chosen as one of the great dragons and blessed with the gift of flight."

Lathaan looked at me, yellow eyes contrite. "It grieves me to say, but even after all that I was given, I still fell to Char's words and turned traitor. The regret has torn at me every day, and I am so sorry. Out of all of the great dragons, I had the most to be thankful for, yet I threw my gift away like trash."

There was a long pause before the dragon continued. "While the orcs and their griffins were the only ones who could give me back the sky, the world was not kind to them. I asked Shal'eth for Faleous. He agreed that I should be her guardian until such time as he needed her again. As her master, I wished for Faleous to combine her abilities with The Gem of Aero and levitate The Isle of Tranquility.

"Thus, I created a sanctuary for the orc race, who were being aggressively hunted by both humans and elves."

"Why were they being hunted?" Wren asked.

"Because individuals are often judged by what they look like and not who they are," Lathaan told us. "I'm sure when you were gathering the other stones you did not resort to sneaking around by night and attempted theft." He gave each of us a stern look.

"Hardly," I scoffed. "The gnomes attacked us several times without even knowing what we wanted. We did attempt to talk to the high elves, then they tried to kill us. Plus, we figured it would be pointless to attempt negotiations with the humans since their stone was making them rich."

"I see the land has grown far more fractured than it was when I left," Lathaan mused, almost to himself, before addressing us again.

"You have gathered many of the stones, then?" he asked.

"Yes," I answered, slightly guarded.

"We have all but one of them," Wren told Lathaan.

"All except The Void Stone," he stated.

"Yes, but we know who has it," I told him.

"As do I," Lathaan replied.

"How would you know?" Ingol asked. "I mean no offense, but you've only just come down off your isle less than a score of days ago."

"Rakus must have told him about that too," Wren guessed.

"Indeed, he did," Lathaan confirmed. "Rakus said the human who used its power to bring the isle down was slain in battle. The stone was then taken by a wizard who was once Rakus's apprentice but abandoned his training in order to seek his own glory and power."

I blinked as all the pieces fell into place.

"Rakus is the same as you, isn't he?" I asked.

Lathaan smiled. His teeth were very pointy. I wasn't sure if that was from the dragon part of him, the orc part, or both.

"You're starting to catch on now," he said. "Rakus is the great dragon Camroc. Like Shal'eth, he is no longer able to take his true form."

"Is Rakus here?" Wren wondered eagerly.

"No, he and the others have been hunting the wizard," Lathaan answered.

"His name is Axel," Wren told the dragon. "We sort of met him, then he killed me."

Lathaan didn't quite know what to make of that and cocked his head to one side.

"Do you know Shal'eth's plan?" I asked before we had to explain the vision we'd seen of the future. "When we've gathered all eight stones, what then?"

Lathaan's yellow eyes fixed on me for a long moment, and I knew he was deciding exactly how much of the truth to tell me, or rather, how much of the truth he needed to tell me to make me do what he and the other dragons wanted.

"I cannot say," he finally replied.

I crossed my arms over my chest.

"Then we have a problem," I snapped. "My friends and I have been all across the land, destruction just a step behind. My brother died, along with hundreds of others. I think we've earned the right to be let in on the plan."

"I don't disagree with you," Lathaan attempted to assure me. "But until the final stone is obtained, even we don't entirely know how things will play out."

There was sincerity in what he said but also a lot of misdirection.

"Why didn't the great dragons gather the stones themselves?" Ingol asked. "Seems like that would have been far easier, especially since nearly half of you already had one. Couldn't you have–"

"It would not have been possible," Lathaan interrupted. "While we had several stones in our possession, we were being watched. Had we attempted to locate the rest, Char would certainly have made her move, which would have cost even more lives. We would not have been able to stand against her."

"But you're dragons," Ingol protested. "Surely, together you could have bested her and her forces."

A sad look crossed Lathaan's face. "Most of us are dragons in name only."

"But Asteropaios alone is strong enough to–" Wren started.

"Asteropaios no longer trusts the rest of us," Lathaan interjected. "And for good reason. We are fallen creatures, deserving of our fate." Lathaan lowered his head, and I could see years of regret and despair in his posture.

"Then why did she give us her stone?" I asked, breaking the heavy silence that had fallen.

Lathaan's attention snapped to me. He remained silent for a long moment, eyes burning with intensity.

"Hope," was the one-word answer he finally gave.

"But is she working with you now?" I pressed. "Is she helping the rest of you find Axel?"

Lathaan dipped his head in assent.

"Then she must trust you somewhat," Ingol said.

"Perhaps," Lathaan mused. "I think it more likely that she has seen the signs."

"The signs of what?" Wren asked, eyes wide.

Lathaan didn't answer but took a deep breath. "You'll have to ask her," was all he said.

"Maybe we should," I agreed. "Do you know where she is?"

"I do not, but the last I heard, Rakus had tracked Axel to Lake Sona," Lathaan informed us. "There is an old tower on the shores where Axel has been seen. I imagine that is where Asteropaios can be found."

"If Axel is there, then the stone will be too, and that's where we need to go," I announced. "I've not heard of this lake. Can you tell us how to find it?"

"I can do even better than that," Lathaan replied. "I will lend you griffins to fly you there along with an escort."

"Will you be coming with us?" Ingol asked.

"Not yet, but I will join you there as soon as I can," the dragon promised. "First, I must escort my people to my old lair. In the caverns there, they will be able to take shelter from whatever comes next. I failed in my duty as a guardian once; now I will not abandon those who took me in when no others would.

"However, I have two able-bodied scouts in mind who will make sure you reach the lake safely."

"When can we leave?" I asked.

"At dawn," Lathaan answered. "I will attempt to contact Shal'eth and let him know your plan."

"I'm not sure that's a good idea," I murmured, glancing at Wren.

"Why?" Lathaan asked.

"Because he's trying to release Char, and we're not completely sure whose side he's on," I admitted.

"It is true he is trying to free her," confirmed Lathaan. "He was the one to bind her, so only he can unbind her."

I raised an eyebrow skeptically at the dragon.

"Why would he do that?" Ingol exclaimed.

"Only once she's free will The Void Stone come into its full power," Lathaan replied. "Until that happens, the eight stones cannot be used together, and her evil will continue to consume the world, polluting and destroying it little by little."

Grudgingly, I nodded. I was certain we still weren't getting the full story.

Maybe once I had all the stones, I would drop them down a hole somewhere, then Shal'eth could go on his own wild goose chase. It would serve him right.

Chapter 25
The Flight

"I'm really not sure about this," I said, skeptically eyeing the griffin in front of me. Even crouched, its shoulders were as high as those of a horse. Speaking of horses, we were leaving Raspberry, Valor, and Nettle with the orcs after Wren had extracted a promise from Lathaan that they would not be eaten.

"You'll be fine," sighed an orc named Daisy, who had mottled gray and brown skin.

Lathaan had told me that there was a time when orcs and humans lived together, and the bloodlines had occasionally mingled. Unlike most half-breeds, half-orcs had no trouble reproducing. Daisy was one of those who still carried a portion of human blood, making her shorter and slighter in frame. However, her massive biceps were still thicker than my thighs. She and her mate, Ralph, another orc with a touch of human heritage, were the ones escorting us to Lake Sona.

I glanced around nervously. Wren and her griffin were getting along great. She was petting him just behind his tufted ears while he gently butted her with his head. A moment later, the creature flopped onto his side, exposing his stomach to Wren for more scratches.

At least Ingol seemed as uneasy as I did about the feathered beasts we were going to be riding as soon as the sun rose.

"Casum won't do you no harm," Ralph promised, gently stroking my griffin's beak. The male orc was half a foot taller than Daisy, with dark green skin. He had a deep, guttural voice and seemed the more reserved of the two.

"I'm sure it will be fine," I replied, trying to sound braver than I felt.

Ten minutes later, Daisy helped me mount Casum. By "helped me mount" I mean she grabbed my leg and thrust up so hard I was almost hurled completely over the griffin's back and off the other side. Clinging to the saddle, I managed to scramble into an upright position.

"Could say 'thank you'," I heard Daisy grumble as she moved on to Wren. Before she reached the half-elf, Wren had nimbly scaled the griffin's back and taken her seat.

I glanced to my left where Ralph had half climbed into the saddle of a third griffin with Ingol thrown over his shoulder. The dwarf, who wasn't even accustomed to riding a horse, took a long time getting situated.

Finally, Daisy and Ralph mounted their own, even larger, griffins. The pair took the lead, guiding the beasts away from the camp and out into the empty plain beyond. Thankfully, Casum followed on his own, even when those in front of him picked up speed and spread their wings.

I leaned forward and tightened my grip on the front of the leather saddle. I'd been warned against holding onto the feathers since they were sensitive, and nothing made a griffin dump its rider faster than feather pulling.

With three mighty beats of his wings, Casum lifted off from the ground and soared after his brethren. The moment we were in the air, a stupid grin spread across my face. It was incredible. The wind rushed through my hair, blowing it straight back. I looked down and felt giddy at how far the ground was below us as we continued to rise.

Glancing back, I saw Ingol with his eyes closed and knuckles white as he clung to his saddle. To my right, Wren peeked a look at the ground and went pale as she witnessed exactly how far down the drop was.

I laughed at them. Why be afraid now? The air was freedom itself!

My griffin lowered one wing as he banked slightly. I leaned into the turn, squinting as we headed straight toward the rising sun. I never wanted the flight to end. I could have sat on the griffin forever, floating above the land, riding the wind, and watching the miles vanish beneath us.

A little before noon, I spotted Shal'eth's shrine going by below. From the corner of my eye, I saw Wren looking down at it with a tormented expression. When I checked on Ingol, he looked like he'd either been sick or was about to be.

Straightening in my seat, I could see Daisy and Ralph ahead of us, their mounts side-by-side. The orcs appeared as comfortable in the air as they were on the ground.

I wondered how they knew the way to our destination. Had Lathaan shown them a map? Or had the pair left The Isle of Tranquility to scout the land in times past? Whatever the reason, they seemed confident that they knew the way. While we had been told the trip would take about a day and a half, we'd been rushed off to griffin riding training before I could ask where Lake Sona was located.

We stopped in the early afternoon for about an hour to let the griffins rest. The creatures drank deeply from a nearby creek, then tucked their heads under their wings and went to sleep.

"You lot stay here," Daisy ordered us.

"Where are you going?" Wren asked her.

"To hunt," Daisy replied.

"But I thought we had farther to go today," I said.

"We do," was her only answer as she took a pair of javelins from her griffin's saddle, then followed Ralph into a nearby clump of trees.

"How are you holding out, Ingol?" I asked the dwarf.

"Badly," he muttered. He was lying on his side, eyes closed.

"Let me get you some water," Wren offered.

"It won't help," the dwarf moaned. "My kind weren't meant to walk on the surface of the earth, much less soar in the skies above."

"You know, you're probably the first of your kind to fly," Wren pointed out.

"That's not a good thing," Ingol told her. "It's– it's unnatural."

My eyes met Wren's, and both of us had to suppress our laughter.

Daisy and Ralph returned three-quarters of an hour later, each carrying an entire deer.

"Do you want us to build a fire?" asked Ingol, who'd recovered considerably.

"Thank you, but no," Ralph told him.

"You're going to eat them raw?" Wren gasped.

"Of course not," Daisy sighed in annoyance. "These aren't for us."

At the orcs' return, the griffins had clustered around the pair. Daisy and Ralph flung the deer corpses to the ground. Without hesitation, the griffins started a feeding frenzy. Somehow, our guides escaped unscathed. Holding hands, they walked over to where we were watching the bloody spectacle in stunned silence.

Shortly after the griffins finished their grizzly meal, we were in the sky once more. Ingol and his mount were positioned behind me again. I glanced back at them from time to time. The dwarf looked slightly better than before, but very slightly. Maybe he was right, and dwarves weren't meant for these kinds of heights. In all fairness, elves hated the oppressive weight of being trapped underground in dark tunnels for long periods of time.

We made camp for the night on the banks of a river. The griffins drank, then did a little grazing, before scratching dead leaves and grass together to make a nest large enough for all five to share. After removing the griffin's saddles, Daisy and Ralph went to hunt again.

I offered to come with them, and Ralph accepted before Daisy could tell me no. Leaving Wren to tend Ingol's wooziness, I shouldered my bow and followed the two into the forest. Despite their size, both walked on nearly silent feet.

"There," Ralph breathed, pointing to where a pair of deer grazed nearly a hundred feet away. We crept closer, and I put an arrow on my bowstring.

I raised the weapon at the same time Daisy began aiming a javelin. We were still at least fifty feet away.

"I'm aiming for the one on the left," I whispered.

She snorted but adjusted her stance.

"On your mark," I told her.

She sighted the distance once more, then gave a nod, and I released the arrow at the same moment she threw the javelin. Both connected, and the two deer dropped dead.

I turned to look at the orc, my mouth hanging open. "That was– that was an unbelievable throw."

Daisy shrugged and walked away, but I saw a pleased expression cross her face.

While we retrieved and cleaned our weapons, Ralph ventured further into the woods. He returned just before we finished with a deer of his own.

"This should do us for tonight," he said.

Daisy nodded. "Grab your kill, elf," she said to me.

"Ummm…" I glanced skeptically at the deer. Mine was the biggest of the three and probably weighed as much as I did.

Still, I had it half hefted onto my back and was struggling to get it the rest of the way up when the weight suddenly vanished. Glancing back, I saw that Ralph had taken the corpse and now carried a deer on each shoulder.

"Please, allow me," he said with a knowing smile.

"Thanks," I told him.

Daisy rolled her eyes. "Delicate, little elf," she muttered under her breath.

"I'm not an elf," I said to her, as I gathered all the weapons.

"Your ears tell a different story," Daisy replied, lifting her own deer.

"I'm no more an elf than you are a human," I countered. Daisy stiffened, and her eyes narrowed. "I have blood from both, but am neither," I went on.

"Are you saying I'm not an orc?" Daisy growled, and I wondered if I'd hit a sore spot.

"It's part of who you are," I said, ignoring her hostility. "But if you were all orc, then you and I wouldn't have any common blood."

The snarl died on Daisy's lips as I continued. "You and me, Ralph and Wren, we all have human blood. We're all kin. Even if we weren't, it's time for all of the different races to stand together, because none of us are going to survive this alone."

"That's kind of beautiful," Ralph replied, showing no strain whatsoever under the weight of the two deer.

We didn't say much more. However, when we made it back to camp, Daisy threw her deer to the griffins, then went to her saddlebag and got out an orange root. She took it to Ingol, who was sitting up propped against a tree stump.

"If you chew on this, you won't feel so nauseous in the air," she told the dwarf.

I couldn't help smiling softly at the exchange.

Ralph also fed his deer to the griffins, then set about butchering mine for us to eat. Wren and I built the fire while Daisy checked the griffins for broken feathers and scratched paws.

At last, we were seated beside the fire, eating from the roasted haunch of my kill. Two of the griffins were poking around the edge of the firelight, hoping for scraps. The others were sleeping soundly in their nest.

"What was it like living on the isle?" Wren asked.

"It was nice," Ralph recalled. "Enough territory for all the clans. The griffins could live up on the mountain tops, and there were plenty of caves and caverns to explore."

"I'm sorry that was ruined for you," Wren murmured to him softly.

"Well, we would have had to leave soon anyway," Daisy grunted.

"Why?" asked Ingol.

Daisy looked down, as though realizing she might have said too much.

"The eggs didn't hatch this year," Ralph finally told us.

"The eggs?" I asked.

The orc nodded. "The griffin eggs. In the last few decades, they've been hatching later and later. Before my time, they were said to have hatched on the first day of spring, but as long as I've been alive, it's been the middle of summer. This year, they didn't hatch at all."

"But why?" Wren gasped, voice and face stricken.

"It was too cold." Daisy was the one to answer. "Griffins sit their nest until it gets warm, then the sun finishes the task. This year, when the mothers flew down from their aeries, the eggs died."

"For the past few summers, the number of eggs that have hatched has dwindled. This year, none of them did," Ralph picked up where his mate left off. "Without the griffins, life would have been nearly impossible on the isle, so we'd already begun preparing for the move, even before the army appeared on the horizon. Their arrival expedited the process."

"Why flee?" Ingol asked. "Why not fight them?"

The two orcs exchanged a quick glance.

"Our leaders did discuss it, but decided that if we were to be seen as anything other than violent brutes, we should not make our first act on the mainland one of war," Ralph explained.

Daisy snorted, and I had a feeling she had not agreed with the choice to flee.

"It was probably for the best," I told them. "Another human army attacked and defeated the first shortly after the isle fell."

"Lathaan said that those who attacked us came for his stone, the one that allowed the isle to float. Is that what the second army wanted too?" Daisy wondered.

"No," I answered. "That was Apricot's army. He is the rightful heir to the human throne.

"The other army's leader, General Greyward, had ravaged quite a few towns before he came to your isle. Apricot attacked him to protect the people of the land. He didn't know anything about the stones.

"However, one of Apricot's closest advisers, a powerful wizard named Axel, knew Greyward had a stone similar to Lathaan's. He wanted it for himself, so he may have pressed for the engagement between the two armies. It is likely he would have come after Lathaan's stone next."

"Isn't Axel the one you're hunting?" Ralph asked.

"That's right," Wren answered.

"If he is a powerful wizard, how do you expect to defeat him on your own?" Ralph wondered.

His words weren't said with malice or condemnation, only curiosity.

"We're still working on that part," I admitted.

"Maybe we should stay and help them," Daisy suggested to Ralph. He met her gaze and nodded slowly.

"No," I said reluctantly. "It is enough for you to take us to the lake. We won't be alone for long. Lathaan has promised to join us, and I think some of the other great dragons are already on their way."

"It doesn't seem right to just leave you," Ralph countered.

"Yet you must," Wren assured him. "Your place is with your people."

Daisy and Ralph exchanged a glance, and I had a feeling they might stay with us despite our protests. However, they said no more on the subject.

None of us sat up much longer. We split the watches and settled down to sleep.

Chapter 26
The Fall

A scream brought me to my senses.

I scrambled to escape my bedding and draw a weapon. Daisy, who had been on watch, was leaning over Wren. I was by her side a second later.

"She's dreaming and won't wake up," the orc said in confusion.

"It's because she's locked in a vision from The Scrying Stone," I explained.

Wren had told me she didn't plan on using the stone anymore, but that didn't mean it wasn't still able to use her, just as it had the night we'd both dreamed of our meeting with Apricot.

Ralph and Ingol came hurrying over, concern evident in their expressions.

"There's nothing we can do but wait," I told them. It was still several hours until dawn, and none of the griffins had stirred from their nests.

After another ten minutes of whimpering and screaming, Wren's eyes flew open. She was panting for air and trembling from head to toe.

"We have to go," she gasped, struggling to her feet. "We have to go now! Asteropaios is in trouble!"

As soon as the words were out of her mouth, Wren sagged to the ground. I caught her and could feel the sweat soaking her body.

I'm all right," she insisted, despite her shaking limbs.

Leaving Wren with Ingol, I helped saddle the griffins as best I could, which mostly meant staying out of the way as Daisy and Ralph worked.

The sky hadn't even started to change color when we mounted and took flight. Daisy had strapped Wren into her seat.

My half-elf friend rode lying forward, with her head on the griffin's neck.

I kept glancing back, hoping that she'd sit up and show me that she was okay. Ingol flew by her side. The dwarf seemed too worried about Wren to remember how much he hated being on a griffin.

However, even the concern for my companions could not distract me from the wonder of flying beneath the stars. They seemed close enough to reach out and touch. I don't know how long I stared at them, but I could have continued for an eternity.

I looked up at The Constellation of the Great Dragons and was shocked to see how pale its stars were compared to the rest. Even the points of light that outlined Asteropaios's form were far dimmer than the last time I had beheld them. In the void, a place where I had never seen stars, was a patch of onyx sky.

A feeling of dread filled me, and I looked forward, checking the horizon for signs of the sunrise. There were none. If anything, the eastern horizon was darker than the rest of the sky, without any light or stars to be seen.

Soon, I knew why. As we neared the darkness, the first crackle of lightning split the dense cloud bank ahead. Five minutes later, a wave of rain hit my face like a shower of pebbles. The griffin beneath me lurched, and I barely managed to stay in my seat. I quickly looked over my shoulder. Wren's tethers had held. She was sitting up now and holding onto the saddle for dear life. Ingol too, but he'd slid several inches to the side and didn't seem able to right himself.

Just then, my griffin began to descend. I straightened and saw that Daisy and Ralph were taking us down. When we were still two dozen feet above the ground, a gust of wind hit us, buffeting the griffins, several of whom shrieked in protest.

A cry from Ingol made me turn again. He'd slid further and was mounted more on the griffin's side than on its back.

"Hold on!" I yelled to him, but doubted he could hear me over the wind and rain. I was so busy willing the dwarf's arms not to give out that I was startled by the sudden jolt as my mount's feet hit the ground.

A moment later, Ingol and Wren's griffins also landed. I heaved a sigh of relief and scrambled to dismount.

"The griffins won't be able to fly in this," Daisy hollered above the gale. "We'll have to wait until the storm passes."

"There's no time," Wren shouted back. She was fumbling to undo the straps keeping her in the saddle.

"We can't ride into the storm," Daisy told her. "It's suicide! And we can't go around it because the lake is just ahead, close to where the storm is centered."

"That's because the storm is coming from Asteropaios!" Wren shrieked desperately. She freed herself and leapt from her griffin. "We must go to her!"

Wren looked at me imploringly. I didn't know what she'd seen in her vision, but she'd never been this shaken, even when she'd lived out the vision of her own death.

"This is where we leave you," I told Daisy. "Thank you for everything. Get out of here before the storm grows any worse."

Daisy appeared torn as our eyes met.

"Go," I urged, freeing my pack from Casum's saddle. "Take the griffins to safety."

"May the winds favor you," Daisy said in farewell.

"You too," I told her.

Flanked by Wren and Ingol, I strode toward the black outline of the storm.

"Can you run?" I asked Wren.

She nodded.

I took off, setting a steady pace that I hoped the others would find manageable. Normally, I enjoyed running. Now, it was not so pleasant. Icy rain pelted me in the face, blinding my eyes and stinging my skin. The wind was a wild force, constantly pushing us back. I hunched my shoulders, trying to narrow my frame, but it didn't seem to help.

The pitch black of night faded to deep gray, and still we pressed on. Behind me, I heard the rasp of Wren's breath. A ridge rose before us. I stopped in its shelter and waited as the others caught up.

Wren looked haggard, and Ingol was puffing, his legs so short he had to take two steps for every one of mine. As she came to a halt, Wren's body gave out, and she ended up on the ground, trembling.

"Stay here," I ordered.

Wren looked up at me, and I felt certain she was about to protest.

"You're only going to be a liability out there," I told her. "You did your part. You gave us a warning; now stay here."

Without waiting to see if she would listen, I began scrambling up the ridge. At the top, I turned back and offered Ingol a hand. After hauling him up, we started running again. The storm ahead grew even more intense, the constant flashes of lightning disrupting my senses. Despite this, I could tell that the level of light was starting to increase as the sun made its way into the sky far above the smother of clouds. It was still dim inside the storm, but even a human would have been able to see the great furrows in the earth that we came across two miles later.

A dragon made these, I thought. *A large one. Probably when it had to take off in a hurry.*

I kept these observations to myself, conserving my breath for running. The gouges were a dozen feet long and created a twisted maze of pits and rises. I leapt the first gully and the second easily, before scaling the mound of churned-up earth beyond.

Turning again to help Ingol, I found that the dwarf was not behind me. I spotted him a dozen yards back. He stopped as he came to the first gully I had jumped. Panting, with his hands on his knees, he looked up at me and shook his head.

I knew what he was saying, that his strength was spent, and I should not wait for him. Without hesitation, I began running once more, faster this time, pushing myself to my limits.

The rough terrain slowed me, but soon I was clear of it, sprinting headlong into the storm. The rain was even colder now. I was completely drenched, and I would have been shivering, but a fire seemed to flow through my veins in place of blood. It roared in my ears and kept even my fingers and toes warm. My feet skimmed across the ground as I ran even faster.

A deafening crack of thunder split the air ahead, closely followed by another. I had to stop as the ground shook, reverberating from the concussion. It nearly cost me my footing, but I managed to stay upright. I covered my ears, then waited to see if more was to come. When it didn't, I began running again.

I was going uphill. The slope of the ground continued to increase until my muscles finally felt the strain I was putting on them. I was forced to slow my pace. When I was halfway to the top of the rise, a blast of wind nearly took me off my feet. Lowering my head, I plowed forward.

Suddenly, a blazing flash of lightning burst across the sky. It left the image of two creatures locked in battle among the clouds burned into my eyes. The first was a powerfully built dragon. The second was also a dragon, but lean and thin. Like a snake, the slender dragon seemed to be wrapped around the first, constricting it.

Doubling my speed, I crested the hill and found the heart of the storm centered over a lake. In the sky above the water, I saw Asteropaios. Her blue and silver scales glimmered as lightning passed through them before exploding out in every direction. I'd been correct about the second dragon. It had a narrow body, long and lithe as an eel. Trailing behind it was a cloud of dark purple smoke.

Horror gripped my heart, turning the fire in my veins to ice. I knew the monstrous creature was Char. Shock held me in place as the two dragons separated.

Asteropaios opened her mouth, sending out a blast of lightning. Char neatly coiled her body and dodged, then darted forward and struck. I cried out as Char's teeth latched onto Asteropaios's neck. Before she could bite down, Asteropaios shook her off, slashing at Char's wings with her hind leg. Her claws connected, and Char dropped toward the surface of the lake.

The slender dragon flared her wings a moment later, halting her descent.

Without hesitation, Asteropaios dove, front claws outstretched. She latched onto Char's back where razor-like spikes protruded. Char twisted her head and sank her fangs deep into Asteropaios's side. Asteropaios let out a growl, and thunder exploded far above my head.

The noise shook me from my stupor. I needed to do something to help. Wren had seen a terrible ending to this battle. What was the point in coming all this way if not to change that future?

I notched an arrow to my bowstring, hoping the pair would drop low enough for me to take a shot. After a moment, they did move closer, but before I could shoot, they rose a hundred feet higher into the air.

What can I do? I thought, desperately wishing for a griffin, not that it would do me much good. The creature would never have been able to fly in this gale.

If only there were another dragon who could have helped me. But all the dragons I knew were grounded. Even had they been here, they would have been as useless as I felt.

The Gem of Aero, I thought suddenly. *It's the gift of flight!*

As I began fumbling through my pouch for the stone, a horrible sound filled the air, like metal scraping metal. Looking up, I realized the sound was coming from Char. Asteropaios had flipped her onto her back in the air and was ripping at Char's pale gray underbelly with tooth and claw.

"Look out!" I screamed, but there was no possible way for Asteropaios to hear me.

While she was attacking Char's vulnerable stomach, Char's tail wound around Asteropaios's wings, binding them together. Suddenly, the two were plummeting toward the ground. As they fell, Char reared back her head, revealing a pair of long fangs. Like a viper, she struck Asteropaios in the head, one fang piercing the dragon's neck and the other puncturing her left eye.

Asteropaios's wild cry of pain filled my heart with panic. I watched their struggle helplessly. Asteropaios fought to free her wings, and Char continued to constrict her coils, holding the larger dragon tightly.

Less than a hundred feet from the ground, Char extricated herself from Asteropaios and pushed off. Char didn't slow but managed to shift her trajectory toward the lake instead of the land. Asteropaios attempted to right herself and spread her wings, but they were bent and torn from Char's grasp.

Char hit the water a second before Asteropaios crashed into the ground beside the lake. I was running before the shockwave had even reached me. When it passed under my feet, I stumbled and went down, but was scrambling back up a moment later without stopping.

Get up! Get up! My mind screamed at Asteropaios. *Keep fighting!* But the mass of scales, limbs, and wings did not stir.

The storm was still raging, which I took as a good sign. I glanced at the lake. Its waters were roiling, and a murky patch marked where Char had entered the waves. I knew I would never be able to stand against a creature such as her, but if she reared her head from the water, I would die before I let her touch Asteropaios again.

Finally, I reached the silver and blue dragon's side. I slowed as I rounded her shoulder and saw her head. Her one good eye was closed. The other oozed silver blood along with a grayish purple liquid.

There were multiple bite marks along the dragon's sides, the same ooze leaking from each.

I walked to Asteropaios's head, the entire scene feeling surreal to me.

"Asteropaios?" I whispered. My voice broke, and I repeated her name louder.

Slowly, I reached out and laid a hand on the dragon's cheek. She felt warm under my fingers, which gave me hope.

I pulled back as a crackle of lightning ran along her scales, and one great, blue eye opened less than a foot from my face.

Chapter 27

The Confession

I froze as Asteropaios's one remaining eye fixed on me. There was a chance that she remembered when we'd met at her hall, but Wren had done most of the talking.

Even in her weakened state, I had no doubt she could kill me in less than a second if she perceived me as an enemy.

"I–" I started, without knowing what words should follow.

"Alora?" Her voice was soft but deep.

"No," I said gently, shaking my head. "No, my name is Candra. Is there anything I can do to help?"

My eyes scanned the dragon's broken body, and then I remembered that one of the stones I carried had healing properties. I pulled out The Heart of Jong and closed my eyes, trying to recall how I had used it the last time.

The gurgling rasp of Asteropaios's laughter stopped me.

"Put that stone away," she ordered. "It can't save me."

"N– No," I stuttered. "No, it– it can help. The stone is powerful. It's a dragon's gift."

"Which is why it will do me no good," Asteropaios explained. "After my transgression, the gifts no longer work for me."

"But you weren't a betrayer!" I insisted. "You remained faithful! That is why you are still strong and– and…" I trailed off, looking at the pool of silver blood surrounding the dragon's body.

"If not the stone, then maybe there is some other way. Some magic or–" I continued desperately until Asteropaios cut me off.

"No," she murmured. "It is too late. Char's poison fills my veins. Nothing can save me now."

I felt my legs sway as weariness and despair dragged me to my knees. The mud was cold, but I didn't care. I wasn't sure if it was tears running down my face or just the rain.

"I'm sorry," I gasped. "I'm so sorry."

"None of this is your fault," Asteropaios replied. "If anything, it is mine. I could have stopped Char long ago, but I did not have faith. All that has happened is my fault alone."

"No." I shook my head, throat too constricted to speak more than just the single word.

"It is true. And someone should know why," Asteropaios went on, her deep voice racked by a wheeze. "I have carried this secret too long. This is my last chance to make the truth known.

"After Char's gift, the gift of light, had been corrupted by void, she seduced the other dragons with promises of a grand future.

"Even Shal'eth, my once-mate, could not see through her lies. The moment he did, he came to me in repentance. Shal'eth told me everything, and I went to stop Char, but I was too late. Seconds too late.

"Char set a trap in a small village. The other great dragons had lent her their gifts, and she used them to attack The Blessing given to Planosia by The Creator many, many years ago.

"When I arrived, Char had already fled. I was helpless to do anything but watch The Blessing–my friend–die in the ruins. That was when I made a terrible mistake."

The dragon's voice cut off with a cough. It sounded weak and wet. Her eye, which had wandered to the horizon, focused on me again. She hesitated, gathering her strength for a few moments before continuing.

"I alone knew of the ninth gift, but I did not trust it. Instead, I tried to use my own power and, as a result, I cursed the world."

Asteropaios fell silent. I wondered if there was more she was going to say or if this was all she intended to share. It seemed she was trying to tell me something very important, but I didn't understand it. Was she even in her right mind? Did she know who it was she was speaking to?

208

The rain had grown lighter. It was a gentle shower now. While it wasn't as cold as before, I still felt chilled to the bone.

"All the inhabitants of the village had fled, except one young elf," the dragon finally went on. "She was sitting in the rubble of her home, clutching the body of her child to her chest and weeping as though her tears could bring the little girl back."

A feeling of dread prickled down my spine.

"You must understand," Asteropaios said seriously, "the child was dead. There was nothing I could do for her. Nothing. I vow that upon the sun and stars."

The dragon's voice faded to a whisper. "Otherwise– otherwise, I would not have even tried. Soul magic is forbidden. It is against nature and all things that are good in this world. Using it tainted me and cost me my gift. As soon as I attempted the graft, I wished to take it all back, but I couldn't. There was no going back. No way to undo what I had done.

"Had Shal'eth not found a way to bind Char with the elemental powers, we would have been as helpless against her as we are now. All because of me. Because I had no faith."

The dragon's eye slowly closed.

"I am sorry, Alora." The last words of Asteropaios were so quiet, I barely heard them.

"No!" I cried. "No! It wasn't your fault! You did all you could! In the years since, you have fought the darkness! Protected the mortals against the evil things of the world! We needed you! We need you still! How can we fight this battle without you?" The words tore from my throat in a ragged plea.

"I need you," I whispered.

There was no answer, except the rain, which stopped falling, leaving the land shrouded in silver and blue mist.

I don't know how long I remained on the ground next to the body of the dragon, but that was where Wren and Ingol found me when they finally caught up.

"I couldn't help her," I told them quietly. "I couldn't change the future."

Ingol looked heartbroken. I expected Wren to come and weep beside me. Instead, she flew into a rage.

"No!" she screamed. "This can't be happening! Where is Shal'eth? He did this! It's his fault!"

"What are you talking about?" Ingol asked her.

"Shal'eth went to the orc camp last night," Wren started. "Lathaan let him use Faleous. His wish was for the genie to release her hold on Char."

"As he's done with the others," Ingol murmured.

"Yes," Wren replied. "And each time he breaks one of her chains, it makes her more powerful. By having Faleous undo her binding, it gave Char access to the air again.

"The dream left me with a bad feeling, so when I woke, I used The Scrying Stone to see what would happen. As soon as Char realized she was no longer confined to water and earth, she attacked Asteropaios, the only creature she feared could stand against her."

"What's going to happen when Shal'eth wishes the last of Char's bonds released?" I asked nervously.

"I'm not sure," Wren admitted. "But it won't be good."

"If I had to guess, I'd say that she'll be just as she was before the binding," Ingol said.

"Brimming with power and ready to consume the world," I breathed.

"We need to stop Shal'eth," Wren spat venomously. "We need to kill him!"

"Easy there," Ingol told her. "We don't even know if that's possible."

"I'll find a way!" screamed Wren, face red and eyes filling with furious tears.

"Shal'eth told me he was the protector of my people, but we were fools! He let my mother die in horrible agony! He is prepared to let all of us die!" A sob broke from Wren, but that didn't stop her tirade.

"He doesn't care who he hurts! He doesn't care what we sacrifice! He's a liar, and I hate him!"

Wren fumbled in her pocket and pulled out her stones.

"He let his mate die!" she shouted, throwing Asteropaios's Gift into the mud beside the dead dragon.

"He gave me this stone so I could see the future, but I couldn't save her." The tears in Wren's eyes spilled over and began running down her cheeks. She flung The Scrying Stone beside Asteropaios's Gift, then fled, sobbing as she ran.

Ingol went after her, leaving me alone with the body of the dragon once more.

I rose to my feet and looked at it sadly. There was no way to bury her. She would lie here for a long time. Maybe a forest would grow over her bones. Dragons' bodies were supposed to be rich in nutrients, and it wasn't unusual for an abundance of vegetation to sprout where they perished.

Except, nothing was growing now, because even though it was the middle of summer, it felt as though winter was about to begin.

I took a deep breath and collected the two stones from where Wren had thrown them. They felt warm in my hand as I tucked them into the pouch that held the others.

Slowly, I walked away, my legs feeling watery. I found Wren and Ingol on a grassy knoll nearby. Wren appeared to have finished her cry and was sitting on the ground, staring out at the lake. The mist concealed most of it from view.

"What is there for us to do now?" Ingol asked. The dwarf, who had always been a very solid companion, seemed as defeated as the rest of us.

"Lathaan said the other dragons would be coming here soon," I reminded him.

"Do we trust them?" Ingol asked.

"I don't know," I admitted. "I don't know what to believe anymore."

"I do," Wren hissed. "I believe they are all evil!"

"Then why would Shal'eth have locked her away in the first place?" I countered.

"No idea," Wren replied hotly.

"Look," I said more softly, coming to sit beside her. "Shal'eth is definitely keeping things from us, but we may still need him."

Wren scowled at my words, and I let the matter drop.

We spent the remainder of the day resting by the lake. Wren slept all afternoon. I felt exhausted, but sleep wouldn't come to me while the sun was up, not that we ever saw it through the thick fog hanging over the water.

Even when night fell at last, I didn't feel that I'd be able to rest, so I took the first watch. Around midnight, I woke Ingol and lay down.

I was almost asleep when a feeling of cold touched my leg. Quickly, it spread through my body, until I was shivering. I sat up and began rubbing my hands along my arms to warm them.

Above, I saw that the clouds had cleared enough for me to see the stars, but there were only a few left.

Chapter 28

The Future

I leapt to my feet, realizing my blanket and bedroll were gone. It was too dark to see much of my surroundings. Only by the smallest trace of starlight could I tell that I was standing on barren ground in a wasteland.

The handful of stars that still remained were all closely grouped together in the very center of the night sky. They were besieged on all sides by a darkness so deep I felt sure no light but the sun itself could banish it.

My warm breath made clouds in the cold air as I turned, looking around the completely empty world in which I had found myself. There was nothing to see. This place was empty, void of all life.

Movement from the corner of my eye made me jump. The creature that walked toward me was almost invisible in the night, save for the glimmering, green eyes. It was a black wolf, the same one I had seen in the forest of the high elves. It approached me calmly, and I felt no fear. This animal was not here to attack me.

I could barely see its outline as the creature turned its head and looked back the way it had come. After a moment, a second figure emerged from the gloom. This one a human and, yet, not a human. He was tall and extremely broad, with white hair, toned muscles, and brilliant, teal eyes.

"Shal'eth?" I breathed, staring at his very human face.

"Hello, Candra," he greeted me.

"What is this place?" I asked.

"It is the end," he replied.

"The end of what?" I pressed.

"Everything," he told me. "The end of time and life and warmth. In a few more hours, the void will swallow the entire

213

planet, and there won't be anything anymore. No future. No past. Not even any darkness. Just void."

"This– this is what's going to happen?" I spluttered. "This is what's going to happen to *our* world?"

Shal'eth pursed his lips. "I'm afraid so," he replied. "Ever since that day, you know the one of which I speak, this is the only future that has been."

"What do you mean?" I gasped.

"As you undoubtedly know," the dragon began, "my gift was the future. It was mine to watch over and protect with the help of The Scrying Stone.

"When Char revealed her plan to me, I rejected it at first, but her words were enough to persuade me to use my gift and see what would happen if I joined her."

"What did you see?" I breathed.

"Joy. Gladness. A world full of life," he admitted.

"How is that possible?" I asked in bewilderment, looking at the oblivion all around me.

Shal'eth hesitated. His next words came very carefully. "I have asked myself the same thing many times. The Scrying Stone only shows the outcome for choices made and the most likely course that will follow.

"Although I walked in the future several times, I never saw this end until it was too late. I couldn't understand how Char blinded me so completely, not until I learned of the ninth gift."

"What is the ninth gift?" I wondered. "I've heard it mentioned a few times, but no one has told me what it is."

Shal'eth regarded me for a long moment. "It is better that you do not know," he decided at last. "Even I do not fully understand it or the role it played in concealing this future. I think Asteropaios does, but she– she never spoke to me after that day.

"As soon as I had played my part in the betrayal, everything felt very wrong. I went to her and admitted what I had done. After that, my visions of the future changed, and this became the new ending," Shal'eth lamented.

"My ability to use The Scrying Stone faded a short time later. However, I did not let that stop me. Century upon century, I have labored to rewrite the future, but I cannot. It always ends here, just like this, in utter darkness.

"I have tried everything I can think of," Shal'eth sighed. "It has cost countless mortals their lives, and for that, I am eternally sorry. But what other choice did I have?"

"You're talking about Wren's mother," I replied stiffly.

Shal'eth nodded. "Her and many others. Too many for most to count, but I know each of their names and have wept for them. Through their use of The Scrying Stone, I have watched thousands of futures play out, trying to change the course of time and avoid this." The dragon gestured to the blackness all around us.

"And you were never successful?" I wondered.

Shal'eth's eyes met mine. "No," he answered bitterly. "Every time we did things differently. Sometimes we made big changes, sometimes we made small changes, but it didn't help. Nothing worked. The void always wins in the end. It consumes everything, and there is nothing beyond it."

We were both silent for a moment.

"Are we in one of those futures?" I asked, then shook my head. "Not right now, I know we are in a vision from The Scrying Stone now, but I mean my friends and me. Has this all been you watching a failed future play out?"

The idea made me feel lighter. We would get to start over. Go back to the beginning and try again. Kraster would still be alive; I could save him this time!

"No." The word dashed my hopes. "I ran out of time."

I opened my mouth, but there didn't seem to be anything to say.

"While I may never have prevented this dark future, I did get closer and closer over the years," Shal'eth explained. "Each time we almost succeeded, it always started with your visit to the shrine."

I shuddered slightly, thinking of how many versions of myself he must have watched die.

"Why didn't you tell us all of this from the beginning?" I demanded.

"Do you think I didn't try that?" Shal'eth wondered. "Sometimes you laughed. Sometimes you drank yourself to death. Sometimes you ran away. A few times, you did agree to help, but you always ended up failing because you didn't believe."

"Didn't believe what?" I asked.

Shal'eth only pursed his lips in a smirk.

"Surely, you can tell me now," I almost yelled. "I have done what you asked. I have gathered all the stones, save one."

Shal'eth remained silent for a long moment as he contemplated me. What changes did he see in my eyes? The months of travel had worn me down, but they had also given me a new strength. The challenges helped me grow, the pain too, much as I'd hated it. My crutches were gone. I couldn't hide behind drink or my brother anymore. I'd thought without those things I would crumble, but I'd learned to stand on my own.

"I will tell you a story," Shal'eth finally said. "You may believe what you will.

"The world was made long ago by The Creator. He shaped it carefully and set the celestial bodies in their places. He crafted plants, animals, mortals, dragons, and other magical creatures, all to live in balance if not harmony.

"And so they did for a great many centuries, until the sun started to go dark, as all suns do. The dragons and creatures grew fearful of the day it would go out completely. Some fled deep into the UnderEarth and became abominations of darkness; the same who would later corrupt Char.

"However, the mortals trusted The Creator. They were right to do so, for something special was given to them, something even greater than a dragon."

A hazy memory of light and warmth filled my mind.

"The Phoenix," I breathed.

For a moment, a look of shock and horror crossed Shal'eth's face, then he carefully forced the emotions from his expression.

"Someone has told you then," he murmured.

"I'm not sure," I admitted, my mind turning to The Constellation of the Great Dragons. I finally comprehended what creature was at its center.

"Yes," Shal'eth said carefully. "She was The Blessing given by The Creator. Her name was Alora. Though not nearly as strong as The Creator, The Phoenix had nine gifts that she used to renew the sun when it went dark and to chase evil from the land. Her gifts were the future, eternity, power, life, guidance, fire, flight, light, and one other.

"In turn, she chose eight dragons to help her, and granted each a boon, a piece of one of her gifts to aid in serving the plan of The Creator.

"I believe you know her fate." Shal'eth looked at me with unblinking eyes, and I nodded. "We allowed Char to use our gifts, and she murdered Alora, then attempted to take the world with void. Using the elemental forces, myself and the others barely managed to bind Char before she could carry out the second half of her plan."

I furrowed my brow.

"But you're freeing her!" I burst out, as the memories of Asteropaios's death came rushing back to me. "Do you know what happened yesterday?"

Sorrow crossed Shal'eth's face. "I do," he replied. "Asteropaios was the first of the great dragons to perish, but she will not be the last. If our deaths can help save the world from this dark future, then we shall gladly give them.

"For us to have any hope, Char must be freed. Only once all eight of the stones are united at their full strength can there be any chance."

"Chance of what?" I asked desperately. "Can you use the stones to kill Char?"

"Not I," Shal'eth told me. "But the stones can be used to avoid the ending you see all around you. They are the only way."

"How?" I demanded. "How can they undo all the damage that has been done to the world? Do you actually know? You've already told me that you have never seen a path to changing this future. Maybe it's already too late. Maybe there really is nothing we can do, and this end is inescapable."

"We must have faith," Shal'eth said. "Just as the mortals once did."

"What if that doesn't work?" I wondered.

Shal'eth's only answer was a sad smile. It was the first time I had ever seen him wear such an expression.

I sighed when it became clear he wasn't going to give me an answer.

"Why does Char even want this?" I asked. "I see no benefit to her if the world is swallowed by void."

"The weight of her corruption is so heavy that she would rather there be nothing at all than bear it any longer," Shal'eth replied.

"We know where all of the elemental vessels are. Can we not simply bind Char again?" I pressed. "If it worked in the past, why not now? That would give us more time."

"Because Char isn't the one bringing the world to an end," Shal'eth explained. "Her void will follow, but the end you see here is coming on its own."

I blinked at him in surprise.

For so long, I'd thought Char was the only enemy we'd have to face, the only calamity we'd have to quell, but I was wrong. Even if we somehow defeated her, it seemed there would be more to do.

Despite how far I'd come, the path forward appeared more impossible than ever before, especially in the destroyed landscape with darkness pressing in on every side.

"If you can't use your gift anymore, then how did you bring me here to see this?" I asked.

"I did no such thing," he told me. "You're the one with The Scrying Stone, you brought yourself."

I scowled. "Are you close by then? Isn't that how others get pulled into visions, like I was with Wren?"

"It didn't work that way this time," Shal'eth admitted. "I wouldn't have been able to find you on my own, but I had a guide."

He glanced at the black wolf, who was sitting quietly a few feet away.

"A guide?" I asked.

Shal'eth nodded. "Yes, one who is very good at finding things."

"Do you always speak in riddles?" I wondered.

"Often," Shal'eth smirked. "I'm afraid it is a tendency of my species."

I snorted.

The wolf rose to its feet and glanced at Shal'eth.

"Apparently, my time is up," he told me. "However, I will see you soon, and we will stand side by side against the darkness."

"Just the two of us?" I half laughed.

"Of course not," he replied. "I'm planning to bring a scorch of dragons along with a king and his army."

With a wink, the dragon turned away and followed the wolf back into the darkness. I didn't feel afraid when they left me in that empty place. Somehow, I knew that as soon as I wanted to, I could wake up in my bedroll safe and sound.

Still, I lingered, watching as the darkness above slowly consumed the stars. A short time later, I sensed a wall of nothing closing in on me.

At last, the final star went out, and there was no more light. I could sense the void closing in, ready to swallow me whole.

Only when its frigid embrace touched my skin did I jerk myself awake.

Chapter 29
The Traitor

The first thing I noticed when I opened my eyes was that the mist had finally faded from the land. The second was that the light of dawn was spreading across the waters of Lake Sona below, turning its waves crimson. I had never been here before, but I knew it from the pictures and stories told of it. The lake was vast, with a lone tower rising from the northeastern shore.

Quickly, I scanned the area for signs of danger. Seeing none, I rolled onto my knees, keeping my head low as I gathered my things into a messy bundle.

"Is something wrong?" Wren asked from behind me. Her words were soft, but in the stillness of the morning, they seemed deafening.

I twisted around and pulled her down beside me.

"What are you doing?" she squeaked out before I was able to get my finger to my lips.

Again, I checked the horizon for signs of movement.

"We are in great danger," I warned. "We have to leave now, quickly and quietly."

Wren nodded at me, eyes wide. However, just as the last word left my mouth, Ingol shifted in his sleep and rolled onto his back with a loud snore.

Both Wren and I leapt for the dwarf. She clamped a hand over his face, while I pinned his body to keep him from throwing her off. There was a momentary struggle, which was far louder than was desirable, but Wren finally got Ingol to settle enough for us to let go.

"What do you mean by jumping me like that while I was sleeping?" the dwarf whispered crossly. It was the loudest whisper I'd ever heard.

Wren turned, looking to me for an explanation.

"This lake, it's Hawnkenquack Lake," I hissed.

Terror flooded Wren's eyes.

"Come again?" Ingol said, looking equal parts annoyed and bewildered.

"The Hawnkenquack is what killed us when we went to see Apricot the first time," Wren tried to clarify, but her words had the opposite effect.

"I've never even heard of such a creature!" Ingol all but yelled. "A Hawnkenquack?"

"Sh!" I shushed him. "It's a very dangerous monster, and it's probably lurking around here somewhere, so we need–"

"No. It's not here right now," a voice cut me off.

All three of us jumped to our feet. Turning, and looking down, I drew my swords. There stood the last person I'd ever expected to see again.

It was Gnombie.

With a twist of my wrist, I had a blade pressed to his throat. It kissed the skin lightly, causing a single drop of blood to slowly roll down his neck. The gnome didn't flinch in the slightest.

"What do you mean by *'it's not here right now'*?" I snarled.

"The creature, the one you call the Hawnkenquack, it's not at the lake right now," Gnombie answered. His voice was weary, and the purplish circles under his eyes spoke of many restless nights.

"Where is it?" I demanded, keeping my blade firmly in place.

"I'm not sure," the gnome admitted. "Axel must have sent him on a mission for Char."

As he spoke her name, an image of Asteropaios falling from the sky flashed into my mind.

Without hesitation, I sideswiped the gnome's legs, dropping him to the ground like a sack of potatoes. He landed flat on his back with a small gasp as the air was forced from his lungs. My sword remained at his neck the entire time, and only the fact that the gnome made no attempt to resist kept me from skewering him.

"Candra!" Wren gasped in shock at my violent action.

I glanced at her sharply, and she took a step back, eyes wide. After my day of sorrows and a night spent watching the world end, I'm sure I couldn't have looked more deranged if I'd tried.

"I am tired of lies," I snarled at the gnome pinned to the ground. "You want me to believe that the Hawnkenquack is working for Char?"

"You really have no idea what the Hawnkenquack is, do you?" Gnombie asked. Despite the situation, he was very calm, while I was practically frothing at the mouth.

"Explain," I managed to choke out.

"When the great dragons fell and lost their powers, some of them handled it better than others," the gnome told me as though it were a perfectly clear explanation.

I raised an eyebrow and pressed down a little harder with my sword. Gnombie gritted his teeth but began speaking again. "One of them, Morazz the Fire Drake, went completely insane."

There was a long moment of silence.

"You expect me to believe the Hawnkenquack is a great dragon?" I scoffed. "It's a giant goose!"

"And how many geese, giant or otherwise, do you know of that can breathe fire?" Gnombie asked. "Morazz was polymorphed long ago by the wizard Azazoth. It was an attempt to quell his vicious nature. Obviously, it didn't work, and the wizard was forced to flee before he could try anything else."

"Actually, that does kind of make sense," I heard Wren whisper to Ingol. "That's probably when Azazoth took Morazz's stone to put in his wand."

"And Char is controlling the Hawnken– Morazz?" I clarified, ignoring Wren.

"No. Axel's magic is controlling him for her," Gnombie replied.

"Because Axel is serving Char," I stated.

"Yes," Gnombie confirmed.

"And so are you," I snapped. "So why would I trust anything you tell me?"

There was a moment of silence. Both Gnombie and I remained perfectly still, the blade between us keeping him in place.

"You're right," he finally admitted, looking away from me in defeat. "I did serve Char, but I don't anymore."

"How can we believe you?" I demanded. "Especially after what you tried to do to me?"

There was another pause before the gnome answered. "I guess I don't expect you to. Although I hoped that you would."

"Because we're stupid?" I wondered.

Gnombie started to shake his head but stopped as soon as he felt my sword's edge under his chin. "No, but please, at least hear me out."

Now it was my turn to hesitate. Carefully, I glanced at the others, making sure to keep the gnome in my peripheral vision.

"I think maybe we should," Ingol finally broke the silence. "I do sense something different about him."

I remained still, wondering what kind of trap this could be.

"I agree," Wren added. "Let's see what he has to say." She paused, then gave me a meaningful look. "And maybe he doesn't need to be at sword point the whole time?"

I glowered at her, then looked down at Gnombie lying in the mud. He'd never posed much of a physical threat, at least, not to those who saw him coming. It was when he snuck up behind his victims that they found their throats cut with no warning.

"Fine," I snapped, stepping back without sheathing my blade. "We don't have much else to do at the moment, so I'll listen to his *story*."

Slowly, Gnombie sat up, one hand moving to touch his neck. The shallow cut I'd given him wasn't bleeding very much, but his hand still came away spotted with red.

I refused to feel bad about it.

"After I left you, I–" Gnombie started.

"No!" I interrupted sharply. "Start at the beginning, just so there is no more *confusion* between us."

"As you wish," the gnome said, dipping his head. "The beginning was many, many years ago. My clan didn't live on The Gnome Plateau but in a small village to the south. It was fairly common then; only in the last decade have the gnomes begun to migrate in force to the plateau.

"One night, our town was attacked by goblins." Gnombie spat the last word with malice, his cool demeanor evaporating.

"They raided the town, stealing all their hands could carry and burning what they could not. They destroyed everything and killed everyone. Everyone except for me, that is.

"My wife, my family, my friends, they were all dead. I was wounded and barely alive by the time help arrived from another clan. They said it was a miracle I survived. I didn't agree, and now, I know they were wrong.

"The other clan nursed me back to health. I stayed with them because I had nowhere else to go. Even though they welcomed me with open arms, I was nothing more than a shell, unable to feel or appreciate any of the friendship they tried to show me.

"That was when I began to hear the whispers. At first, I thought I was imagining things or going crazy, but, eventually, I discovered it was her, calling to me from the river close to the village. I didn't even know who she was, but her voice touched me deeply and promised me a better future. She made me think she could bring my family back and return my wife to my arms."

"And you believed her?" I asked.

"It took several months," Gnombie explained. "But Char assured me that all she wanted was to help. She told me of how she had once tried to remove death and suffering from the whole land, but the dragons had stopped her and imprisoned her unjustly.

"Her words finally swayed me because I wanted them to be true so badly. Char started giving me small missions, sometimes leaving a loaf of bread on a random doorstep, sometimes repairing the cartwheel of a stranger, all small things that she said would make the world a better place.

"Eventually, these missions required me to leave my new clan. I met with others who Char had also called. All of us were fully committed to the beautiful new world she promised.

"Slowly, the tasks she gave us grew strange. I was asked to spy, steal, and set traps. Over time, some of the others began to change. It seemed to me that they became more interested in gaining power than in building a better world. Axel was one of these, as was Greyward, though I only met him a few times."

"And we were just another mission?" I guessed.

"At first," Gnombie admitted. "I was ordered to keep an eye on you and report on how many stones you gathered. Char was impressed by how quickly you managed to track down the first four. She told me that she would find a way to delay you while she gathered the others, two of which were already in the hands of her agents."

Gnombie gave me a sorrowful look before continuing. "I promise I didn't know what she had planned. I still believed she was trying to save the world. However, when we reached the fort, and I saw that it was full of goblins who were also following her orders, it was like the veil was lifted. I could see and think clearly for the first time in many years. I began to question all that I was doing and to doubt the promises Char had made me. I didn't tell her when you recovered the fifth stone or where we headed after."

The gnome hung his head. "Yet, I am ashamed to admit I was frozen with indecision. That is why I did not tell you the truth or attempt to remove the shade. Then you discovered me, and I fled.

"Not knowing where else to go, I returned to Char, but her hold on me was broken. I saw her lies for what they were. However, I remained by her side long enough to learn her plans. I have come now to fight her as best I can in the hopes that it will make amends for the time I spent in her service."

Gnombie fell silent. His keen eyes studied us, trying to gauge our reactions.

"So what's her plan then?" Ingol prompted.

"This is where she was bound. Thus, this is where she will emerge once freed," Gnombie explained. "About two decades ago, her chains began to loosen. That was when she started whispering and claiming followers. Then, shortly after summer began, she grew stronger and– and unless I am mistaken, it happened again two nights ago."

I nodded. "Shal'eth has been using the elemental genies to release her."

Gnombie furrowed his brow. "I'm not sure Char is aware of that. I think she believes she is breaking free on her own."

Wren scowled darkly, but I just shrugged.

"Char has her plans and Shal'eth has his," I said. "Now, we need to make ours. Please continue." I looked at Gnombie expectantly.

"Once Char emerges, she will kill the other dragons first, and then take the stones for her own. After that, nothing in the world will be able to stand against her," Gnombie told us.

"But the dragons don't have the stones," Wren protested. "We do."

I wished she hadn't shared that piece of information. Just because Ingol said there was something different about Gnombie didn't mean I trusted him.

"Not all of them," I reminded the others. "But we can use the ones we have."

"It won't be enough," Gnombie replied. "Individually, the stones are too weak to have any large-scale effect against Char."

"Then we need to get the last stone before she breaks free," I concluded.

Gnombie hesitated. "I don't know that I would recommend that."

"Why not?" asked Wren.

"I knew Axel before he found his first stone, the one called Azazoth's Wand. He was always interested in becoming powerful, but he was still Axel.

"I saw him again after he claimed The Void Stone, and he was a completely different person. The stone changed him. Axel is

226

her creature now, completely subjugated to her will. He is cruel and malicious even to Char's other followers. I fear that anyone who touches The Void Stone may fall to the same fate."

"Then what are we to do?" wondered Wren.

"We'll need to get it from him without touching it," I said.

"And then?" she pressed.

I looked at Gnombie, but he shook his head.

"Shal'eth will be here soon," I told them. "I'm sure he'll know what to do."

Before Wren could object, Gnombie spoke up. "There's no time! That's why I came to find you. Axel is in the tower now. You must defeat him before Morazz returns. I can't imagine The Fire Drake will be gone for long. This could be your only chance. I can show you the way."

Instantly, I sensed a trap and gave the gnome a hard look.

"I promise I'm not setting you up," he tried to assure us. "The tower has magical protections, and you'll never find your way through without my help."

"We have no reason to trust you," I reminded the gnome. "In fact, we have many reasons *not* to trust you."

Gnombie opened his mouth but couldn't seem to think of anything to say.

"There is something else I want to know," I pressed on. "Was Kraster also working for Char?"

"Not really. It was more subconscious for him," Gnombie explained. "As you know, Char saved his life when he was a child."

Guilt washed over me as I recalled the day my brother had nearly died trying to keep me safe.

"Kraster would have drowned," Gnombie continued. "But Char wrapped him in her power, and it preserved him. That's why he was able to use magic even though it didn't run in his bloodline nor had he studied it.

"He told me once that his magic sometimes spoke to him, telling him to trust certain people or take certain missions. That is how Char used him to do her bidding."

"And she put him in the path of people like you and Greyward so he would be putty in your hands," I added darkly.

"It's true," Gnombie admitted shamefully. "Char used her influence to make him trust me."

"Then why did she kill him?" I demanded.

"She wasn't trying to kill him. That was a miscalculation," Gnombie said softly.

"She threw a hydra at us and didn't expect anyone to die?" I snapped.

"I didn't say she wasn't expecting one of you to die." The gnome spoke the words haltingly. It took me a moment to grasp his meaning.

"It was supposed to be me, wasn't it?" I asked.

Gnombie nodded. "You had too much influence over your brother, and you never would have willingly given the stones to Char. At least, that is what she told me. I sensed a lot of uncertainty in her. It was like there was something about you that Char couldn't quite understand."

The gnome's words made me shudder.

"Char assumed you would die, and the others would flee," Gnombie went on. "Then she could have Kraster bring the stones to Greyward unhindered.

"Axel was also supposed to give up his stone after killing Apricot, but Char underestimated the wizard's desire for power. He kept Azazoth's Wand and took The Void Stone from Greyward. In doing so, he went from Char's servant to her puppet.

"I've always been able to fight her influence to a certain extent, but no one who has touched The Void Stone can. Except your brother."

"What?" I gasped. "Kraster touched The Void Stone?"

Gnombie nodded. "I heard the rumor that Char tried to give The Void Stone to a mortal boy. She put it in his hand, but he recoiled from the evil within.

"I didn't know if it was true. However, when I met Kraster, it all made sense. He was strongly touched by her power but not controlled by it."

"That is fascinating," mused Ingol. "Amazing even, but I have learned to never underestimate the ability of an innocent child to resist evil."

"She still managed to use him," I pointed out. "He was the one who led Greyward to The Void Stone."

"I don't understand how Char was able to influence so many while she was bound by the elemental powers," Wren said.

"It is because Shal'eth had already broken the bond the water elemental put on her," Gnombie answered. "As a result, she was able to manifest small amounts of her essence through the waters that ran out of the deep places where she was imprisoned. This allowed her to save Kraster and offer him The Void Stone.

"Similarly, she was able to move her armies through the earth and begin attacking cities once the bond of the earth vessel was broken."

"That means it really was Shal'eth's fault that Asteropaios died," Wren hissed. "He released Char from the bond of the air, and she instantly took to the skies and attacked."

Gnombie nodded grimly. "When he releases the final bond, the one of fire, she will be completely free, able to fully walk in this world again."

"Then we should–" I was cut off as the ground started quaking beneath our feet.

Chapter 30

The King

As the ground continued to tremble, we looked to the west and saw a vast host marching toward us. At their front rode Apricot, armored in gold and riding Lamasku. The flaming lion's head was held high as he led the grand procession.

This must be the army Shal'eth promised, I thought.

As they grew closer, I saw others I recognized. Lucille was mounted beside Apricot on a buckskin stallion. The note I'd received had made it seem the high elf's death was imminent, but it appeared she had made a full recovery.

There was also Rakus, who I now knew was really the great dragon Camroc. He was riding close behind Apricot and Lucille on a shaggy ram. In his hand was a short staff of golden wood.

A second ram kept pace with the first. This one also carried a gnome, Doctor Phillis Nithe. I had met her in Gnomonly where she'd confirmed I was cursed as The Oracle of the Three Sisters had said. She had also been the one who sent us to see Rakus, her brother.

Understanding bloomed in me. They weren't just any siblings; they were twins. She was the great dragon Zaydia, twin of Camroc. How had I been so blind to the dragons all around me?

Movement from the air made me look up. I saw a pair of griffins soaring above the approaching army. They carried Shal'eth, still dragon-headed, and Lathaan.

We cleared a space for the massive beasts to land.

"Hello," I greeted the two dragons as they dismounted.

"Good to see you again so soon," Shal'eth told me with a twinkle in his eye. Despite the dragon head, his eyes were the same as they had been in our shared vision of the future. Somehow, they fit both of his faces perfectly.

Wren looked at Shal'eth, then turned away. I knew her feelings were tied in knots, but there were more important things going on. In all the excitement, I hadn't had the chance to tell Wren and Ingol about the vision I'd seen.

"Come," Shal'eth said to us. "I would like to formally introduce you to the king."

He led us down the hill to where Apricot and his troops had come to a halt. The army flew the flags of the three major human cities: Lion's Hill, The Coral City, and Kempt. There were also hundreds of banners stitched with the crest of Apricot's house, a golden tree laden with fruit set on an emerald backdrop. It was something I had only ever seen in the history books.

When he saw us, Apricot dismounted and headed toward Shal'eth. Lucille walked beside him with Camroc and Zaydia following.

"Your highness," I said, attempting my best bow. It was not particularly graceful, but I usually fell down when I tried to curtsy.

"There's no need for that," Apricot insisted, flushing with embarrassment.

I straighten, slightly confused. There was a crown of golden metal on his head, nestled among the similarly colored curls. Clearly, he'd claimed his title, but maybe he was still feeling awkward in the role.

"It is a pleasure to meet all of you," Apricot told my companions, then glanced at me specifically.

"And I would like to apologize for my less-than-cordial behavior at our last meeting," he went on. "Your warning saved my life, along with the lives of many others. For that and for the assistance you have given in gathering the stones, we owe you a great debt."

The stones are for him, I realized with a twinge of disappointment. I'd considered it before. However, some part of me had always been convinced Wren was chosen to wield them. Now, it was obvious Apricot was the one. He was from an anointed line and probably the only mortal left alive who could resist the evil of The Void Stone.

231

"Yes, here," I said, fumbling to pull the stones out so I could offer them to him. "We have all but the last one, which–"

Shal'eth's hand fell on my wrist, stopping me. "Not in the open," he murmured. "There may still be spies around."

It took all of my self-control not to look at Gnombie.

Shal'eth removed his hand as Apricot turned to Lucille. "I was planning to introduce you to my chief advisor, but she's informed me that you have already met."

I nodded, trying not to cringe at the memory. I'd been drunk, of course, and had probably said something stupid. The amused glimmer in Lucille's eyes told me she remembered everything. Something about the orange of her irises stood out to me as odd.

"We have met," Lucille confirmed at the same moment I blurted out, "You're a dragon too?!"

She laughed, a beautiful sound. "My true name is Karradin," she told me.

"Karradin the Wise," Wren breathed behind me.

A sad expression crossed Karradin's face. "I was once called that. However, my part in the fall of the great dragons would certainly suggest otherwise."

In the moment of silence that followed, I carefully counted the great dragons in my head. They were all accounted for now, if the Hawnkenquack really was Morazz. Once Char was released, the eight would be united again.

Except for Asteropaios, I reminded myself. Her body still lay on the shore of the lake, but her soul had departed back to The Creator.

"We have some information for you," I spoke up, then motioned Gnombie forward. "Our friend, Gnombie, was once an agent of Char."

Apricot and all of the dragons, except Shal'eth, flinched when I used her name.

"Sorry," I apologized, making a note to refrain from speaking it in the future.

232

"Gnombie believes Axel and The Void Stone are in the tower on the far bank and that they are unguarded," I went on.

"I wouldn't say unguarded exactly," Gnombie mumbled. "Just that he is there, and Morazz isn't around."

None of the dragons reacted to Morazz's name, and I started to wonder if I was literally the only person who hadn't known the true identity of the Hawnkenquack.

You were never very good at figuring out secrets, I reminded myself. *That was Kraster's job, while you used your blades and fists.*

"But– but there is a creature in the lake by the tower," Gnombie continued, glancing quickly at me.

"You didn't mention that before," Ingol said.

"I was going to," Gnombie promised.

"What kind of creature is it?" Wren asked.

"A hydra," the gnome answered.

My insides went cold, then hot anger tore through my body.

"*The* hydra?" I demanded in a quiet voice.

Gnombie nodded.

My hand went to my sword.

"Candra, wait," Shal'eth ordered.

I paused, blade half-drawn.

"This is no time to throw away your life needlessly," the dragon told me.

I wanted to argue that this was the perfect time to throw away my life needlessly. There was a hydra that needed slaying, and I was probably the least important person here. In fact, it was laughable that I was even permitted to speak when I stood beside five dragons, the long-lost heir of the human kingdom, and two mortals who had been trained since birth to serve in sacred orders. The only person I might be more important than was Gnombie, and even he had insight and knowledge of the enemy that I could never provide.

I released the hilt of my sword and took a step back, suddenly aware of how ridiculous I must seem to them all. My only role should be to take orders and carry out the will of others.

"There is no point in finding The Void Stone while Char is still bound," Lucille, or Karradin rather, announced. She glanced at Lamasku, who was watching us with his great cat eyes.

"No!" Wren protested. "You can't release her!"

"I must," Shal'eth told her grimly. "I am the only one who can, and I do not believe I will be alive much longer. If Char is never freed, the world will end."

Confusion clouded Wren's face.

"It's true," I murmured softly. "Char isn't the only threat we are facing."

Before I could say more, Karradin addressed Wren. "Shal'eth has not been thoughtless in his actions when releasing Char's bonds. Each time, he has waited until the precise moment of necessity. Only by his foresight have we even made it this far. While we are still not guaranteed success, Shal'eth and the mortals who sacrificed their lives beside him have given us a fighting chance. Our only chance."

A hundred different emotions played across Wren's face.

"Time is short," Karradin said to the rest of us. "As we speak, an army of Char's fel creatures is marching on our position."

"Gnomex is preparing our generals and troops to engage them," Apricot assured her.

"I do not know that it will be enough," Karradin told the king with a sad look.

"A flight of orc warriors is headed this way on their griffins," Lathaan announced. "I know they may not arrive before the enemy, but they won't hesitate to join the battle."

Apricot nodded to Lathaan as the twins, Camroc and Zaydia, stepped forward.

"Axel is our first problem," Camroc began. "He was always a very gifted student. He will not be easy for any of us to defeat."

"Especially if he has taken control of Morazz's mind," Zaydia put in with a glance at her twin. "The Fire Drake was always fierce in battle."

234

Camroc nodded vigorously. "Taking them both down will be all but impossible for anyone besides me."

"I will go with you, brother," Zaydia vowed.

"I am quite familiar with the tower," Gnombie piped up. "There are many magical traps, and it is a maze on the inside. If you will have me, I can come along and show you the way."

"Excellent!" Camroc exclaimed. "And will the rest of your team be joining us as well?"

All of the dragons turned to Wren, Ingol, and me.

"If you don't need us somewhere else," I replied.

"I think the tower will be a challenge worthy of your talents," Shal'eth said. "You will have an hour before I release Char's final bond. Once she is free, I will hold her off as long as I can.

"Apricot, you and Karradin will lead your army against Char's. As soon as the orc reinforcements have arrived, Lathaan and his troops will provide relief to the human ranks."

I had more questions, but the others were all nodding and heading to their posts. Camroc and Zaydia nimbly clambered onto their rams.

My companions and I were given mounts. I didn't bother with my bedroll or anything from our campsite. What was the point? We were probably all going to die horribly. If that didn't happen and we needed to make a hasty getaway, I didn't want to be weighed down with the extra gear. The only things I needed were my weapons, which were never far from me.

I mounted and guided the horse to where the twins waited. They'd produced another ram from somewhere, which Gnombie rode. Wren and Ingol joined us as we headed toward the lake and the tower on the far bank.

Zaydia let out a soft cry as we crested the hill leading down to the water's edge. Even I, who was prepared for the sight, felt a pang of sorrow when I once again beheld the broken body of Asteropaios.

We rode past in silence. I glanced at Wren and saw tears on her cheeks. I might have wept too, if I'd had any tears left after yesterday.

I'd ridden into many battles but none like this, where death seemed all but inescapable. It felt like the day Kraster had discovered his powers. We were pinned down and surrounded on all sides. We should both have died. We knew that. The enemy knew that. There were no options open to us. No way to escape.

Until there was, a voice whispered in my head. *It could happen again.*

Not a chance, I told it. *Miracles like that only happen once in a lifetime.*

Despite their short, stocky build, the rams set a fast pace as we rounded the lake. Normally, I would have suggested we try to stay out of sight and use the undergrowth for cover, but the area was far too overgrown. Instead, we remained close to the water, traveling along its stony shore.

I kept my eyes peeled for signs of Morazz. I'd seen the carnage he could cause once before and hoped he would remain far away until the battle was over.

At last, after nearly forty nerve-wracking minutes, we saw the tower looming ahead of us.

Zaydia, who was in the lead, stopped her mount. The rest of us followed her as she got down and took her ram into a nearby thicket where she tethered it.

Leaving the animals, we moved stealthily through the trees until the base of the tower came into view. It was a dozen yards away, set on a cliff overlooking the lake.

Gnombie was in front now. As he reached the stairs leading up to the tower's only door, a scaly head broke from the surface of the water. It was instantly followed by another and then another, all glaring at us with immeasurable hatred.

Chapter 31
The Tower

I stood there, rooted to the spot as I stared at Kraster's killer. It emerged from the depths of the lake, clawing its way up the shore to cut us off from the tower.

The hydra was even bigger now than when I'd seen it last. However, instead of five heads, it had only three, all of them with gaping mouths full of knife-like teeth. The cruel, tawny eyes of the leftmost head turned in my direction. The neck attached to it bore a scar where I had cut it open from chin to sternum.

The other two heads had undoubtedly grown after the one that had been blinded in our fight was severed. Whether it was done by the goblins, some of Char's other servants, or the hydra itself, I couldn't tell. All I knew was that the creature seemed intent on finishing the fight we had started in the dwarven fortress.

I drew my swords, ready to engage.

"Candra, no!" Zaydia yelled. "I will distract it. The rest of you get to the tower."

I tried not to laugh at the ridiculousness of the situation. Zaydia might be a dragon somewhere deep down at her core, but right now, she was trapped in the body of a gnome.

Still, she planted herself firmly and pointed a finger at the beast blocking our path. A tendril of green sprouted from the ground beneath the hydra's feet. It thickened and began wrapping itself around the creature's legs.

The hydra noticed too late. It tried to rear back, only to be pulled earthward. More vines were growing from the ground now, spreading over the monster like a net.

"Go!" Zaydia called to us.

Gnombie sprinted up the stairs. Camroc, Wren, and Ingol hurried after him. When I tried to follow, the scarred head lashed out, breaking free of the plants.

I leapt back as teeth snapped close to my face. As soon as my feet touched the ground again, I sprang forward and dropped to one knee. Quickly, I brought my blades up into the soft underside of the hydra's scarred head. The maneuver brought me inches from the enormous fangs.

The hate-filled eyes seemed utterly shocked, but their light didn't die. I dragged each of my hands in a different direction, making them cross over my body as the swords sliced through skin and flesh.

The head lurched, and dark blood began to seep out of the scaly lips. I retreated once more as the head convulsed and died. The other two let out cries of pain and rage. They renewed their struggles and began pulling loose of the thick vines that held them in place.

"We have to burn–" I started, only to be cut off by a screech of fury.

It didn't come from the hydra but from the skies far above where a small, red shape was diving straight for us and rapidly growing larger.

The blood drained from my face as I realized The Fire Drake had returned. Axel must have removed the goose enchantment on him, because he appeared as a dragon once more.

"Everyone, get inside!" Camroc screamed.

Zaydia and I began to rush forward. The others were already at the arch of the entryway, but the hydra lunged, again blocking our path.

The head I had slain was dangling uselessly to one side, making the whole creature unbalanced. Both Zaydia and I noticed it at the same time, but she was somehow faster. Without any hesitation, she launched herself at one of the hydra's front legs. From her hands, I saw more vines sprout and wrap around the beast. With their help, Zaydia managed to pull the leg out from under the creature.

The hydra slipped, tumbling back down the slope toward the lake. As it fell, one of the two remaining heads struck out and caught hold of Zaydia's side. She screamed in pain as the teeth bit deep into her body.

I lunged forward to sever the head, but something pulled me to a stop. I glanced down and saw more vines twisting around my own feet.

Desperately, I looked up at Zaydia, her emerald eyes meeting mine.

"I'm sorry," she whispered, then she was gone, pulled into the churning depths of the water by the hydra.

A moment later, the binding on my feet vanished, and Camroc cried out in agony. I looked at him and saw that he had dropped to his knees.

"She's gone," he whimpered. Horror washed through me.

"Candra, come on!" Wren called, desperately motioning me forward. Her eyes were fixed on the sky.

I glanced up and was immediately sprinting, because Morazz wasn't just a small speck anymore. He was now the size of a cottage and still growing larger. Just as I made it through the archway, the floor shuddered with the impact of The Fire Drake's landing.

The first level of the tower was mostly empty. The only feature in the circular, stone room was a staircase built along the wall, which led to the level above.

"Take cover!" Ingol bellowed, pulling Wren behind the stone staircase. Gnombie and Camroc followed them. I raced to join and threw myself forward, narrowly avoiding being engulfed by an inferno.

The Fire Drake was well named. Despite the fact that only a fraction of his flames were able to make it through the archway into the tower, the intensity of the heat quickly began to grow. Soon, it became unbearable.

"He's not going to stop," Wren gasped in panic.

"I will try to make him," Camroc said, rising from where we crouched, huddled as far from the stream of fire as possible. He clutched his staff for a moment, about to step out into the torrent of scorching flames.

"What are you going to do?" I demanded. "We need you to defeat Axel."

He looked at me with sad eyes, and I knew he was thinking of his dead twin. Before he could do anything stupid, I grabbed his shoulder and pulled him back toward us.

"Ingol," I said, turning to the dwarf. "Use Baarthagon's Collar on Morazz."

"I don't know how! I've never used any of the stones before." The dwarf thrust his hand into his breast pocket and drew out both of the stones he carried. "Someone else will have to do it."

There was no time to argue. I grabbed the stones from Ingol's hand. The temperature had risen another five degrees, and I didn't want to accidentally conjure fire, so I shoved Azazoth's Wand into my pocket.

With no real idea of what I was doing, I clutched Baarthagon's Collar and bent my thoughts toward the dragon that was trying to roast me and my friends alive. In my mind, I could see him clearly. I sensed that another presence was commanding him. Wrestling control would have taken too long and wearied me too much, even if I could have managed it. Instead, I took a leaf from Kraster's book and directed my will at the beast's subconscious.

Sleep, I thought to the great dragon.

The fire stopped.

Sleep, I commanded again.

The ground trembled slightly as Morazz shifted his bulk.

Sleep, I breathed once more to The Fire Drake. *Sleep and do not wake until you have found peace.*

I am sorry, something whispered back to me, then I felt darkness close off the dragon's mind. I let out a sigh of relief.

"He's down for now, but I don't know how long it will hold," I told the others.

We were still forced to wait several minutes to allow the floor to cool before we could venture out from behind the staircase. I glanced through the archway to see Morazz's large head resting on the grass. His eyes were closed, and smoke was trickling from his nostrils.

The stairs led up one level to a sitting room but went no further. The room was dusty, and the stuffing was falling out of the chairs, leading me to believe it was never used. Just as in Camroc's tower, there were three doors set equidistant in the room's walls.

"What is it with wizards and magical towers?" I muttered under my breath.

"They are terribly practical," Camroc told me. "What better way to hide or lure your enemy into a trap than to make your home a maze only you can solve?"

I glanced at Gnombie. "But you know the way, right?"

"Mostly," he replied.

"Mostly?" I asked.

"Only Axel knows where every door leads," Gnombie admitted. "But I have watched him for many days."

"So which way first?" Ingol asked.

"This one." Gnombie moved to a door directly opposite the top of the stairs. We clustered around as the gnome turned the knob. The door opened into a library. Swords drawn, I stepped inside first. While this room appeared more used, there was still no sign of Axel.

"What's your next guess?" I asked.

In answer, Gnombie closed the door we had just stepped through and opened it again, revealing a study. I gaped in surprise, completely confused by how this tower worked.

We tried three more rooms–a bedroom, an armory, and a potion laboratory–with no sign of the wizard. Gnombie opened another door. This room contained a long table with a dozen chairs.

"He knows we're here," Ingol grunted, looking around the empty space. "Why doesn't he show himself?"

"I think he's waiting in hopes that Char will come," Camroc said.

"Does he fear facing you alone?" I asked.

"Perhaps," the dragon answered. "He hasn't beaten me in a duel yet."

"How come you and Zaydia can use magic?" Wren wondered. "I thought the dragons lost their powers."

"We did," Camroc admitted, voice quivering slightly as he continued. "My sister– and I– we learned the old-fashioned way. Study and hard work."

Wren let the topic drop, and we all looked at Gnombie, who was staring around the room uncertainly.

"One of these two doors will lead us to the top of the tower," he announced. "The other will activate the tower's defenses."

"And what are those?" Ingol asked.

"I'm not sure," Gnombie said, shaking his head. "But they won't be good."

"And you don't remember the right door?" Wren pressed.

"It's not that. I've never seen Axel use either," Gnombie explained. "There wasn't any reason to."

"Then make your best guess," I told him. "Whatever happens, we'll deal with it."

Gnombie nodded and chose the door to the right. As it swung open, the foul stench of death and decay washed over me, and I knew he had guessed wrong.

A pair of skeletons, and something that still had a bit too much meat on its bones to be considered a skeleton, charged us.

Wren reacted before I did, darting forward to kick one of the skeletons in the head. The creature stumbled but didn't seem damaged by the blow. I slashed at the next one with my swords. Their bones were so hard that my blades didn't even leave a mark.

Ingol fared far better. Using his staff like a mace, he smashed the leg of the one Wren had struck. The skeleton stopped moving, unable to walk. It glanced down and then looked at Ingol and lurched forward, hopping unevenly toward the dwarf. I would have found the sight funny, if the outstretched hands hadn't been so close to my friend's neck.

I twisted away from the skeleton in front of me and lashed out at the meaty creature behind it. My aim was true, and one of my swords sank into the monster's torso. However, the abomination continued moving in an unbothered fashion.

Behind my foe, I caught sight of Gnombie trying to close the door. As he struggled, another pair of skeletons pushed through.

"Someone get to the door!" I cried, fearing we would soon be overrun by the undead.

Just then, the room lit up with a golden glow as Camroc sent a searing ray of light into the first two skeletons. Their bodies trembled then disintegrated. I didn't have time to cheer as the meaty creature advanced on my position.

I dropped my second sword, holding the other one in both hands as I leapt up to bring it down with all my might. I caught the monster in the shoulder and swept my blade inward, managing to cut it from the base of the neck to the opposite side of the ribcage. With a sickening slurp, the head, shoulders, and half of the chest spilled off the top of the body and splattered on the floor.

The putrid odor made me gag. If there had been any food in my stomach, I'm sure I would have retched it up. Instead, I suffered only a few dry heaves before I was able to scramble away from the cloud of noxious fumes.

Ingol was at the door with Gnombie. The pair had almost managed to get it closed. A skeletal hand was reaching around from the opposite side, trying to force its way into the room. With a heave from the dwarf, the door clicked shut. The skeletal hand broke off at the wrist. It dropped to the floor where it lay twitching.

At some point during the battle, Wren had ripped the arm off one of the two remaining skeletons and was using it to bludgeon the creature. The other was advancing on Camroc. Before it could reach him, I darted forward and slammed the flat of my sword against the side of its skull, which promptly popped free of the neck. The skeleton's body took a few steps, but they were jerky and uncontrolled.

I attacked again, this time with the edge of my blade. It lodged in the backbone, right over the hips of the creature. The headless skeleton tried to turn, but I held on tightly and managed to keep the monster from pivoting more than a few inches. After taking a deep breath, I wrenched my weapon free and then slashed with all my might. I struck it in the same spot, and the spine snapped. A moment later, the skeleton began breaking into pieces.

I turned, looking for more foes, but Wren had finished subduing her opponent with Ingol's help. We all stood there for a moment, breathing hard.

"So, shall we try the other door?" I asked, retrieving the sword I'd dropped.

Chapter 32
The Apprentice

The second door opened to reveal a curving staircase, which led upward. It was enclosed, but several arrow slits allowed light inside.

I was prepared to charge, but Camroc's voice stopped me. "I shall go first."

I hesitated, wanting to argue. However, there was a serious expression on his face that revealed the powerful dragon within. When I compared him to Gnombie, I was surprised I'd never noticed the difference.

Camroc walked forward, pausing at the base of the stairs to wave a hand in front of him. The air he touched glimmered with a golden light for a moment before fading. Even after the light was gone, I could still sense the aura of magic coming from around the wizard.

Taking a deep breath, he began to climb the stairs. I followed on his heels, with the others right behind me.

We emerged onto a small landing with a pair of doors before us.

"Whatever happens," Camroc whispered to me so quietly I didn't think my friends could hear him, "do not sacrifice yourself on my behalf."

"What—" I started, but the wizard had already flung the doors open, revealing the sky above and half a dozen more steps leading to the tower's top.

A wave of metal spikes flew toward us, ready to pin us to the stone wall. We would all have been killed instantly if not for the shimmering shield of golden light, which was illuminated briefly when the metal shafts struck it.

Once the last of the spikes clattered to the floor, Camroc confidently strode up the steps, every inch of him carried like the dragon he was. I followed, my mouth gone dry with the realization of how close we'd come to dying.

The steps brought us out onto the top of the tower, the rest of which was a flat surface without any walls or turrets to protect against the long drop to the ground below.

Far across the lake, I could see the flash of weapons as Apricot's army engaged that of Char.

"Hello, Master," an unpleasant voice greeted us. It came from Axel, who stood a dozen feet away, watching as we emerged from the staircase.

In one hand, Axel held a new staff. The other, I was surprised to see, was nothing more than a nub. It was all but hidden in the sleeve of the robe he wore, which was a venomous shade of purple, patterned with dark swirls.

"Hello, Apprentice," Camroc replied. His voice seemed weary and sad. "I see you have finally found what you were looking for."

"Indeed, I have," Axel sneered. "I always knew there were things you were keeping from me, secrets you would never share. Now, I know them all! I understand why you have lived so long and what the source of your power truly is."

"These are things I would have told you in time," Camroc replied. "You weren't ready."

"I'd spent over half of my life learning from you!" Axel exclaimed. "You were never going to think I was ready. So I decided to seek the answers on my own."

"And has it made you wiser?" Camroc asked. "Was it worth the price you have paid?"

"The price?" Axel chuckled darkly. "The only price is that I have to kill you, which is more of a privilege if you ask me."

Curls of gray smoke began to appear around the human wizard as his speech grew more animated. They matched the pattern on his garment, blending together to make his robe seem alive.

"When Char rises, I will be the first to greet her, and I will offer her your head as tribute. She shall appoint me as her champion and grant me more power than you have ever had."

A smug smile curled over Axel's lips.

"You always had such great aspirations, my apprentice," Camroc murmured. "And you could have achieved them the right way, but you have chosen corruption. That is why you are on the wrong side today, and why your legacy will burn to ash."

"You're wrong!" Axel snarled, great clouds of purplish gray billowing out from him.

"Am I?" Camroc challenged. "Many things you could have accomplished had you dedicated yourself to study and discipline. Alas, you did not. You fled from your training to seek power that wasn't yours to take. You found Azazoth's Wand and paraded yourself as a hero. You acquired The Void Stone, which fed into your ambition. However, its promises are lies that you are unable to see through. Karradin defeated you, taking both your hand and Azazoth's Wand, so you fled here to hide behind Morazz's broken mind.

"These are not the doings of a great man, much less a great wizard. Of all the students I have guided over the years, you showed the most promise. Thus it is that your fall shall also be the greatest."

Axel let out a screech of fury. He waved his staff, and several bolts of dark power streaked toward us. They broke against Camroc's golden shield, but I could see the strain on the dragon's face as each blow fell.

"We need to separate Axel from The Void Stone," I told Wren, Ingol, and Gnombie as Camroc sent a brilliant ray of light flashing at the other wizard.

"How?" Wren asked.

"By killing him," Gnombie replied.

There was a moment of silence, then all of them turned to me. I dipped my head and pulled a short knife from my belt.

An arrow from Gnombie's bow raced for Axel a second later. The purplish gray clouds twisted to intercept, and the arrow crumpled into dust.

I threw my knife with the same result. Ingol muttered something under his breath, and several glowing balls of white light converged on Axel. They began to dispel his cloud. Quickly, I pulled out another knife.

I was preparing to throw it when a sudden roar erupted from the middle of the lake. Glancing down, I saw that the waters were churning wildly.

"He's done it," I heard Camroc say from what felt like a hundred miles away.

The lake's center began spinning, turning into a whirlpool as dark fog rose from the raging waters. The fog filled the sky, blotting out the sun.

A sharp pain exploded in my chest. It felt as though my heart was shattering into a million pieces. I think I let out a cry, but all of my senses were deadened as a searing agony filled me, spreading from my chest to each of my limbs.

When I opened my eyes, I was lying facedown, my body drenched in a cold sweat. After a moment, I recovered myself enough to look back out at the water.

The center of the whirlpool was pitch black. No, it was darker than black. Out of it emerged the eel-like body of Char, her scales mottled purple and gray. She was even larger and more horrifying to look at than when I'd seen her slay Asteropaios.

My hands rushed to cover my ears as she threw back her head and screeched to the sky before launching into the air. Instantly, she pointed herself toward the far bank where Apricot, his army, and most of the dragons were.

"We need to get The Void Stone now!" I tried to yell, but my throat was completely dry, and the words came out only as a whisper.

With Char free, Apricot would need the stones to defeat her, but how were we supposed to get them to him?

Shal'eth must have a plan in place for that, I told myself. *We must be ready.*

Dragging myself to my feet, I saw Camroc bent and kneeling as though a heavy weight was pinning him down. Gnombie was emptying his quiver at Axel while Ingol continued to send white spheres of light to dispel the wizard's dark magic.

I raised my swords and charged, trying to shake off the pain that still clung to my bones. Every step was a struggle as I closed the distance between Axel and myself. Wren was already there, forcing the wizard to dodge the blows from her fists.

Just before I reached them, a wave of power pulsed out from Axel, throwing all of us back. I scrabbled at the stony tower top, stopping myself just inches shy of a devastating drop.

Gnombie had been thrown off but clung to the tower's edge with one hand. Ingol hurried toward him. However, another blast of magic from Axel shoved him away. Wren was faster than the dwarf and managed to reach Gnombie, despite another of Axel's attacks. She heaved the gnome back onto the tower, and the pair darted away quickly, dodging more blasts of dark magic.

A shriek from Char on the far side of the lake made all of us freeze.

Camroc let out a gasp of shock.

"Shal'eth," I heard Wren cry in despair..

"He's dead now," Axel sneered. "The dragons are all going to be dead soon. Char will be the only one who remains, except maybe Morazz, who will be kept in chains. They will be nothing but a memory of a past age, and you shall join them!"

Axel unleashed a flood of power. It came as a great cloud, flowing out from him and spreading wide over the entire top of the tower.

"Get close to me!" Camroc called.

Quickly, we darted to the dragon's side. The magic of his golden shield deflected the black cloud.

"We have to retreat," Gnombie panted. "How can we stand against his power?"

"If we don't stand against this evil here and now, we will never have another chance because it will win!" Ingol declared.

"But what can we do?" Wren asked, eyes searching each of our faces for an answer.

My hand went to my pouch, and I withdrew Baarthagon's Collar. It felt hot. Extremely hot. Any more and it would have burnt my flesh.

Wake up! I thought.

Without seeing anything, I knew Morazz had opened his eyes.

Fly! I commanded, and then felt the creature unfurl his mighty wings.

As best I could, I formed a picture of Axel in my mind and sent it to the dragon. *Kill! Fire! Death!*

With a rush of massive wings, the clouds around us were blown away, and the head of Morazz appeared over the edge of the tower.

"No!" shrieked Axel, turning to face the red dragon.

Beside me, Camroc let out a gasp of relief, as though he'd been holding a great breath. His shield flickered and went out, as he sagged to the floor, his magic spent.

Even as I held the stone, I felt another will contesting with me for control of Morazz. It was a strong mind, schooled in the ways of dominating others, and I had only a stone meant to guide, not control, but it was still a gift from a dragon. I didn't know what I was doing. However, I channeled all of my resolve and desperation as I fought to maintain control.

Then, from behind me, I heard Camroc cry out. "Karradin! Lathaan! My friends!"

I didn't have to ask, because I knew that they were dead, just as Zaydia and Shal'eth and Asteropaios were dead, just as we would soon be dead if I could not take control of Morazz.

My vision started to go dark as I struggled. If only I could kill Axel right now and take the stones to Apricot, then the world could still be saved!

Sluggishly, I took a step forward, then another. My body seemed to weigh three times as much as normal. Every ounce of will I possessed was locked in combat with the treacherous wizard. All the while, the eyes of Morazz watched the two of us, ready to devour the loser.

After the first few steps, I managed to build a little speed. I wasn't running but moving as quickly as I could toward Axel with the stone in one hand and a sword in the other. He hadn't noticed yet, his eyes closed as he fought me for control of the dragon's mind.

At the last moment, he opened his eyes, and they went wide with surprise. It was too late. I was already there.

The instant before my sword would have sliced the wizard in half, a gust of air threw me backward as Char landed just in front of me.

Chapter 33
The Ninth

I scrambled away from the dragon's claws as Char latched onto the tower. Her long, black talons pierced the stones, tearing several of them loose. A swirl of dark clouds had followed her, blocking out the sun.

Camroc stared up at Char in horror.

Fire! I thought desperately to Morazz, but nothing happened. The dragon's mind was no longer held by me. From a place within the coils of Char's body, Axel leered at us.

"Where are the stones?" Char demanded of Camroc. Her voice was a thunderous roar. The words didn't come from her mouth but from her mind.

While her focus was elsewhere, I shoved Baarthagon's Collar back in my pouch and drew my second sword.

"We hid them!" Camroc shouted. "We hid them where you will never find them!"

"Liar!" Char hissed.

She struck at him with her spiked tail. The blow glanced off of Camroc's golden shield, but sent him to the ground.

Char turned to Axel. "Mine is here, and I sense the others are close."

She reached out a long claw to Axel, and he pulled The Void Stone from inside his robe. It was glowing with purple light.

No! I thought. *We'll never be able to take it from her!*

In my head, I saw again the future of void. Shal'eth had tried so many times to stop it, but he never could. Asteropaios, Zaydia, Shal'eth, Karradin, and Lathaan had all died without being able to prevent it.

What else could be done? What else could I do?

Without knowing the answers to those questions, I lunged for Axel. Camroc was quicker. With a greater speed than I'd known he possessed, the dragon raced for his apprentice.

Char whipped her head toward Camroc. He dodged her teeth but did not see that her tail moved at exactly the same moment. One of its spikes pierced Camroc through the chest.

Our eyes locked for just a moment.

"I'm sorry," he mouthed as his eyes closed.

With a flick of her tail, Char flung Camroc's body into the lake below, then her gaze turned on me. She had no light in her eyes, only void, the promise of a future that wasn't a future.

"It seems there is one more task for Morazz before I end his suffering," Char growled, looking at Axel. "Kill them all."

Instantly, The Fire Drake rose into the air above the tower. I'd seen this before. I knew how it would end. With my friends dead and all hope burnt to cinders.

"Take cover!" I shouted as I started to move back toward the others.

Wren hesitated, looking over her shoulder at me, but Ingol and Gnombie each grabbed one of her arms and pulled her in the direction of the staircase. I didn't see if they made it before a wall of flames cut me off. I swerved, running in the opposite direction. I could feel the heat at my heels following me as I ran back toward Char and Axel.

The lake, my mind thought, and I had to laugh at the irony of it all. There was a small chance I could escape the attacks of the two dragons and the wizard, then jump far enough to make it into the water, but when had water ever been my friend? My whole life, it had tried to snuff me out as had so many other things, and people, and just the world in general.

No! I thought sharply. *I will not die like this! I will not run! I will fight!*

Both of my swords were still in my hands, so I charged my enemies.

I sprang over a thick coil of Char's body, striking down at her as I did. She let out a hiss, probably more from surprise than pain, and lashed her tail at me. I dropped to my belly, rolling out of the way.

Springing to my feet again, blood and adrenaline screaming through my veins, I twisted to the left and slashed at Char's outstretched claw. I wasn't sure how I'd known it would be there, but I also sensed that her next strike would come from above. I lowered myself and spun away, then leapt upward, scissoring my blades and clipping off the very tip of Char's tail.

The snarl of rage that came from her set my teeth on edge, but I didn't back down. I was going to die. I knew it. She knew it. If any of my friends had survived the flames and were watching, they knew it too. Death was only a few heartbeats away for me, but I was going to make them the most fantastic heartbeats I had ever lived.

I dodged a ball of fire from Morazz then sprinted for Char's exposed flank. I never reached it. She opened her mouth, and a wave of poison spewed forth. I darted to the right, my retreat bringing me within reach of Axel.

He started to shift out of the way as I approached but was too slow to avoid me as I slammed into him. I doubted Char would cease her attack to save the wizard, but it was my only option. As we both went down, something small and purple dropped to the ground.

Instantly, I dove for it. My hand closed around the stone just as a blast of fire engulfed me. Axel shrieked in pain, and I saw his robes catch as his skin cracked and peeled in the blaze.

Without Axel controlling Morazz, he turned on Char, but she was too strong for him. She grabbed The Fire Drake by the throat and finished him off with a slash of her claws, then let his corpse fall to the ground far below.

I didn't feel any pain as my body burned. All I felt was a great, searing heat. I was scared to look at myself, sure that my clothes and hair were incinerated and my flesh was black and charred.

As I died, the heat grew even more intense at eight points across my body, one of them the stone gripped in my hand. Not that I thought I had a hand anymore, exactly.

In a haze, I felt the eight points move away, each a glowing light as they began to rotate in front of me. Their pattern was not a circle, but a sideways eight. Faster and faster they went until their colors were so mixed they were white, then there was a flash and they were gone, shattered into a million little pieces, which fell around me like pure snow.

This was my death. My end. The last breath I would take.

But in death, I found something else. Something greater.

I found life.

I found the ninth gift.

Rebirth.

In an instant, everything changed. I was no more a creature of flesh and blood, but one of fire and fury. Radiant light poured from me as my shape shifted from that of a half-elf mortal to one with wings of flame. I felt the power in them as I pumped the air, rising from the ashes around me.

The dark clouds retreated from my light, revealing a cold, red sun, very near the end of its life.

Alora, a voice not my own whispered in my heart. *Use your gifts. Fulfill your purpose.*

I launched myself upward. Char's dark shape was between me and the sun, but that did not stop me. I obliterated her as though she were nothing more than a shadow melted away by a beam of pure light.

My destination was the heavens, where I was called to complete the task I had been created for, but I paused. All nine of my gifts were thrumming in my chest, strong from my rebirth.

Quickly, I circled the lake on wings made of feathers and fire.

I was remembering many things as my past lives came back to me in flashes. My soul had lived for so long it was no wonder I had chosen eight friends to be my immortal companions.

Some had betrayed me, it was true, but they had also died to redeem themselves. Their sacrifice had to count for something. They had been the fallen, but now they could be the forgiven.

Epilogue
The Song

The sky was rose pink as the golden sun lingered on the horizon. In the air above, beautiful music could be heard trickling down from the heavens.

A half-elf woman, along with her two companions, a dwarf and a gnome, climbed a ridge to look at the sunset.

"It's the most beautiful thing I've ever seen," the half-elf murmured.

"I have to agree with you, Wren," the dwarf breathed.

The gnome only nodded.

"How long do you think it will last?" Wren wondered.

"How long will what last?" the dwarf asked.

"The beauty of this moment, Ingol," she replied dreamily.

"The sun will set soon," the gnome said. "But I have a feeling that isn't going to be the end."

"Gnombie is correct," Ingol breathed in wonder. "I think we all have many more sunsets yet to come."

Movement from the trees nearby caught their attention. A man and a woman stepped out holding hands. Together, they began climbing the hill.

"Shal'eth?" Wren asked uncertainly of the man as the pair grew closer.

He smiled at her. "It is I."

"But you died," Wren said, then turned to examine the woman. She had silver hair and rich blue eyes. "You– you're Asteropaios. But how? You both died."

"We did," Asteropaios confirmed. "But Alora chose to give us rebirth. We will serve her again now, as we once did, only better."

"Only I need to do better," Shal'eth told his mate.

257

A grim expression crossed Asteropaios's face. "You are wrong, for I doubted. I doubted the ninth gift, the one Alora used to save us. Everything would have been all right had I trusted, but I did not. Instead, I locked Alora's soul–her immortal soul–in a prison of flesh. My actions caused the suffering of many."

"What about the others?" Ingol asked. "Camroc, Zaydia, Morazz, Karradin, Lathaan. What of them?"

"They are around," Asteropaios said with a smile that wasn't human at all. "Camroc and Zaydia have already left for the plateau. Karradin has gone with Apricot and will continue aiding him in rebuilding the kingdom of his great sires. Lathaan was testing out his wings when last I saw, but I'm sure he has plans to find a land where the orcs and their griffins can settle. And Morazz is heading for The King's Forge of the dwarves."

A look of joy came into Ingol's eyes. "He shall relight it?!" the dwarf exclaimed.

"Indeed," Shal'eth told him.

"What are you both going to do?" Wren asked the two dragons.

"There are other places to be rebuilt and peoples to be gathered," Asteropaios replied.

Wren beamed at them and nodded happily.

"May I ask a question?" Gnombie piped up.

"Of course," Shal'eth told him.

"There were eight great dragons before; are there only to be seven now?" the gnome wondered.

"No," Asteropaios replied, a knowing smile playing on her lips.

"You don't mean Char–" Ingol started.

"I do not," Asteropaios cut him off. "Char has been eradicated. None of her essence remains in this world."

Slowly, the dragon turned her head and looked down the hill to where a solitary man stood.

"Kraster?!" Wren gasped. The half-elf raced to the man and threw her arms around him. She was laughing and sobbing all at once.

"How are you here?" she gasped, pulling back to look at the face of the friend she'd thought lost forever. He appeared different to her now. His eyes were a bright purple, and his skin was smooth and unmarked.

"I was chosen to replace Char," Kraster softly explained.

"I don't understand," Wren admitted. The dwarf and the gnome had come to stand behind her and were staring at Kraster in wonder.

"Candra– Alora– The Phoenix, whatever you want to call her, she brought me back along with the others," he explained. "I'm the eighth great dragon."

"She can do that?" Wren gasped.

"I think she had a little help from The Creator," Kraster admitted.

"And is she– still Candra?" Ingol asked.

Kraster nodded. "In some ways, yes, but in some ways, she's much more too. She is all of the different lives she's lived, both as a mortal and an immortal.

"Listen, and you can hear her voice singing everywhere throughout the entire land. A song of fresh beginnings because she has renewed the sun and restored hope to all–" Kraster cut off as a fiery, avian shape soared over them.

Everyone turned to look back up the hill as the creature landed on the top and transformed into a half-elf woman. Her eyes were burning like embers speckled with gold, her hair shimmered with inner light, and there was a warm glow to her skin.

"Candra?" Wren asked at the same moment Asteropaios breathed, "Alora?"

The Phoenix smiled at them, because they were both right. Her eyes turned to the golden sun about to slip below the horizon. It would rise again in the morning, promising a new day and a radiant future.

Runes

Future

Eternity

Power

Life

Guidance

Fire

Flight

Light

Rebirth

Void

The Elemental Spirits

Puvva of the Pot
Element: Water
Vessel: Teapot
Colors: Mint & White
Gender: Female
Mortal Form: Finfolk

Sif of the Sand
Element: Earth
Vessel: Hourglass
Colors: Copper & Brown
Gender: Male
Mortal Form: Stone Elemental

Lamasku of the Lamp
Element: Fire
Vessel: Oil Lamp
Colors: Orange & Charcoal
Gender: Male
Mortal Form: Winged Fire Lion

Faleous of the Flute
Element: Air
Vessel: Flute
Colors: Navy & Steel
Gender: Female
Mortal Form: Kitsune

The Great Dragons

Asteropaios
Queen of the Dragons - Queen of Storms
Colors: Blue & Silver
Gender: Female
Gift: Power
Stone & Gift: Asteropaios's Gift
Mortal Form: Human

Shal'eth
The Great
Colors: Teal & White
Gender: Male
Gift: Future
Stone: The Scrying Stone
Mortal Form: Human

Karradin
The Wise - Lucille
Colors: Orange & Copper
Gender: Female
Gift: Guidance
Stone: Baarthagon's Collar
Mortal Form: High Elf

Lathaan
Great Wing
Colors: Yellow & Tan
Gender: Male
Gift: Flight
Stone: The Gem of Aero
Mortal Form: Orc

Camroc

Twin of Zaydia - Rakus
Colors: Gold & Green
Gender: Male
Gift: Eternity
Stone: Dimble's Legacy
Mortal Form: Gnome

Zaydia

Twin of Camroc - Phillis Nithe
Colors: Green & Gold
Gender: Female
Gift: Life
Stone: The Heart of Jong
Mortal Form: Gnome

Morazz

The Fire Drake
Colors: Red & Brown
Gender: Male
Gift: Fire
Stone: Azazoth's Wand
Mortal Form: Dwarf

Char

The Corrupter
Colors: Purple & Grey
Gender: Female
Gift: Light/Void
Stone: The Void Stone
Mortal Form: Dark Elf

About the author and the party

Danielle N. McDonough is an author who loves all things to do with imagination, fantasy, and storytelling, so it is no surprise that she enjoys playing Dungeons and Dragons. In fact, it was one of her party's adventures that inspired the story for The Cursed Half Moon.

Although Danielle (Candra) has been friends with the members of the party for many years, D&D has brought her closer to each of them in a special way. Anna was the one who first invited Danielle to try D&D in 2017, where she instantly fell in love with the game. This is also when she met Charles (The Dungeon Master). The two have been in an active D&D group together ever since.

In turn, Danielle introduced Makenna (Wren) to D&D when she put together a small game for her birthday party. Afterward, Danielle got Collin (Kraster/Ingol), an experienced player, invited to the D&D group Makenna was joining, as she knew Collin had a crush on Makenna. With a little coaxing, the two started dating, fell in love, and got married.

When everyone came together for the adventure that inspired this book series, The Teapot McGuffin, as it was originally called, Joe (Gnombie), Danielle's brother-in-law, was invited to join. This was Joe's first D&D campaign, but not his last. All of them look forward to playing together many times in the future!

www.daniellenmcdonough.com